EXTRACTING EMMA

A NOVEL BY

ANNABELLE WINTERS

Copyright Notice

Copyright © 2022 by Annabelle Winters
All Rights Reserved by Author
www.annabellewinters.com
ab@annabellewinters.com

If you'd like to copy, reproduce, sell, or distribute any part of this text, please obtain the explicit, written permission of the author first. Note that you should feel free to tell your spouse, lovers, friends, and co-workers how happy this book made you. Have a wonderful evening!

Cover Design by S. Lee

ISBN: 9798443167275

0 1 2 3 4 5 6 7 8 9

BOOKS BY ANNABELLE WINTERS

THE DARKWATER MILITARY ROMANCE SERIES
Avenging Amy
Breaking Brenna
Capturing Cate
Delivering Diana
Finding Fay
Guarding Gale
Hiding Hannah
Interrogating India
Jacking Jill
Killing Kay

THE CURVES FOR SHEIKHS SERIES
Curves for the Sheikh
Flames for the Sheikh
Hostage for the Sheikh
Single for the Sheikh
Stockings for the Sheikh
Untouched for the Sheikh
Surrogate for the Sheikh
Stars for the Sheikh
Shelter for the Sheikh
Shared for the Sheikh
Assassin for the Sheikh
Privilege for the Sheikh
Ransomed for the Sheikh
Uncorked for the Sheikh
Haunted for the Sheikh
Grateful for the Sheikh
Mistletoe for the Sheikh
Fake for the Sheikh

THE CURVES FOR SHIFTERS SERIES
Curves for the Dragon
Born for the Bear
Witch for the Wolf
Tamed for the Lion
Taken for the Tiger

THE CURVY FOR HIM SERIES
The Teacher and the Trainer
The Librarian and the Cop
The Lawyer and the Cowboy
The Princess and the Pirate
The CEO and the Soldier
The Astronaut and the Alien
The Botanist and the Biker
The Psychic and the Senator

THE CURVY FOR KEEPS SERIES
Given to the Groom
Traded to the Trucker
Punished by the Principal
Stranded with the Psycho
Wifed by the Warlord
Late for the Landlord
Vanquishing the Viking
Disciplining the Duke
Saving the Sinner

ANNABELLEWINTERS.COM
WNTRS.CO/READ

Extracting Emma

A Novel By

Annabelle Winters

I
HONG KONG

Tom Edgerton blended in with the crowd of protestors like a ghost at Mardi Gras. His dark green eyes scanned the spaces between the heads of men and women as he moved farther away from the White Lotus cafe and the gray haired ex-CIA man who'd been on his trail from Egypt to Macau and now Hong Kong.

"Coming through, kids," Edge muttered in Cantonese Chinese as his broad, heavy body almost knocked over an entire group of Hong Kong teenagers wearing American brands colored so bright they made Edge wish he hadn't left his sunglasses at that underground fight venue two nights ago.

He'd also left his burner phone and a cheap money clip that held about six hundred Hong Kong dollars. Edge had made a hasty exit. He'd won the fight but broken the rules.

Story of his damn life.

Not a huge loss, Edge thought as he glanced back through the crowd and saw no sign of John Benson. The burner phone was locked and had nothing personal on it. The money clip was something he'd picked up from a street vendor near Kowloon Park.

As for the six hundred in local currency . . . well, he could make that up in about an hour once he got back to Macau, where the laws were looser, the police more corrupt, and the payouts much higher.

Though the payout at the fight the other night had been raised way beyond what Edge had seen in the Hong Kong arenas before. Edge was already in the ring when that vicious asshole General Trung and his ruthless consort Emma Chang showed up and turned his fight into a Chinese deathmatch for their viewing pleasure.

It tripled the payout for the winner, changed the odds for the gamblers. A deathmatch was a different kind of fight. A superior fighter might lose a deathmatch simply because he lacked the hardness to finish the fight.

Edge stayed the hell away from those matchups. It wouldn't be fair to the other fighters. Edge was a trained killer. Hardened before he even landed at BUD/S training. And the stakes only increased as he moved up in the Teams until he was given command of SEAL Team Seventeen despite several strong objections saying he wasn't ready, would never be ready.

Of course, none of those objections came from the Navy. They all came from the spooks running those CIA-owned off-the-books Special Forces missions. Edge was a born leader, but his ability to manage upwards was . . . lacking.

Edge's SEAL commanders understood him and trusted him well enough to stay out of his way. But the CIA

Extracting Emma

guys were control freaks who sometimes exercised poor judgment and extreme reluctance to admit a mistake.

Bad combination.

The kind of combination that got soldiers killed.

And got CIA dickheads punched in the face.

Edge got through the crowd and stepped up on the curb of the opposite side of the street. He was almost all the way down to the end of the block, a safe distance away from the White Lotus Cafe.

No John Benson in sight. Edge didn't think the old guy could keep up with him through the crowd. Hopefully he wouldn't even try.

After all, Edge had made his intentions pretty damn clear.

No.

Fucking.

Way.

Now Edge rubbed his beard that was getting to bushman levels of wildness. It was thick, dark, and long. Softened the blow if someone managed to land a punch. It also completed the image of the American Warrior Monk that seemed to have become part of his reputation on the Hong Kong and Macau fighting circuit.

Edge didn't mind it. He was a hothead when it came to incompetent bigshots trying to give him orders, but he was cool like a mountain stream in a fight. He could slow his heartbeat to the point where a doctor would pronounce him dead even though his green eyes were focused and his dark red lips curled with an easy smile of lazy confidence. Edge had trained in mixed martial arts since he was a teenager, and he could move around his opponent with the grace of a Burmese tiger.

But this guy Benson had gotten Edge worked up, uncomfortable, maybe even a bit curious. Benson had been calling him relentlessly for months now. Didn't matter how many burner phones Edge went through. Benson always tracked down the new number and sent him a chirpy message asking if he'd like to meet for a glass of coffee in Egypt or a bowl of rice-wine in Macau or a cup of green tea in Hong Kong.

Edge had asked around the small circle of CIA contacts he actually trusted. Turned out John Benson was a legend in the Agency. He had moved up through the ranks alongside CIA Director Martin Kaiser before abruptly quitting a couple of years ago. There were some rumors Benson was running his own outfit called Darkwater. It wasn't clear if it was just a dark ops cover funded by the CIA or if it really was something new and different.

Either way, it was enough to make Edge curious. Touring the underground fight circuits was more of a vacation to Edge than an actual career. It wouldn't last long. Best for Edge to get out before he killed some guy by mistake.

Or on purpose.

And then what would Edge do for work? He'd lost his insurance and pension after getting BCD'd out of the military. He'd been kicked out of his home when he was thirteen, so there was sure as hell no trust fund or inheritance to support his ass. He'd worked his way through college only because he knew it would give him a leg up on getting into the Teams. Didn't remember a damn thing those idiot professors tried to teach him in their brown tweed jackets and polka-dot bow-ties.

So yeah, Edge was curious about what Benson wanted. And since Benson himself had a reputation for doing things his own way, without regard for rules and authority, Edge had finally agreed to a meeting.

A meeting that didn't even make it to the handshake part.

A new record for Edge.

Edge took a long, slow breath. He ran his fingers through his thick hair. Thought back to the other night when General Trung and Emma Chang had showed up at the fight. Then he exhaled hard and thought about Benson's newspaper open to Emma Chang's photograph.

The coincidence was jarring. Edge wasn't sure what to make of it.

He heard a jarring electric chime to his right. A woman had just walked out of the store on the corner. She was unwrapping a maroon-and-gold pack of Indonesian cigarettes. The door was closing slowly behind her.

Edge grabbed the door and went into the little corner store. It sold cigarettes and snacks and lottery tickets. It also sold newspapers.

Edge grabbed the top copy of the *Hong Kong Chronicle* off the stack. He dug into the right pocket of his black cargo pants, hoping to find some change.

Nothing. He cursed when he remembered he'd left

his foreign cash at the fight venue and all his American dollars were in a train-station locker with his American passport and IDs and a couple of bank cards.

Edge huffed out a breath as the cashier peered at him from behind the hard plastic counter. The store was the size of a shoebox. It wasn't the kind of place where you could read the newspaper and then drop it back on the stack and leave. Sure, the black-haired wide-eyed girl behind the counter probably wouldn't stop him, but it wasn't that important. He didn't need to read that article right now. He needed to get to his locker and pick up some cash for a plane ticket back to Macau anyway. He could get the paper at the train station or at the airport later.

"I got it," came a smooth American voice from Edge's left. "*Gàn dé hao.*"

Edge stared in annoyed disbelief. It was John Benson. He was paying for Edge's newspaper. He spoke Cantonese with a shameless American accent. He was smiling like a damn wolf.

Edge scratched the tip of his nose and tightened his jaw. He considered his options. There weren't many.

He could walk out the door without saying a word to Benson. But the old CIA dog seemed to be able to sniff out Edge's trail like a bloodhound. Perhaps Edge should just talk to the guy. It was the logical thing to do.

Too bad Edge trusted instinct over logic.

He walked past Benson, straight out the door.

"Thanks, man," Edge said coolly without even glancing into Benson's shining gray eyes.

Benson nodded calmly. He waited for his change as

the electric door-chime played its high-pitched tune. Edge had to give the old guy credit for being so damn relaxed. Like he wasn't in any hurry. None at all. Like it was inevitable that Benson would get to Edge.

Edge strode out into the Hong Kong sunshine. The protestors were still crowding Lee Street. Edge could disappear again. Benson still hadn't emerged from the store. Perhaps the miserly old bastard was counting his change. Spooks obsessed over details like that.

Edge stepped away from the door. He glanced back inside through the small store window and saw Benson chatting with the girl behind the register. She was giggling. Benson was grinning as he jabbered away in Cantonese.

Edge wasn't sure whether to groan or laugh. The guy was good. He had poise and patience. He was playing Edge like how you wait for a cat to come to you. He was probably a damn good spook. Maybe working for the guy would be interesting.

So long as it had nothing to do with General Trung and Emma Chang.

Edge wasn't dumb. He knew how the CIA worked. He understood that today's spooks were going deeper into the shadows with their dark ops stuff. Maybe they wanted General Trung bumped off and were looking for a patsy to do the job and take the fall.

It was entirely possible Benson was working with one of the CIA guys who'd helped get Edge kicked out of the Navy. Maybe the CIA figured they could kill two birds with one stone.

Get Edge to kill General Trung. It would be great for

plausible deniability. A hot-headed ex-Navy man kicked out of Special Forces. Edge was already known in the local fight scene. He'd fit the off-the-rails lone gunman profile just fine. Everything would check out if anyone looked up the records.

After all, the bad stuff was true.

Of course, Edge knew enough about Trung's history that he wouldn't lose sleep if the General was found in a Hong Kong backalley with a broken neck. But General Trung's network went deep in many directions, from the People's Liberation Army on the Chinese Mainland to the Macau gangs that ran the casinos and brothels. Even if someone got to Trung, they weren't getting away alive. If the CIA wanted Trung dead, they'd expect the assassin to die too.

He would have to be disposable.

Two birds with one stone.

Ruthless and efficient.

The CIA way.

Or maybe *three* birds with one stone, Edge thought darkly as he remembered how Emma Chang had looked down at him from up on her perch above the unwashed masses in the arena.

She'd looked directly into Edge's eyes, then leaned to Trung and whispered something into his ear.

Three seconds later Trung declared the fight was to have a Chinese deathmatch finish.

And a second after that, Emma Chang was added to Edge's personal grudgematch list.

Hell, Edge thought as he felt the hairs on the back of

Extracting Emma 9

his neck bristle at the memory of Emma's full-figured, silk-clad body leaning towards Trung and whispering out what was basically an execution order for one of the two men in the arena.

For some odd reason Edge's cock moved at the memory of Emma's red lips parting in a whisper. Perhaps a reminder that sex and violence came from the same place in a man's heart.

Edge was suddenly hit with a vivid image of Emma screaming for mercy, on her knees before him, her jet black hair open and wild, her dark maple-brown eyes wide with the realization that Edge was now in control, in command, in charge.

It took a long minute for the image to fade. An even longer minute for that hardness to subside. When Edge finally calmed himself down, he realized he was still in the same damn spot even though it felt like he'd been transported somewhere else.

"All right, Benson," Edge muttered through a loud exhale. "Guess I'll wait."

He leaned against the exposed brick wall of the building. Opened up the newspaper. Flipped to the article about General Trung and Emma Chang.

Edge's gaze went straight to the photograph. It was in black-and-white but in his mind the colors were bold blues and gaudy greens, ripe reds and vivid violets.

She was in that form-fitting blue satin Chinese style tunic-gown that went up to her neck and down to her ankles. But there was no hiding the fullness of her breasts, the girth of her healthy hips, the thickness of her thighs beneath the tailored watered silk. Her hourglass shape was as deadly as the look she'd given him from above the arena. Her hair black as oil at midnight. Those red lips parted slightly in a treacherous slit.

General Trung was in the background of the photograph. His right arm was raised, palm open like the photo had captured him in mid-strike. He was out of focus, but it was clearly him.

General Trung was a big man, well over six feet tall, broad like a building, with arms like cannons and a chest like two quarter-barrel kegs stacked sideways. Edge had heard about him years ago, when Trung had been kicked out of the Chinese Army. It had been reasonably big news in military circles around the world. The man was a General in the PLA. And the Chinese Communist Party cared deeply about appearances, so they wouldn't have authorized it without a damn good reason.

Of course, the reason was never made public. There were some rumors about Trung's role in sex trafficking from the Chinese Mainland to Macau's gangland-operated brothels. But there were also rumors that it was a smokescreen for Trung to move from the Army to the Ministry of State Security—China's version of the spooks who worked in the shadows.

Maybe both rumors were true. Spooks around the world were the same when it came to breaking the rules.

"Spooky, isn't it?" came Benson's voice as he stepped out of the store but stayed in the shadow of the building.

Edge glanced up from the newspaper. Asked the question with a raised left eyebrow.

Benson chuckled. Took a sip from a brightly labeled plastic bottle that had an image of two drunk panda bears dancing on their hind paws. It was a kiwi-fruit cocktail. No alcohol.

"Spooky that I find you just as you find your mission," Benson explained. He took another sip of his panda-bear kiwi drink. Gestured towards Edge's open newspaper. Chuckled again. "Who is she?"

Edge frowned, wondering what kind of game Benson was playing. He glanced at the photo of Emma with Trung in the background.

Then he sighed, folded the newspaper, rolled it into a tight baton, and javelined it into a metal-wire trash can.

Edge straightened to full height, crossed his arms over his chest. The thin black fabric of his merino wool tee shirt stretched over his muscles. Benson was maybe six foot and change. Edge was a good four inches taller.

"You know I got kicked out of the Navy for breaking some bigshot spook's jawbone, right?" Edge said coolly.

Benson shrugged. "He got some new dental implants and an alignment procedure. Looks better than before. Tells everyone he killed fourteen Taliban with his bare hands. He's cleaning up on the dating scene with the new scars and smile."

Edge couldn't help breaking a grin. Benson grinned back at him. The sun was very bright. Edge considered asking Benson to buy him a pair of sunglasses.

"You guys want General Trung dead, don't you?" Edge said.

Edge was a straight-ahead kind of guy. No bullshit. No games.

Benson blinked. Then he shrugged coolly. "Do *you* want General Trung dead?"

"I want a lot of people dead," Edge said. "Which

means I need to stay alive so I can get to them all. Taking out Trung is a suicide mission. Tell the CIA to blackmail some offshore asset into doing it. Torture someone's puppy. Poison someone's kitten. Whatever you sneaky assholes like to do these days."

"And what are you doing these days, Thomas?" Benson said, smoothly answering Edge's question with another question. "Besides avoiding the barber."

Edge stroked his long beard and grinned. "Really? You working directly from the CIA psy-ops playbook? Calling me Thomas is supposed to trigger something in my damaged mind? Make me think of Mommy or something?"

"Oh, you want to talk about your mother?" Benson said innocently. "She's still working in Vegas. Doing all right, according to her bank records and tax returns." He blinked, looked directly into Edge's eyes. "No need to worry, kid. She isn't breaking any laws. After all, prostitution is legal in Nevada."

Edge's grin changed shape. He licked his lips and glanced off to the side. Considered realigning Benson's jaw, then decided against it.

After all, he knew what Pam Edgerton did for a living.

Same thing she'd always done.

"Not sure this is the best recruiting strategy, Benson," Edge growled.

"Don't need one anymore," said Benson merrily. "You're already being pulled into the game. Good luck, kid. You have my number. Call me when shit starts to get weird."

Edge frowned. He tried to read whether Benson was for real, or if he really was a bit fucked up in the head.

One screw loose. One brick short. Couple ounces light.

That was what one of Edge's CIA contacts had said. There were rumors Benson had been secretly married to a State Department official named Sally Norton. She'd been murdered a couple of years ago in Dubai. Benson had quit the CIA soon after that. Maybe he'd lost his damn mind.

But then Edge thought of Ax, Bruiser, Cody, and Dogg. The former members of SEAL Team Thirteen. They'd all quit the Teams around the same time. Rumors were that they were part of this Darkwater outfit Benson was supposedly running in the shadows.

Edge hadn't worked with those guys much in the recent past, but he knew they were some of the best SEALs in the field. They certainly weren't out of their minds. So it meant something if they'd all chosen to work for Benson.

Follow his rules.

Play his games.

Who is she, Benson had asked.

Now Edge felt a shiver go through him even though Hong Kong was in the tropics and it was the middle of a summer day. He thought of Benson's open newspaper on the cafe table.

Was it just a coincidence that the paper had been open to that page?

Was Benson genuinely asking who Emma Chang was?

Or was Benson trying to lead him to General Trung in that sketchy way the spooks brainwashed folks into becoming assassins.

Maybe it was all in Edge's own head. A web being spun by his own imagination. A game unfolding from someplace within him instead of the external world.

Edge blinked three times and shook his shaggy head to clear it.

When he looked up the sidewalk was empty.

Benson was gone.

Just the echo of his words swirling through the sweltering summer air.

Who is Emma Chang?
Who the hell is she?

2

"Who are you?" General Trung shouted again.

Emma blinked away the blood that was dribbling from the cut above her left eyebrow. Trung had backhanded her with his knuckles and sent her flying across the Hong Kong Mandarin's Presidential Suite like she was a doll. The gold ring he wore on his middle finger would leave a mark on her face.

It is just a battle scar, Emma told herself as she got back up to her feet and straightened her blue silk gown. She knew there was blood on her bosom, but it would wash out well enough. The intricate embroidery bordering the long line of cloth buttons would hide any faint leftover stains.

Trung stayed where he was in the center of the room. He stood in the middle of the large circular rug with a dragon-themed design. Bright yellow on crimson. Hot colors.

They matched Trung's personal color scheme. He still wore red tunics with gold embroidery years after being relieved of his command in the Chinese Army. Still liked being called General Trung even though he held no military rank. A hot-blooded man, but with the cold heart of a snake in winter. Still, hot colors worked well for his image.

Emma herself preferred a cooler palette. Blues and greens, mostly. It helped balance the red rage in her heart. Helped to keep it hidden. Locked away until she unleashed it in one savage explosion that had been building for years, gathering power until the day she would use it.

But today was not that day. Emma was no closer to her goal now than a year ago, when she'd first arrived at General Trung's doorstep with an offer he could not refuse. She had learned nothing useful about him from almost a year by Trung's side.

She had, however, learned a few useful things about herself.

She'd learned she could survive anything to get what she wanted.

She'd learned she could take pain and rage and store it away to use later.

She'd learned that the longer she waited to use those pent-up emotions of violence, the better it felt.

Perhaps that was why she'd impulsively whispered to Trung and asked him to declare that American Warrior Monk's fight a deathmatch at the last minute, when the fighters were already circling, when the bets were already placed.

Emma had gotten a sickeningly luscious thrill from feeling the instant change in the energy of the arena. She'd felt it in every part of her body when she looked into that bearded man's dark green eyes.

She'd done it on a whim, casually, without thought or

Extracting Emma

planning. But somehow it felt like it *had* been planned, Emma thought now as Trung undid the gold metal clasps along the front of his red tunic and shrugged the jacket off his powerful shoulders.

Trung's well-lined face was unreadable. Those golden eyes alert. He was forever on his guard. Never switched off. Never left an opening. Even if Emma had wanted to make her move, she'd never have been able to get past those eyes which were wary and watchful, equal parts a leopard prowling for a kill and a buffalo watching for the wolves.

Emma knew Trung had survived at least six assassination attempts, perhaps one of them by the Chinese Communist Party itself. This little scene was supposedly about the most recent plot on Trung's life. It had been discovered before Trung was in any danger, but now came the aftermath.

If there was a traitor in Trung's troops, his man Zhu would flush him out and flay him alive. But if Emma was the traitor, Trung would handle it himself.

It was terrifying, but also strangely gratifying. It meant Emma had moved up in the ranks. She'd proved herself an able manager of the women, an astute judge of new recruits, and a commanding presence in the Macau brothels.

Emma had worked with prostitutes all over the world. She treated them with respect and understanding. She accepted that many women treated the work as casually as an office job, with neither shame nor revulsion, sometimes with enjoyment and appreciation.

Not all of them, of course. But Emma had to stay

firm and focused, and she kept her head down and her eyes on the prize. The world's cities teemed with women who'd been tricked into turning tricks, lured by ads offering employment and ending up with a different set of duties from what the brochure said. Emma felt for those women, but she stuffed that hurt inside her along with everything else to be used later.

Emma told herself she couldn't fix everything for everyone. To try would be a sign of weakness. She'd be stopped before she got very far. A day later she'd be floating face-down in the South China Sea. It wouldn't accomplish a damn thing.

So Emma stayed on course, did her job, trusted in what she believed was her fate—or at least her duty. It had taken years, but she was here now. Within smelling distance of General Trung himself.

Things were turning in her direction. A year ago Emma was still not close enough to the General to hope to find what she was looking for, but Emma held the faith that the universe hadn't gotten her this far to let her down now.

And Emma was right.

Three months ago she'd been photographed with the General, the two of them walking out of the Macau Metropolitan Hotel. Emma wore a fitted long gown of black silk, her hair perfect like a black helmet, her makeup immaculate like a doll in the store window.

Immediately the tabloids had called them a couple, and when Trung saw that it enhanced his own image, he made her his official consort.

It had been a fortuitous turn of events. A coincidence

Extracting Emma

that felt like a miracle. After all, Trung had never bothered to take a wife or a girlfriend. He used his Macau women when he needed his release. He mostly continued to use them even after taking Emma as his public consort, though he did his thing with her too when he pleased.

It was not a big part of Trung's life, it seemed to Emma. If sex and violence came from the same place, then Trung's needs leaned far to the side of violence.

Emma watched now as Trung came closer. She wondered in which direction his needs were tilting. She was not a small woman, but Trung still loomed over her like a wall as he got close. He pulsed his massive pectorals through the red silk undershirt he wore beneath the red tunic as he approached her like some lumbering dragon.

His fists were big like boulders. Emma had watched him beat a gangland assassin to death a few months earlier with those fists. Trung had given the man permission to fight for his life. It had seemed vaguely honorable, even though the mismatch was clear to anyone watching.

Still, Emma wasn't worried for her own life right now. The backhand swat was a lazy, casual swipe. Emma had backpedaled and stumbled as Trung connected, which was why she'd hit the wall so hard. And if not for his ring, she probably wouldn't be bleeding.

No, Trung wasn't going to beat her to death.

Not today, at least.

"Who are you, Emma?" he hissed through his signature smile that showed two rows of sharp white teeth that were aligned with machinelike precision.

"You know who I am, General," she replied respectfully in Mandarin, which was Trung's preferred Chinese dialect. He considered Cantonese beneath his dignity, and chose to speak English to the Hong Kong natives, a mocking reminder of their British colonial history. "Your staff took my fingerprints and photographs and blood and urine for their background checks. You know more about me than my own mother does."

"Your mother who was an American citizen?" Trung said, still holding the unnerving smile which was exactly the same whether he was pleased with a dance performance or in a psychotic rage at some imagined betrayal or insult. "Your Chinese mother who rejected the land of her birth?"

Emma kept her back straight and her feet together in her rope-soled cloth shoes. She clasped her hands in front of her, just beneath the swell of her breasts. She stayed silent and listened. None of it worried her. After all, Trung had known all of this from the beginning. Emma's family history wasn't a secret.

Not that part of it, at least.

"I cannot be blamed for my mother's decisions before my birth," she said in Mandarin, making sure to keep her tone respectful without crossing over to where Trung might think she was being patronizing. "And you know of the decision I made when I was old enough to understand who I am inside, where my heart and loyalty lies."

Trung stroked his clean shaved jaw that was almost comically square. It went well with his square military-style haircut. His black hair was still lush and thick, but with flecks of gray betraying the fact that he was well into his fifties now. His belly was larger now than in photographs of Trung from a decade earlier, but the heavy gut only added bulk to his massive frame, did not seem to take away from his immense strength or slow his surprising speed.

"Hah, yes, that part did check out," Trung said somewhat grudgingly. "Your American citizenship was renounced legally. No indication that it is part of the ruse."

"Part of what ruse, General?" Emma asked as a chill of dread slithered down her spine, down past the string-elastic of her turquoise thong underwear, all the way through her bare thighs, calves, and toes.

Emma could feel her heart speeding up beneath her blue silk dress.

He couldn't know, could he?

No. If he knew, she'd already be dead.

Gutted like a fish, her carcass floating in the South China Sea, all bloated and blue like a belly-up tuna.

"Do not *lie* to me!" Trung roared. "Who do you work for? The Russians? The Thais?" He blinked his cold yellow eyes three times. "The CIA?" he hissed.

He turned his body and kicked at the room-service cart, sending leftover tuna and whitefish all over the hand-woven carpet. Soy sauce dripped black like drying blood onto the rug. A soggy sprig of broccoli stared forlornly up at Emma as she gulped and stayed still, fighting the urge to either run for her life or scream for it.

She calmed herself down. Stood her ground. It was a good sign he'd kicked the cart instead of her, Emma told herself.

It meant he wasn't sure. This was a demonstration. A sudden outburst meant to shake her up. Trung's own ruse to get her to confess anything she might be holding back. It meant he didn't truly believe she had betrayed him. This was his ruse, not hers.

"Your records are too clean," Trung finally said as he crunched his way over the white crockery and red caviar, grinding millions of fish-eggs into the carpet. "Almost like they have been sanitized. Perhaps manufactured. It is a pattern we have seen before. CIA used to do it, but they are more sophisticated now. This seems more like the work of the Thailand gangs. They overdo it when creating fake identities or cleaning up real ones."

Emma relaxed even more. This was the final stage of Trung's purity test. He was accusing her of betraying him to one of the rival gangs that fought over gambling and prostitution in Macau.

There were Chinese, Russian, and Thai gangs. General Trung ran the Chinese gangs. The Russians were almost as powerful as the Chinese. The Thailand groups were the weakest, so if Trung was ranting about Emma betraying him to the thugs from Bangkok, this test was over and she had passed.

Emma watched in relief as she saw Trung unclench his fists and exhale noisily like he was satisfied for now. She felt her eyebrow throb. It meant the adrenaline was draining away. Adrenaline was a natural painkiller, and now she felt the pain make her face twitch.

Trung bent down and picked up a black cloth serviette from the remains of their meal. He tossed it at Emma. She caught it and pressed it against her cut.

Extracting Emma

Her gaze moved down to the floor. Along the way she saw the bulge beneath Trung's belt.

She knew what was coming.

What always came after Trung got angry and there was no one to beat to death.

"Turn around," Trung said. "Go to the window. Raise your dress."

Emma blinked and nodded once. She turned and padded in her cloth shoes to the floor-to-ceiling dark-tinted window. They were seventy floors above the city streets. The sun was low in the sky. The window's dark tint made it seem like there was a solar eclipse over Hong Kong.

Emma did as she was told. She raised her blue silk dress over her bottom, then leaned forward and placed her palms against the thick glass.

She kept her feet tight together. Trung had made it clear he liked this view the best. It was how he always made them stand.

His shadow fell across her from behind. She could see a faint reflection of him in the window glass. He undid his belt, unzipped his trousers, let them drop down to his knees.

He pushed down his silk boxer shorts. Emma closed her eyes. She felt her eyebrow throb. She heard Trung start to mutter in Mandarin.

She heard him touch himself. Heard him move his fist back and forth over his shaft. Heard him lick his fingers and then massage his circumcised cockhead.

She knew all the sounds.

She knew the routine.

She started to count.

One hundred and twelve seconds later Trung let out a long, guttural groan and came all over her raised rear. Emma didn't even flinch when she felt his warm semen spurt on her lower back and slowly roll down and begin to soak the thong-string wedged in her rear crack.

Trung's routine was military precise. He rarely took longer than two minutes. Sometimes he touched the women when he did it, but mostly just to get them in the right position.

He was a purely visual man, it seemed. Emma wondered if he had no feeling in his rough fingertips. No sensation on his skin. It would explain why he showed no sign of pain when someone cut him in a fight.

Emma thought of the only time Trung had touched her naked body. When she first presented herself to him he'd made her strip bare, pressed her breasts like he was checking to see if they were real.

Emma hadn't flinched. She knew Trung was evaluating whether to put her to work in one of the Chinese-run brothels in Macau or to give her a management role like she'd asked.

That first evaluation had been more tense than anything else she'd experienced over the past year. If she'd misjudged Trung, she would end up in a brothel and never see him again. She'd be given a room in one of the hotels like the other girls. There would be a contract and payment, but there would also be curfew and guards.

Of course, it wouldn't have been the same kind of hotel where the trafficked women were kept, so Emma wouldn't have had much trouble getting out.

But the point wasn't to get out.

It was to get in.

And so Emma had thanked her stars when Trung declared she was too old for the brothels and perhaps her experience would indeed suit her for the role she'd asked to fill.

Good. Because she'd waited years to be old enough where she'd be "too old" to be a moneymaking whore in General Trung's domain.

Which meant she was past the threshold.

Inside the dragon's lair.

Now all she had to do was survive until she found what she was looking for.

Stay strong even if she felt weak.

Through hell and fire.

Through thick and thin.

"You are a thick woman," Trung had said thoughtfully on that first day, pressing her heavy breasts again and then squeezing each of her large buttcheeks with his big rough palms. "If you were a few years younger I would have rented you to the men who like to be rough and hard. But they are picky. Nobody over twenty-five for them. You miss the mark. Just as well, I suppose. Those women do not last long in the business. With your experience and education, you are destined for grander things, Emma Chang. All right then. Once Zhu completes your background check, we can try you out, see if there is a permanent role for you in the Macau businesses."

Then he'd made her lie down flat on her back, naked on the floor of the Macau penthouse.

He'd called in his right hand man Zhu, a lean, long-faced killer from Guangdong Province. Zhu had eyes that were like black pearls. He kept a goatee that was groomed to a savage point. His fingernails were painted black, just like his eyes and hair.

Zhu had looked at Emma without any reaction at all. He simply stood there.

It was a strangely sick moment. Neither man spoke. They just looked at Emma as she lay on the floor, her legs tight together, her hands folded over her triangle of short, straight black hair.

It was humiliating, but Emma had been prepared for much worse. She stared calmly at the ceiling of the Macau penthouse. It was black tile, like a bathroom. Perhaps things spattered all the way up to the ceiling. Tile wiped off easy.

"Is the background check complete?" Trung had finally asked Zhu after exactly three full minutes of that humiliating silence, like it was part of their interview routine.

Zhu had nodded. "UCLA graduate. Mandarin and Cantonese language major. Las Vegas and Reno residences check out. Two years in Amsterdam's Red Light district. One year each in the Bangkok and Tokyo whorehouses. She has worked with whores for nine years. Her references are real. She might be good for us. We can use her for settling in the recruits. Might help with managing the bitches who get restless and think they have some bargaining power. My men do not have the patience to discipline the badly behaved cunts without leaving marks on their faces."

Trung had grunted. "And you are sure she has renounced her American citizenship?"

Zhu had nodded. He said nothing more.

"You want to use her?" Trung had said, showing that signature smile for the first time.

Zhu had snorted. He said nothing. Just leaned forward and spat on Emma's bare chest, then turned on his boot heel, saluted his General, and walked out of the room.

Emma had kept staring at the ceiling. But in her mind she added Zhu to her list.

Now Emma thought of that two-person list as she used the black serviette to wipe Trung's mess off her back and butt. She tossed the sticky black cloth onto the stinking pile of whitefish and tuna. Then she glanced at the General.

Trung had his back to her. He was on the phone with Zhu. They were talking about Trung and Emma's appearance at the underground fight arena in the Hong Kong Warehouse District the other night.

Zhu was upset about it. In Macau Trung could do anything, Zhu was saying, but in Hong Kong caution was wise.

Emma could hear Zhu's sharp, halting voice loud and clear. Trung always used the speakerphone even though he held the phone to his ear. His eardrum had been blown during a border skirmish with the Indian military. One of Trung's own men had fired too close to Trung's ear. Apparently Trung had cut off the man's ear and fed it to a mountain goat as the man was made to watch.

Emma watched as Trung strolled past her and stood facing the dark tinted window. He asked Zhu about the supposed plot to kill him. Zhu replied that the weekly search of the trafficked women's rooms had turned up a single-dose vial of Black Ivy poison.

It was taped under a woman's bed frame. One of the women Trung had used last week. She claimed to know nothing about it. Zhu reported that they'd held the whore down and dripped the poison into her eyeballs to make sure she was telling the truth.

It appeared she was, Zhu reported casually. Because she died blind and screaming.

Emma felt something tug inside her as Trung grunted like it was just another day at the office. She'd seen and heard things over the past year. Things she hadn't been completely prepared for. Emma could feel herself changing inside.

Getting cold inside.

Numb inside.

Dead inside.

"My enemies want me dead," Trung said to her as he tapped off his phone, slid it into the left pocket of his black trousers, then smiled his chilling smile at her. "If only they knew that each attempt makes me feel more alive. Like the saying goes, if you are not making new enemies, you are not doing anything of significance with your life."

Emma blinked and looked down. Then she glanced into Trung's yellow eyes. He stared coldly at her face. Dispassionate but smiling. It was like those demon-face masks used in some traditional dramas and dances.

Extracting Emma

"Did you see the newspapers?" Trung asked as his phone vibrated again.

He didn't answer it. It just made his trouser fabric shiver like there was something alive in there, trying desperately to get out.

Emma nodded once. Trung had shoved her roughly on the street after they'd left the fight arena the other night. He'd sent her stumbling against a trashcan. Someone's cell phone camera had captured the moment just as she found her balance. The photograph had Trung in the background, his arm completing the follow-through motion of the violent shove.

It had looked like a staged scene, but Emma had been surprised. Trung cared about appearances, especially in Hong Kong. Something like this was unnecessary drama.

And there was also something about how Trung had looked at her before lashing out. It was not cold and careless. It was hot with emotion.

It could have been the supposed plot to kill Trung. But as far as Emma could tell, the news from Zhu only arrived this morning.

So what had set Trung off that night?

What had made him turn his sharp jaundiced gaze on her, smile that sickening smile, show an uncharacteristic flash of real emotion instead of the cold ruthlessness that was his default state?

"The American Warrior Monk," Trung said just then, studying her face like he was watching for a reaction. "You know him from somewhere?"

He kept his gaze on her, slid his hand into his pocket, pulled out his phone again. Slowly he dragged his gaze down to his phone. Tapped the screen with his big rough thumb. Scrolled slowly as his smile inverted to a scowl.

Emma stared at Trung's massive body in his red silk undershirt. The scowl on his face was real displeasure. Perhaps even something else.

It surprised her. She wasn't sure what was happening. She couldn't understand why he would ask her something like that.

"Of course not," she replied somewhat hurriedly as a flash of heat rose up along her smooth neck to her cheeks before dissipating. "No," she added in a calmer tone. "I don't know him."

Trung looked up from his phone. He stroked his clean shaved cheek with his knuckles. "Zhu contacted our man at the Hong Kong Airport. Matched the American's photograph to inbound travelers." He paused and swallowed. His big Adam's apple moved like a massive pustule beneath his leathery neck-skin. "He was American Military. Special Forces. Navy SEALs. Recently discharged for Bad Conduct."

Emma blinked three times, not sure what to say, not sure what Trung was trying to say.

"The two of you looked at each other," Trung said quietly. "Three seconds of eye contact. That is a long time, Emma. A long time to look into a stranger's eyes."

Emma's heart thumped beneath her breasts. Panic started to rise in her throat.

Did Trung think there was some secret plot involving her and the bearded fighter who was a Navy SEAL?

Was this the end of Emma's private mission?

Should she cut her losses and try to kill Trung now before she never got the chance again?

But if Trung suspected her then she would already be dead, Emma reminded herself when she thought of that poor woman's poisoned eyeballs. There was no fair trial in General Trung's domain. He was the final judge and often the executioner too.

Her heart keep hammering behind her breastbone, but Emma held her peace, held on to the faith that Trung had been a brilliant military strategist and would have figured out that if Emma and the SEAL were working together, certainly she would not have called attention to it by asking Trung to declare the fight a deathmatch.

Trung exhaled slowly as he watched her expression. He stayed silent for almost a full minute. Then he shrugged those big shoulders, grunted from his heavy gut.

"So you will not object if I have the man killed," he said quietly, still watching her eyes for a reaction. "After all, he broke the deathmatch rules by not finishing the fight. He defied my declaration. Created a mess with the bookies and gamblers. He defeated his opponent, but forfeited the fight by granting mercy. By rule, he also forfeited his own life. Do you agree with my judgment?"

Emma gulped. She nodded quickly. Flashed a tight, trembling smile.

"Of course, General," she said, surprised when the words caught in her throat. "Those are the rules, and without rules we are no better than animals, yes?"

Trung's trademark smile flashed back onto his face. But she saw something flash behind those eyes too. The same uncharacteristic flinch that Trung had revealed earlier when he brought up the American fighter who'd looked into Emma's eyes for three long seconds.

Oh my God, Emma thought suddenly.

Was General Trung . . . *jealous?*

She wasn't sure whether to laugh or vomit at the idea. In the three months that she'd been his consort, Trung had shown few signs of normal human emotion.

Of course, having a man killed for looking into your consort's eyes wasn't *normal* by any stretch. Neither was treating a woman as your physical property.

But the knowledge that he could feel jealous was useful, Emma decided. It might make Trung hesitate to kill her during some future showdown. Even a fraction of a second might give her enough of an opening when the time came to end this game.

But that time had not come yet.

She still had to play this game.

Still had to do whatever it took to survive.

She could do it, of course. Emma was not the first woman in history to endure a monster to get what she wanted, and she would not be the last. She would survive for as long as it took.

"You have thirty-six hours," Trung said as he strolled to the teakwood chair where he'd draped his heavy red tunic.

Emma frowned. "For what?"

Trung patted his left jacket pocket, then the right. He slipped his hand inside and pulled out a dark glass vial sealed in a plastic bag.

Trung tossed it at her.

Emma missed the catch, gasping when it fell to the thick carpet with a silent thud.

"Black Ivy resin," he said casually. "Pick it up."

Emma's heart almost stopped. Was he going to make her drink it? Hold her eyelids open and burn her blind?

Why did he even have it with him?

Wasn't it an odd coincidence that Zhu had found the same poison in the supposed plot to kill the great General?

Unless . . .

Trung's smile broadened. He chuckled. "Yes, it was I who placed the vial in that whore's room," he said. "A test to make sure my men are searching properly. A ruse to make sure the people around me can be trusted. These are old tricks, Emma. Every emperor from the great Chinese Dynasties had elaborate practices such as these to flush out traitors." He chuckled again. "And so this is your test now, Emma. Thirty-six hours."

Now that sickening feeling of dread was thick in her throat. "I do not understand," she whispered hoarsely.

"I think you do," Trung said. His gaze flicked down to her bosom, then to her hips, finally back to her face. "I saw how the American looked at you. You will not have a problem getting close to him. He has been fighting mostly in Macau, Zhu tells me. He will likely go back there rather than show his face on the Hong Kong circuit again. Go to Macau and wait for him to show up. Zhu will keep you informed. I have business in Hong Kong, so you will have until I return to finish what you started with your sultry gaze and your delicate whisper." He thought a moment as Emma swayed on her feet. "And since you seemed so very enchanted with the American's mysterious green eyes, I would like you to bring them to me."

"Bring . . . bring what to you, General?"

"His eyes," snapped Trung savagely, letting a flash of rage escape like he couldn't help himself. "When I return to Macau, I want his eyes in the teakwood jewelry box that sits atop the dresser in my penthouse bedroom. I want him watching when I reward you for proving your loyalty, for earning my trust, for showing me who you really are inside."

3

Edge peered inside the blue metal locker at Hong Kong's Hung Hom Train Station. All his stuff was still there, untouched in a neat stack. American passport, Wells Fargo Credit Card, Nevada Drivers License, two thousand U.S. dollars in hundreds, all secured by a thick black band of military-grade rubber. Nothing was missing. That wasn't the problem.

The problem was the black unmarked phone sitting silently on top of his neat stack of personal effects.

"Benson," Edge muttered in disbelief when he put the pieces together. "You sneaky son of a bitch."

Edge placed the passport, cards, and cash into his left cargo flap, then stared at the phone and debated with himself. Finally he exhaled noisily and grabbed it, slammed the blue locker door shut, then strode out of the busy train station.

He walked outside to the line of blue-and-white taxicabs. Got into the backseat of a Toyota Camry and told the driver to head to the airport, to the small side terminal with the short runways where the shuttle flights to Macau and Guangdong took off and landed.

Edge turned on the black phone and waited for it to start up. There were messages waiting for him. They were from a three-digit number, which meant it was a hard-coded redirect that was routed via U.S. military satellites with space-age encryption. Benson might have left the CIA, but he was still connected.

Edge thumbed through the messages. Files and photographs. Three sets of each.

A military-posed photograph of General Trung.

Another military mugshot of a mean-looking fucker named Zhu.

And a passport photograph of Emma Chang.

From an American passport.

Cancelled three years ago.

Edge glanced up at the rearview mirror. The driver's eyes were on the road. He was talking casually on a Bluetooth earpiece. His voice was low, but clearly out of regard for his passenger's comfort rather than secrecy. Edge picked up some words in Cantonese. He was talking to his daughter.

Traffic was moving briskly along the Kowloon Expressway, and Edge slid down against the cool leather seatback and focused on Benson's messages.

There were no instructions. Not even a personal note. Edge still wasn't sure whether Benson gave a damn about General Trung. And Edge certainly wasn't sure what Benson had meant when he claimed Edge had already found his mission, was already being pulled into the game.

But Edge couldn't stop himself from scanning those files. He thought about that strangely intimate look that he and Emma had shared in that crowded, bloody arena. It had lasted maybe three or four seconds, which was actually a pretty long time to look into someone's eyes. It was more than a glance.

It was a connection.

Now anger ripped through Edge's muscled frame when he thought of how she'd leaned close to General Trung and whispered into his ear like she was some sick weirdo who got her thrills from watching men beat each other to death.

Edge wondered if her pussy got all sticky and wet when blood spattered on the dirt of the arena. The thought was vicious and vivid, and again Edge saw Emma in the theater of his mind, imagined those deadly pretty eyes looking up at him as he held her down and showed her what happened to wicked women like her.

The thoughts were savagely dark, and Edge had to blink himself back to the real world. When he looked down at himself, he realized he was peaked like a damn mountain, hard like a concrete wall, uncomfortably bulged, obscenely erect.

Edge shot a glance at the back of the driver's head, then adjusted his package. He hadn't taken a woman to bed in months now. There'd been no shortage of willing participants back in the States, and of course in Macau and Hong Kong he could easily get a release from a squeaky-clean, government certified working girl who was well paid and well treated.

But Edge had been channeling everything into the fights, and so far his energy had been balanced perfectly.

There was a reason folks were calling him the Warrior Monk, and it wasn't just the sage-like beard. Edge was enjoying doing battle with his fists, and it took supreme control, both physical and mental, to win his fights without doing any permanent damage to his opponents.

Though now that discipline had made him *persona non grata* on the Hong Kong underground fight scene. Edge knew the deathmatch rules. You don't show mercy. The fight only ends when one man dies. If you show mercy, it means you've forfeited the fight.

And it means *you* have to die.

Of course, no fighter ever chose that option. It sounded noble, but when it's you or the other guy, nobody chooses to let the other guy live.

So Edge had technically forfeited the fight—and his life along with it.

The only reason he'd gotten away was because this wasn't a deathmatch arena. The gatekeepers weren't prepared to enforce those sorts of brutal rules. The gamblers were too busy arguing with the bookies, trying to change their bets after General Trung changed the rules at the last minute.

And so Edge had finished the fight in eight seconds flat, then barreled his way out through the back alley before anyone realized the other guy was out cold but still alive.

Now Edge felt alive in a different way, like that moment had changed the path he was on. His mind swirled with the jarring coincidences that had started with a silent moment of eye contact with Emma and had led to Edge flipping through CIA files in the backseat of a Hong Kong taxicab.

It felt like something was happening, taking shape in the swirls of space, the torrents of time. Edge couldn't deny that Emma's beauty had struck him in a way that was disconcerting, uncomfortable, maybe even terrifying.

Because Edge had never been entranced by a woman's beauty like that. It wasn't his thing at all. He was not particularly moved by visual beauty.

Maybe it was those early years growing up in Las Vegas, surrounded by strippers from the first day he opened his dark green eyes. Maybe he'd been numbed by those early days of learning the harsh truth that a woman's beauty could be bought and sold like any commodity, was valued in dollars and cents, could be used and abused, rented and then discarded by men with power and money.

Edge's gaze drifted down to a discarded candy wrapper on the black floor mat of the taxicab. It was neon green and bright orange. Kiwi fruit gummies.

It made Edge think of Benson coolly sipping that kiwi drink outside the corner store on Lee Street. He grinned and shook his head. Edge knew he was being drawn in by whatever mystery was brewing.

Edge knew he was *allowing* himself to be drawn in.

He could feel the excitement in his bones.

Taste it in his throat.

Hear it in the way his heart thundered inside his chest.

It was the same feeling Edge got the night before a new mission. That trickle of adrenaline. That intoxicating mix of danger and anticipation. The gambler's rush when you bet it all on red and roll the dice.

Edge dreamily watched the cars float by as the taxicab took the Hansui Bridge to the small island where the airport was located. He glanced down at the black phone again. Started reading about Emma.

Born in East Los Angeles to Chinese parents. Varsity tennis star in high school. Graduated UCLA with honors in Chinese and Economics.

Then moved to Vegas. To work for a non-profit that specialized in supporting sex workers around the world.

Now Edge sat up straight, alertness ripping through his brain. He feverishly read through Emma's work history.

Las Vegas.

Amsterdam.

Tokyo.

Bangkok.

They all had one thing in common.

Legalized prostitution.

Just like Hong Kong.

Just like Macau.

Edge frowned as he went through Emma's details in Benson's files. She'd quit the non-profit almost two years ago, shortly after renouncing her American citizenship and reclaiming her right to be a Chinese national.

It was all very strange. There was no sign that Emma was anti-American or anything like that. No record of her being involved in any radical groups in high school or college. No particular evidence of her being a gung-ho Chinese nationalist either.

Really damn strange. It was almost like Emma care-

Extracting Emma 41

fully planned the entire thing to paint a particular picture of herself.

Or maybe someone did it for her.

And as the thought came to Edge, the phone rang in his hand.

"Benson," said Edge with a sigh. "You saw that I just read your messages. Hell, you're probably watching and listening through this phone. Don't you have anything better to do with your life, old man?"

Benson snickered like a schoolboy on the other end. "Doesn't get better than this, kid," he said cheerfully. "Listen, I've got a call in to Martin Kaiser. Checking to see if Chang is a CIA asset."

Edge did a double take. Martin Kaiser was the Director of the CIA.

Edge swallowed hard, then nodded. The thought that Emma might be an asset had occurred to Edge when he saw how carefully engineered Emma's background seemed to be.

The CIA recruited from a lot of the top U.S. universities. Her Chinese skills would make Emma a good match if the spooks wanted to send someone into Macau or Hong Kong.

Send someone after General Trung.

"Can the CIA fake a renounced American citizenship?" Edge asked quietly, glancing at the taxi driver, then putting down the window glass to let some traffic noise into the cab.

"Sure," said Benson. "But the renunciation appears to be real. And there's nothing about her in the CIA files that I can see. So if she's with the Agency, she's off the books. Totally dark. Or maybe even on her own. Off the reservation."

Edge's frown cut deeper. "You mean like maybe she defected to the Chinese?"

Benson exhaled. "It's possible, but then Kaiser would already know her name. He wouldn't bullshit me and say he needed to check into it." He took another breath. "So my gut tells me she's not with the Agency at all." Benson paused a beat. "But maybe she should be. Not with the CIA per se, but with Darkwater. We could use her skills. You get my drift?"

Edge blinked rapidly as Benson's words registered. He took a moment to think it through. Then he nodded.

"She's been with General Trung for almost a year," Edge said as he stayed close to the whoosh of the airstream coming through the open window. "Three months ago Trung made her his official consort, which means he trusts her. She might know a lot about his gangland operations in Macau and elsewhere. Even his ties to Chinese Intelligence. She's close enough to Trung that she can get to him if that's ever needed. So if she isn't a CIA asset, then maybe it's worth trying to turn her into a Darkwater asset." He paused. "Is this my first Darkwater mission, Benson?"

Benson was silent for a long minute. "Nah. But it might be worth feeling her out," he said finally. "Get a sense of what her motives are. She's worked with prostitutes for years. Maybe she joined Trung to help out some of the trafficked women that are rumored to pass through Macao or even work in some of the General's hotels."

"Or maybe she's just a cold-hearted criminal working her way up to executive management in the flesh trade," Edge offered.

His eyes narrowed when he thought back to that shared moment in the arena. There was something in her eyes that he couldn't quite place. Strange but also familiar. Like déjà vu.

Something else in those eyes too, though. A flash of the glint he and the other guys in SEAL Team Seventeen would get in their own eyes before a fight to the death.

That flash of pure adrenaline, the sickening thrill of darkly intoxicating pleasure.

The same thrill that made Edge love the arena more than sex.

"Maybe," said Benson. He paused a moment. Edge could hear him tapping on another phone. "Hell, she's probably exactly that. Just moving up the ladder. Kaiser just confirmed that Emma Chang is not and never was a CIA asset or agent or anything. She's not on any watchlist. Not any kind of target. And neither is General Trung, for that matter."

"You're kidding," muttered Edge. "I thought everyone in China was a CIA target."

Benson chuckled. "Yeah, well, Trung is mostly involved with managing the Macao gang scene around gambling and prostitution."

"What about the trafficking?" Edge snapped. "Or do we not care about that anymore?"

"He only deals with adult women," Benson said. "And doesn't ship from or to the United States."

Edge sighed. No further explanation needed. Bad shit went on in the world every day, everywhere. The United States wasn't the world's cop anymore.

Was that why Emma cancelled her American passport and worked her way all the way into the General's operation?

Because she knew nobody else was going to do it?

Edge didn't know for sure. Hell, he didn't know a damn thing about her.

But he was curious.

Intrigued.

Interested.

And now he understood that Benson was right.

Edge was being pulled into the game.

Invited into the arena.

Was about to meet his match.

4
MACAU

NO MATCHES.

Emma stared at the screen of the black laptop. It was perched on the blue steel-framed table set against the red wall of her private office on the fortieth floor of the Macau Metropolitan Hotel on Wanbau Street. She glanced at the closed door behind her, then back at the laptop.

She hit ENTER. Ran the search again.

NO MATCHES.

With a sigh Emma pulled the glass slide out of the boxy little device connected to the laptop. The spot of blood she'd carefully dripped onto the glass plate was still bright red and wet. She wiped it off with a clean white tissue. Pressed the tissue against the little pinprick on her left index finger. Then she replaced the slide, deleted the searchbar history, closed the little DNA matching program that had been custom built for Trung's digital record keeping.

"How are we progressing with digitizing all our records?" Trung had asked Zhu the last time the General was in Macau.

Emma had been sitting by the window of Trung's top-floor penthouse, waiting for the caterers to bring the food so she could serve it to the General and Zhu. They always had their weekly briefing over live wriggling shellfish and dark-fermented rice wine. Her ears burned as she awaited Zhu's answer.

"We are ninety two percent done with fingerprinting all the staff and soldiers," Zhu replied in his sharp monotone. "Forty three percent done fingerprinting the women."

Trung had grunted. "What about blood samples and DNA?"

Zhu shifted on his cane stool. "It is a slower process. DNA sequencing takes longer. Also very expensive." He grinned, showing off his small sharp teeth that were so misaligned there were gaping black triangles between the yellowed exposed roots. "Why bother cataloging the DNA of all the whores? It is a waste of time and money, General."

Trung had shaken his head. "Technology is our friend, Zhu. Once the women know we have their DNA in the system, they understand that they can never truly leave the profession. Even if they start new lives in some far off corner of China, they will live in fear that someday their DNA will be entered into the China main-net and we will be able to expose them, find them, punish them if they are runaways." Trung had flashed his broad dragon-like smile. "And remember how DNA works, Zhu. Even if the women themselves stay out of reach, their blood-relatives might not. Children, parents, and siblings will share some percentage of their DNA. We can track a runaway woman's families if we want to. Cast a wide net that will bring back any fish that try to swim away. The fear is enough to command obedience. You have to get inside a woman's mind to control her, Zhu. Learn from me, old friend. Perhaps then you will be ready to take an official consort yourself, maybe even a wife."

Both Zhu and Trung had glanced over at Emma. Thankfully the caterers arrived just then, and Emma hurried off to tame the shellfish before they escaped their fate between Zhu and Trung's teeth.

Emma ran her tongue along the inside of her teeth as she watched the digital clock on the laptop screen. She glanced at the carefully sealed vial of Black-Ivy resin on the table. Looked at the clock again.

Trung was due back from Hong Kong in two days. His instructions had been clear as glass. But his motives still bothered Emma.

She was certain she'd seen emotion in those dead yellow eyes that always looked hard like marbles, the pupils never dilating, like there was no soul inside the man.

Her first impression had been that it was jealousy, but now she told herself it was ridiculous. He'd run that dangerous gaze up and down her curves, implying that Emma was free to use all her assets to bring back the SEAL's eyeballs on a tray like the day's raw entree.

Was Trung testing *that* part of her loyalty to him? After all, it was not unheard of for powerful men to use their consort's bodies as weapons.

It was hard to tell with the man. Emma finally decided

that Trung was simply being his paranoid, suspicious self. After all, the bearded fighter was a former Navy SEAL. He could still be working for the U.S. government.

Zhu had said his name was Thomas Edgerton. Zhu had informed Trung that Edgerton had been discharged for bad conduct. Repeated incidents of insubordination, culminating in a violent attack on one of his superiors that left the man with permanent damage to his face. In their typical paranoid fashion, Trung and Zhu had both decided that it could very well be a CIA ruse to transfer a Special Forces man to undercover dark operations.

Of course, Trung and Zhu were well aware that China was probably crawling with CIA assets—along with agents from every other major intelligence service in the world, from India to Israel, Malaysia to Madagascar. Even if Edgerton was CIA, he might be on a completely unrelated mission, or even on vacation.

After all, there was no indication that Trung was a high priority target for the Americans. Indeed, the fact that Edgerton was travelling under his real name and fighting on the Macau circuits and making a name for himself was an indication that Trung was almost certainly *not* a target.

So although Trung was a paranoid madman when it came to things like this, it was not just about testing Edgerton's motives or testing Emma's loyalty. That was part of it, but not all of it.

It was also about that moment of eye contact between Emma and Edgerton.

A moment that seemed to trigger something in Trung. Maybe something in Emma too.

A strange chill went through Emma as she returned to that moment in her mind.

Edgerton's bearded face was clearer in her memory than it had been in reality. His eyes were brighter in her mind than they'd seemed in that dark, smoky arena. She even thought she could smell Edgerton's scent. Hear the heavy beads of sweat roll down his hard, marbled muscles that shone dark in the golden spotlight of the arena.

The memory was so vivid Emma gasped and pushed her swivel chair away from the desk. She shook her head to clear it. Glanced at that vial of poison to remind herself that reality was out there, not in her swirling mind.

Slowly the real world edged out that green-eyed, bearded beast staring up at her from the spotlight. Emma thought of that dead prostitute who was just a prop in one of Trung's drills. This was no different, she told herself. A game born of Trung's paranoia. An amusement that satisfied whatever was behind the man's unreadable smile.

Which meant there was about a seventy percent chance she would be dead when this was over.

Maybe more, since there was no guarantee that Edgerton would not break Emma's neck himself if she did get close enough to administer a dose of the venom.

For a moment Emma wished she'd used the poison on Trung. After all, if this was the end of the line for her, she should at least try to take the General out with her.

But of course it was too late now. If Trung arrived in Macau and did not see the American's eyeballs sitting on his jewelry box, Emma would die before she ever got close enough to try.

And death wasn't an option.

Not until Emma found what she was looking for.

Which meant she needed more time.

Needed to survive long enough for Zhu's men to get all the women's DNA into the system.

And for Emma to survive, Edgerton needed to die.

No way around it.

No way out of it.

5

"You think I am out of my mind, Zhu?"

General Trung strolled to the balcony seventy floors above downtown Hong Kong. The sun had set and the streetlights looked like strings of pearls lining the bottom of a dark canyon. He glanced at his phone when Zhu did not reply immediately.

"It is not my place to say a thing such as that," Zhu replied from the other end of the line after an uncharacteristically long pause. "All I am saying is that it is better not to poke the bear. Edgerton's dismissal from the Navy looks legitimate. He has been travelling with his real passport, under his real name. There are no unusual deposits to his bank accounts. Even if he is working for some government agency, surely you cannot be a target. He has been openly fighting in Macau and Hong Kong, and has shown zero interest in our organization. No attempt at infiltration. No record of excessive presence in our casinos or brothels."

Trung was silent. Zhu was correct. If it was the CIA, it was an elaborate ruse that was a stretch even for Trung to take seriously, despite priding himself on his healthy levels of paranoia.

"What about Emma?" Trung asked after a breath. "You saw how they looked at each other, Zhu. Like they knew one another." He paused. "Is there a connection between them?"

Zhu exhaled through his teeth, making a disharmonious whistling noise, like wind passing through disjointed slats of rotting wood.

"Well," he said. "Emma spent four years in Las Vegas. Edgerton was born in Las Vegas. But the timelines do not match up. Edgerton left when he was thirteen. Emma was still a pre-teen in Los Angeles at the time. There is no evidence their paths ever crossed, General."

Trung sighed. "So I am imagining it? Seeing things that do not exist?"

"Perhaps you are seeing things *before* they exist, General."

"That is the art of war," said Trung. "Know what your enemy will do before he knows it himself."

"What I mean is that you are now sending Emma to Edgerton," said Zhu. "Perhaps there was never any connection between them. But now you have *created* the connection, General. Set events in motion. Poked the bear. There are other ways to test Emma, if you so desire. You could have her slit one of her precious whore's throats in front of you."

Trung exhaled hard. Zhu was correct again. Trung respected a man who dared to disagree with him.

Trung prided himself not just on his paranoia but also

his self-awareness. He understood that a great General can sometimes get trapped in an echo chamber, surround himself with spineless sycophants telling him only what he wishes to hear. It was why Zhu was valuable. Priceless, even.

Trung paced on the open balcony in his red silk undershirt. The wind was strong, but the day's heat and humidity was still heavy in the air.

Trung could smell the sweat from his armpits. Silk was not supposed to trap moisture to the point where it would stink. Trung felt a flash of anger as he imagined his tailor stealing from him by weaving polyester into the silk. Perhaps Trung would arrange a little test for the wrinkled old tailor from Shanghai someday.

But not today. Today Trung needed to think about this Emma situation. He had to admit that he'd been uncharacteristically affected when he saw the way she and Edgerton had looked into one another's eyes like they were on a movie billboard outside the Macau Bijou theater.

In fact the entire scene had been theatrical, Trung thought. The fight at the arena. The whisper from Emma to change the rules. The vicious but controlled way Edgerton put down his opponent without cracking the man's skull or breaking his neck, which surely the SEAL could have done.

Yes, Edgerton had broken the deathmatch rules, but this was Hong Kong, not Macau. Trung was not responsible for enforcing such rules outside of Chinese controlled arenas in Macau. Trung's reputation gave him considerable power in Hong Kong, of course, but it was not his domain, not his duty, not his problem.

So then the problem was Emma, Trung conceded as a shadow of embarrassed rage passed behind his savage yellow eyes. There was something about her that made him lash out in this uncharacteristic way that even Zhu had noticed.

Zhu breathed into the phone as Trung paced in the hot night.

"Just let it go, General," Zhu hissed. "Let Edgerton go on his way. I do not believe he is a threat, so let us not turn him into a threat. General, listen, I will handle Edgerton our way if any intelligence indicates he is not just a disgraced ex-SEAL taking out his frustration on the fighters of Macau and Hong Kong. And besides, Emma is too useful to send to a pointless death. She is good with the women. Even the Russians have taken note of how conditions in our brothels have improved since Emma arrived. Call it off, General. There is no shame in retreat when the strategy calls for it."

Trung stepped back into the air-conditioned room of the hotel suite. He slid the heavy glass doors of the balcony shut behind him.

The room smelled of oyster sauce and dried squid. He sniffed his fingers, then walked to the bar and poured himself a cup of dark rice-wine.

"You think Edgerton will kill her?" Trung asked as he held the tiny cup between his thumb and index finger, took a delicate sip, then drained the cup and smacked his lips.

Zhu made a rasping sound that Trung recognized as a

sigh. "Perhaps. But more likely he will catch her in the act of trying to poison him. Certainly he will want to know more. Even if she says nothing, it is common knowledge that Emma Chang is the consort of General Trung. Perhaps Edgerton will take it personally. Perhaps he comes after you. Naturally he will not get to you. Naturally he will die by my hand. But things could get messy, General. Why unnecessarily kill a former American Navy SEAL if there is no urgent need, if we are not threatened by the man? It might provoke retaliation from American agents or freelancers. It might complicate our ties with the Ministry of State Security on the Mainland." One more sigh from Zhu. Trung could almost hear the man shrugging his wiry shoulders. "And then of course we will need to kill Emma anyway, because she will have failed to do what you asked. So messy. So unnecessary. I advise immediate retraction of orders. Strategic retreat is the optimal solution, General."

Trung took a slow breath. Zhu's logic was impeccable. He was a solid strategist, a crafty tactician. Why start a chain of events that had very little upside and much downside? The best outcome would be that Emma weaseled her way past Edgerton's defenses, poisoned the man to death, and returned to Trung like the loyal consort she was. Maybe she would fuck Edgerton and then kill him. Maybe just fuck the Edgerton and fail to kill him. Was either such an enticing outcome?

Maybe, came the answer from some dark place inside Trung.

The answer was accompanied by a stab of emotion. A streak of arousal. It took the General by surprise.

He placed his left hand over his heavy pectorals and cocked his thick neck to the left.

Why did the idea give him such a thrill?

Why did the thought of Emma seducing that SEAL give Trung an erection that made him dizzy with lust, giddy with arousal?

Trung closed his eyes and thought of Emma's big round bottom split down the middle by that turquoise thong, his white semen flowing lazily down her lower back like the Yangtze River in summer. The sight of a woman with her rump obediently raised and her feet tight together had always been enough for him to get the quick release that he knew was important to keep a man's head clear.

Except now his head was anything but clear. Now he was imagining taking Emma the way a man takes a woman. Emptying himself into her instead of onto her.

The need startled Trung, it was so unusual. Trung had no patience for love-making in any traditional way. He had never married. He had never wanted to be married. His father had died in Mao's Army before marrying Trung's mother. She was already pregnant with Trung, and so no other man in the village would take her as a bride.

So Trung's mother never married. They lived in a two-room hut on the outskirts of a village so small it did not even have a name. The village was not far from a Chinese Army outpost, and so Trung's mother had taken up the most ancient of professions, available to any able-bodied woman.

She did have three more children. Perhaps they were

Extracting Emma

from the same father, perhaps they each had many fathers. All were girls.

Trung's step-sisters never married either. They were born into the profession. It was steady work. It kept the family alive.

It was why Trung never thought of whoring as unnatural or shameful. Yes, he never saw women as anything other than whores. But it was not a moral judgment in Trung's mind. Boys were soldiers. Girls were whores. That was the division of labor by gender.

Indeed, all of humankind revolved around the twin desires of sex and violence. All other desires and emotions boiled down to those two primary drives.

It was easy to see with the animals, Trung thought. Harder sometimes with humans, because most humans tried to pretend that a man shouldn't kill to get what he wanted and a woman shouldn't spread her legs to get what she wanted.

Trung despised that sort of hypocrisy. And it was why he enjoyed the trafficking business. He loved to watch the fake-horror on the young women's faces when they realized they weren't going to be teaching Mandarin in Macau or selling handbags in Hanoi like the recruiters promised.

He savored their expressions as they were made to understand that their most prized asset was between their trembling skinny legs, that their most valuable skill was to maximize the market value of that slippery little slit.

Yes, he had to lock them up and hold them down sometimes to show them the truth about how the world worked, but he was setting them free in a way, was he not? Returning them to nature. Showing them that sex and violence were the twin engines that kept the universe chugging along.

Trung poured more wine and relaxed on the cream sofa which was set flush against the dark green wall. He put his boots up on the teakwood coffee table and stared up at the ceiling. Zhu was still on the other end of the line, awaiting his General's decision.

Trung felt the rice-wine burn its way down his throat to his heart. He let his mind relax into a meditative state.

He had learned to do it during China's campaign in Tibet. One of the Buddhist warrior monks in the Tibetan Himalayas had shown Trung how to gaze inward and relax his focus so that the boundary between himself and the universe blurred. Trung had thanked the monk, then beheaded him and burned the monastery.

Now he thought of that American Warrior Monk looking into Emma's eyes. Certainly something about that moment had affected Trung in an unexpected way.

But it was not just jealousy.

It was not pure possessiveness.

It was the thrill of competition.

Suddenly Trung stood from the sofa, excitement burning through his bulk. He was a student of evolutionary history. He knew that in many ancient tribes the women were shared commodities, available to all men in the tribe.

It was not sexual slavery, but a way of tightening the bonds within the tribe. It was in the women's interests as much as it was the men's.

Perhaps even more so in those brutal, violent days

Extracting Emma

when a man's protection mattered. After all, if every man in the village had spilled his seed inside a woman, her children were said to have many fathers. It was a profoundly uniting arrangement that ensured protection for all women and children because each man considered every woman his wife, every child his own.

But of course this did not truly eliminate sexual competition. The competition to pass on your genes over another man's essence was instinctive, built-in, unstoppable.

And so in tribes where men shared the women, sexual competition was driven underground, into the shadows, into the darkness.

Those competitive battles were now fought within a woman's womb.

Which man's seed would prevail?

Which man's swimmers would arrive at the far shore first?

Which man's soldiers would capture the high ground and plant his nation's flag?

It was the ultimate test of a man's vitality, his strength, his power, was it not?

And it explained the instinctive arousal that Trung felt right now.

After all, evolution might have favored the men who got most aroused and erect when they knew there was competition in the air, a fight brewing in the night, a struggle for the prize.

Yes, evolution indeed might have favored the men able to spurt their seed deepest into the hidden folds of a shared woman's valley.

Was that why Trung was feeling this intoxicating mix

of both possessive rage and dark arousal at the thought of Emma being taken by a worthy competitor, then handed back to him to compete for the ultimate prize of nature?

Was Trung being drawn into a different sort of battle, fought on a different sort of battlefield?

Trung had read of such matters, but had dismissed them as academic nonsense. Still, he had spent his entire life around prostitutes and the men who paid dearly for them. Trung could not deny that while virgins were supposed to be the ultimate prize, in secret many men preferred well-fucked whores to clueless innocents.

And so did General Trung.

Indeed, nothing about a virgin was interesting to Trung. He'd gotten hints of his preferences in the early days, watching his step-sisters come of age in the two-room hut in his village south of the Yangtze river.

For years he'd watched them bathe nude in the river or squat bare-bottomed thrice a day in the grass. Trung had witnessed all of that without experiencing even the hint of sexual arousal.

It was only when their mother began to rent them out to the Chinese soldiers who came down from the Kwangchow Fort that Trung felt his arousal suddenly ratchet up to frightening levels as he watched his step-sisters learn to ply their trade.

He'd watch from between the slats of the hut walls, his throbbing need firmly in his right hand, that manic arousal surging through his rapidly developing muscles.

This was the same feeling, Trung realized as he blinked three times and almost gasped out loud.

Yes, that feeling he'd gotten of possessiveness mixed with arousal back then was similar to what Trung was feeling now. It was a long forgotten feeling, but of such depth and power that Trung could not resist it.

Trung was worried now. He knew it was dangerous to follow through on something this powerful.

A great man's sexual energy was like a blade that could cut both ways. He'd carefully channeled that power into violence for years, making sure to expel his seed regularly and with little fanfare or indulgence.

But to proceed along this path was indulgent at best, more likely reckless, perhaps even suicidal.

You should listen to Zhu, Trung told himself as he stared at the spider-shaped brass light fixture on the ceiling. You are not thinking with a cool head. Something has surfaced from long ago. You do not remember those early days clearly, and it could be a blind spot that will lead to your destruction. Who knows precisely what happened in that little hut forty years ago. Memories take on new lives in the recesses of a man's mind. Who knows precisely what you saw, what you heard, what you smelled, what you felt.

Now Trung felt a sharp pain at the back of his head, and he winced. Blood throbbed in his temples. His cock was still hard. His balls felt heavy.

He wondered if he was coming apart as his age progressed. They said a woman hears her clock ticking louder as the years roll on. Perhaps it was the same with a man.

Perhaps it was Trung's destiny to fight this ancient

battle for the right to seed a woman, pass on his line, then fade away like a great soldier.

Perhaps it was Trung's fate to fight this American warrior in the halls of a woman's heart, the coliseum of her cunt, the stadium of her soul.

Trung almost howled with laughter. The thoughts were insane. So insane that Trung could not speak them out loud. Zhu might decide it was time to retire the old General, put the old bull out to pasture, let him chase the dragons in his mind.

But the imagery in Trung's mind right now was too vivid to suppress. The excitement too overwhelming to control. The draw too irresistible to ignore.

He could hear the call like a battle cry that rang through the millennia.

It was a battle cry that Trung could not silence.

A challenge he could not turn from.

A fight he could not run from.

And so Trung settled back on the sofa, put his feet back on the coffee table, leaned his big head on the cushion and stared up at the brass spider on the ceiling.

"All right, Zhu," Trung said softly into the phone. "New orders. Go to Emma's suite in Macau. Take back the poison from her." He paused, took a breath, let it out slowly. "And tell her I want him brought here alive."

Zhu paused on the other end. "I do not understand," he said. "If you want the American alive, I can have him brought to you within hours. He is already on his way to Macau. I can have a man meet him at the airport,

Extracting Emma 63

perhaps simply invite him to one of our hotels without any need for Emma to get involved."

Trung was quiet as he thought. The blood thundered in his head. His heart pumped like he was transforming into that Chinese mythical dragon with ten heads and testicles the size of the sun. He could feel him passing some threshold, like he was making a choice that would change the trajectory of space and time.

But he couldn't stop himself. He had never been the sort of General who stayed in his bunker. He lived to fight on the battlefield. He couldn't turn back now.

He crossed the threshold. Stepped into the arena. Issued the order.

Made his choice.

"I want Emma to do it," Trung said with the calmness of that Tibetan monk who knew he was about to lose his head. "Tell her to use any methods at her disposal. She is to return to my Macau Penthouse with Edgerton by her side, or not return at all."

6

Edge's return flight to Macau was turbulent and the landing was bumpy. He glared at the pilots as he exited the plane. They wore mirrored Aviator sunglasses even though they'd taken off after sunset. The shades looked like Ray Bans, but upon inspecting the logo Edge noted they were in fact Roy Bons. This was the discount airline. The restroom cost three Hong Kong dollars. You had to pay the three bucks in advance.

The Macau airport reminded Edge of Vegas International. The only difference was the digital slot machines were all in Chinese. The bulk of tourists were from Mainland China, but Macau was once a Portuguese colony, and there was steady traffic from Europe as well.

Edge nodded instinctively at three uniformed Chinese PLA soldiers in battledress. They carried no weapons and were clearly on furlough. They grinned at him and nodded earnestly. Nodding was not a common Chinese greeting. They seemed excited to be able to show off their knowledge of western manners. They were young men. Their faces were smooth and fresh. They clearly hadn't seen combat.

Edge silently hoped they never would see combat. Any

major military expedition by the Chinese would somehow involve the United States, Edge knew. No General on either side of that great divide wanted to see that happen. A commander's directive was to save lives, not sacrifice them.

Besides, Edge had no problem with the Chinese. He was very much a live and let live guy, despite the number of kills he'd notched up in ten years of SEAL missions.

Edge accepted that violence was part of the world, had always been part of the world and always would be. He accepted it was part of him too. Accepted it and loved it.

But that didn't mean he was a damn psychopath. He just happened to accept that every human being walking around today had ancestors who'd had to fight for their lives as part of a day's work. Living in safety and comfort was a pretty new development.

New enough that most people on earth still didn't have that luxury.

Edge's face tightened as he thought back to what he'd read about General Trung's trafficking business. Benson was right in that the good General didn't deal in underage girls.

But Edge suspected that was mostly a business decision, not Trung taking a moral stand or something honorable like that. Trafficking kids puts you on every human rights watchlist, every international agency's radar, every nation's hit-list. Trung was still connected to the Chinese Communist Party after years in the PLA. He couldn't go too far off the reservation without being reined in, perhaps even put down.

And that was probably why nobody had hunted Edge

down after that scene at the arena. It was off Trung's reservation. In Macau's underground fight circuit the punishment would be death, and if Edge had pulled that crap in an arena within Trung's domain, certainly the General would have enforced the law.

But Hong Kong was technically outside General Trung's territory according to Benson's files. Which meant Trung wasn't compelled to enforce the rules. And perhaps he'd run a check on Edge and realized he was ex-Teams. A cautious strategist would have chosen to let sleeping dogs lie, let hibernating bears stay unpoked. Killing a former Navy man wouldn't be good for business.

Wouldn't be easy either, Edge thought with a tight smile as he strolled to a refreshment counter and ordered a chilled ice coffee. He waited while the barwoman blended the black coffee and white condensed milk into a creamy mixture of sticky sweetness. Then he quickly slurped it down, wondering what his buddy Fox would say if he saw Edge with a wildman's beard slurping a smoothie through a red-striped straw.

"Wouldn't have pegged you as a teenage Korean girl with a Hello Kitty obsession," came a woman's voice from behind him. The accent was American, with the faintest hint of Asian inflection. "But based on your choice of smoothie, it's the only reasonable conclusion."

Edge turned slowly, the empty smoothie cup still in his right hand, condensed milk and sweet cream on his beard-framed lips.

It was Emma Chang, but not the Emma Chang who'd

Extracting Emma

been in that lotus-pattern fitted dress with the oriental collar.

This version of Emma was in hip-hugging blue jeans buttoned above her belly-button. She wore a sleeveless black blouse with a halter-collar that showed zero cleavage.

It was high-quality silk. Edge could see the outline of her black bra beneath the cloth. It was perhaps the most conservative bra ever designed.

But the blouse was tailored perfectly. Tucked into her jeans, it showed off her deadly hourglass. Edge felt his breath catch in his throat.

He coughed a little from the sickeningly sweet residue of his drink. Glanced at the red-and-white candy-cane themed straw. Shrugged and tossed the cup into a open-mouthed brown plastic trash can.

He was about to snap out a response, but managed to catch himself. He swept his gaze up and down the busy main drag of the airport. Glanced past Emma towards one of the flight gates. There was no scheduled departure at the gate, so the waiting area was mostly empty.

But not entirely empty. Edge studied the dozing man at the end of a row of blaze orange plastic seats. He glanced at the kid with a hoodie slouched down and staring at a phone screen the size of a billboard. Then listened hard to see if the middle-aged woman with a Bluetooth headset was having a real conversation.

She was. Edge relaxed a little. Emma was alone, best he could tell.

Alone for now, Edge told himself as his sharp mind

worked through scenarios where there was a carload of Trung's thugs in a panel van outside baggage claim waiting for his dumb ass.

Maybe Edge had misjudged the situation. Maybe he was in more danger than he thought.

Yeah, maybe Trung had decided to enforce those rules after all, especially now that Edge had shown up in Macao. Perhaps Trung saw it as an insult. Maybe a challenge.

Either way, Edge needed to stay sharp. Wary. Alert.

There were a hundred ways to get rid of a dead body in this part of the world. So much open ocean. So many little islands. The General could do it and nobody would ever know for sure. Even Fox and the guys might never be able to put the pieces together. As they say, no body, no crime.

But most of all, Edge reminded himself that this woman was not his damn friend.

She was a Chinese criminal's consort three days ago and now she was an all-American girl-next-door in blue jeans and a damn training bra?

Nah.

She was a chameleon.

A shapeshifter.

A trickster.

Be careful, Edge, he warned himself. Watch your step. Do not relax for one damn second around this woman.

"Relax, will you," said Emma with a sideways smile that looked genuine and perhaps even a little cute. Emma stood right where she was like she'd decided getting too close to his body might be dangerous. Maybe for both of them. "The General just wants to talk to you. It's just an invitation. No big deal."

"Yeah, I think we have different definitions of what's a big deal and what isn't," Edge drawled. "Like turning a regular fight into a deathmatch."

He kept his hands loose by his sides, feet slightly apart, just in case something unexpected showed up and he needed to fight his way out of here.

He measured the space between them. Decided he could get to her in two strides, slip his arm around her waist, pull her hard against his body, use her as a human shield in the low-but-not-zero chance this was a public hit.

Emma blinked twice quickly. She glanced down, swallowed, then looked back up at him. There was faint blush on her cheeks.

She touched her jet black hair, then nodded once and shrugged her shoulders. Edge couldn't help notice how her wonderfully heavy breasts moved as she shrugged.

"The fight the other night," she said, blinking twice more, the blush brightening. "I apologize. I don't know what came over me. I . . . I'm sorry. Don't know what else to say, really." She shrugged again, touched her forehead, rubbed her elbow like she really was affected.

You can fake a lot of things, but it's pretty hard to make yourself blush like that, Edge noted.

Also, he was somewhat taken aback by her blatant honesty. After all, no way Edge could have heard what she whispered into Trung's ear up on that arena balcony. She could have pretended like she didn't know what

Edge was talking about. She could have said she had nothing to do with declaring that fight a deathmatch. She could have glared at him, tried to make him feel like an asshole for insinuating that she was anything other than a well-behaved woman who didn't enjoy watching men beat each other to death.

But Emma hadn't done any of that. She just came right out and admitted she'd done it.

More than that, she admitted she couldn't quite explain *why* she'd done it.

And that made Edge perk up and pay attention.

There was something about this woman, he realized. Something that tugged at a place inside him. Urged him to take a step closer.

Edge took that step and stopped. Now he was one long stride away from her. There was no place for passers-by to walk between them.

Edge looked down into her eyes. They were luminous red-brown and iridescent like drops of maple syrup in the sunlight. Edge blinked and swallowed again. His throat felt dry. His vision was vivid.

In fact all Edge's senses were vivid right then. He heard the swish of her long straight hair against her silk-covered shoulders. He could smell the fragrance of her shampoo. It was green apple, fresh from the orchard just like she was fresh from the shower.

Emma curled a strand of hair around her ear, and Edge caught a hint of her scent from beneath her bare arms. Macau nights were warm, but the airport was air-conditioned and dry. If she was perspiring, it wasn't from the outside heat.

Extracting Emma

"Why does Trung want to see me?" Edge asked finally.

He was not sure how much time had passed. Edge was feeling vaguely out of sorts, slightly off balance from being this close to Emma.

She was very beautiful, he thought. And the forthright admission about the deathmatch had gotten him to let down his defenses a bit.

She seemed so genuine. So real. Like even though this woman was a walking talking smiling mystery, she was also totally open in a way he could feel in his heart.

Hell, she might be that way with everyone she meets, Edge warned himself.

He'd grown up with women who knew how to get a man's guard down. The best ones had natural talent perfected by practice.

Just like any elite professional, a great woman of the night learns how to make any man feel perfectly at ease, makes him think only he can open her up, make her bare her soul, reveal her secrets.

Edge had grown up around strippers and prostitutes. He knew that the best of them loved their work, took it as seriously as a great artist takes her craft, a great sniper puts in the hours, a great singer keeps extending her range.

Of course, Edge wasn't sure exactly what Emma was to General Trung. Consort wasn't the same thing as a lover, wasn't quite a prostitute either.

But the real question Edge needed to answer wasn't *what*.

It was *why*.

"I don't know why the General wants to see you,"

said Emma. She blinked again, but without blushing this time. She'd blinked with purpose. To hide something behind those secretive red-brown eyes. "It is unusual, I will admit."

Edge frowned again at how forthright she was being. Like she was on his side. Or at least pretending to be on his side.

"Does he want me dead?" Edge asked, deciding to match her forthrightness with his own bluntness. It was his preferred method anyway. None of those CIA mind-games for him.

Emma shrugged again. She didn't say anything.

She was smart. And she was loyal. She wasn't going to admit that General Trung was the sort of man who had people killed.

Edge stroked his beard, nodded grudgingly. He felt a stab of something inside him. Like some part of him was ruffled that Emma had a shred of loyalty to a man like Trung.

"All right," Edge suddenly said. He shrugged. "Let's go."

Emma fluttered her eyelids like she wasn't sure how to react. Edge realized she wasn't completely prepared for this meeting. Perhaps there'd been some last minute changes to her orders. Maybe she'd been expecting him to say no.

Even hoping he'd say no. Edge thought back to what he'd read about her in Benson's files. She'd clearly *wanted* to get close to General Trung. But it was also possible she wanted to get away from him now.

Was she sending him a message? Asking for help without saying the words?

Had she come here on her own?

But then why offer the invitation?

Edge couldn't read it clearly.

Maybe he should just ask, he thought.

He let his gaze move over every inch of Emma. He was looking for any sign that she was wired for sound. General Trung might have access to Chinese military high-tech stuff that even the Department of Defense hadn't heard of yet. After all, half the shit the American Military used these days came from China. Made sense they'd keep the best stuff for themselves.

Edge's visual search turned up nothing. He wouldn't have minded patting her down slowly and carefully. Maybe a strip search and careful inspection of the secret spaces where a woman kept things hidden. Edge had to close his eyes tight for a long hard blink to stop his thoughts from going where his body wanted them to go.

"Do you need help?" he said softly, deciding to take the chance that General Trung wasn't listening somehow, his gnarled finger on the button of some kind of body-bomb that would cause Emma's heart to explode and kill them both.

Color rushed to Emma's face again. This time even her ears turned red. Edge could feel the tension rip through her curves even though she barely moved on her feet.

She was quiet for a moment. Then she shook her head firmly. Looked at him directly. Smiled politely. Glanced down at the carpeted floor.

"No, thank you," she said, still looking away from his eyes. Then she glanced up. "Do you?" she asked brightly.

Edge cracked a sideways grin. "Why the hell would *I* need help?"

Emma shrugged. "You received a Bad Conduct Discharge from the Navy. You're fighting underground arenas in Macau. Also, you haven't visited a barber in perhaps a thousand years. There could be all sorts of prehistoric creatures growing in that forest of a beard."

Edge couldn't hold back a laugh. Emma's maple eyes were dancing as she smiled up at him. There were the tiniest traces of lines in the makeup beneath those eyes.

Not from age but from hours of focused concentration. This woman had something going on behind those eyes. Something that played over and over again. Some kind of personal mission.

"Can't be a Warrior Monk without the beard," Edge finally said, his own eyes smiling down at her as the traffic of passengers flowed around them like water around two immovable rocks. "Anyway, thought I'd ask since you sound American and maybe you're in over your head with whatever this is."

"I'm no longer American," Emma said, sidestepping the comment about being in over her head.

"I know," said Edge before he could stop himself.

He winced inwardly as Emma frowned at him. She didn't say anything. Didn't ask him how he knew. Maybe she didn't want to know.

"I mean I figured, since no way Trung would hire an American citizen," Edge said, wondering if he was dig-

Extracting Emma

ging himself deeper, if Emma was a master interrogator without even knowing it.

"What makes you think I work for the General?"

Edge felt that stab of emotion again. Possessive emotion. Totally illogical. Absolutely unjustified.

But dangerously powerful.

"Don't you?" Edge said, not sure if his tone betrayed the hopefulness inside.

Emma smiled. She nodded once. "A year ago I was hired to manage some parts of his business, yes. Then three months ago the General took me as his official consort."

That possessiveness shot through Edge's chest and up his throat until it almost throttled him. He had to fight it back down like it was one of those prehistoric beasts that Emma had mentioned.

He forced himself to nod stiffly, pretend like it didn't shock him, didn't surprise him.

Pretend like it didn't matter to him.

"Does that bother you?" she asked softly as they stood there amidst the everflowing stream of nameless and faceless people.

"Doesn't it bother *you*?" Edge said, feeling the blood burning in his cheeks. He winced and shook his head quickly. "That didn't come out right. I didn't mean to imply there's anything wrong with being a consort or even a . . ."

"A whore?" Emma said when Edge trailed off. She raised both eyebrows but kept her tone casual and nonchalant.

Edge chuckled once and shook his head quickly. "Hey, forget I said anything. None of my business. Anyway, shall we go meet Trung, see if he wants to kill me for not killing that guy in Hong Kong?"

Emma smiled. Then her eyebrows twitched like she was restraining a frown.

"The General won't be back until tomorrow evening," she said, letting that frown come through on her smooth brow. "Where are you staying?"

Edge shrugged. "You got any recommendations? You must know the hotels pretty well."

He winced inwardly again, wondering if she'd think he was implying something he wasn't.

Emma was quiet a beat. She wasn't insulted. She was thinking. Debating. Deciding.

Once again Edge got the sense that this wasn't a well thought out plan. That either Emma got pulled into it suddenly or her orders changed at the last minute.

Also, why would Trung send her when he wasn't even back in town yet?

None of this made sense to Edge. He thought of what Benson had told him about feeling her out to see if she could be useful as an asset to Darkwater.

It wasn't really a *mission*, Benson had remarked off-handedly when they'd spoken before Edge boarded his flight from Hong Kong. Edge could take it or leave it, Benson had said. After all, Edge didn't work for Darkwater yet.

Now Edge wondered if the best course of action would be to turn around and just walk away from this whole damn situation. He had no responsibility here. There was no duty involved.

He had some money, and his U.S. passport still got him into pretty much any country in the damn world without a visa. There was nothing keeping him in the Far East. No reason he should get himself involved in something that was murky at best, deadly at worst.

Anyway, he'd asked Emma if she needed help and she'd clearly said no. Hell, she wasn't even an American citizen anymore. She'd given it up by choice. She'd started working for Trung by choice.

And she was also fucking him by choice.

Now that possessive flame almost made Edge explode like that body-bomb was inside his own damn chest. He clenched both fists, tightened his jaw until his teeth squeaked against each other, blinked away the red cloud invading the corners of his vision.

It made no damn sense that he was feeling this way, but Edge knew better than to turn his back on instinct this raw, energy this primal, power this hot.

Like any elite warrior he understood that the body had an intelligence that was profound and powerful. It was just a different sort of intelligence than the kind that produced detailed battle plans and tactical logistics.

Yeah, Edge knew the body's intelligence was fine-tuned to the task of survival. And survival boiled down to two basic things.

Two fundamental forces. Two primal impulses.

Sex and violence.

The impulse to fight.

The need to fuck.

But it wasn't a dumb, blind intelligence that drove a man towards those things. You don't just fight anything that looks at you funny. You don't just fuck anything that moves.

No, you pick your battles.

And you pick your mate.

Now slowly that burst of possessive fire settled down to a steady simmer. Edge frowned and blinked as he tried to make sense of what he was feeling.

He looked into Emma's eyes, his frown deepening as he tried to shake the overpowering feeling like they'd both been drawn to this one point in space and time by all the tiny choices they'd made over the years.

Choices totally unconnected in any logical sense, but somehow profoundly connected in this strange frame of mind that was messing with Edge's thoughts and vision, making things feel both vividly clear and sickeningly surreal.

After all, neither of them would be in this spot right now if Edge hadn't broken that CIA guy's jaw.

Just like neither of them would be here right now if Emma hadn't whispered those words to Trung up on that balcony above the arena.

And the fucked up thing was that both those choices were made without any planning or thought.

The mind wasn't involved at all.

It was instinct, the primal intelligence that lives within the body.

The kind of raw nameless energy that leads whales to

swim a thousand miles to rendezvous with their mates, leads every animal on a quest into the unknown, a search for something that lies at the core of life in the world of flesh and blood.

Or maybe even beyond the world of flesh and blood.

"You have many choices," came Emma's voice through the roar of blood in Edge's ears. "About the hotels, I mean. Why don't you stay at the Macau Metropolitan? It will make the meeting easier when the General returns. He uses the top two floors as his office and residence."

Edge blinked himself back to reality. He knew the Metropolitan. It was lavish like the best Vegas had to offer.

He wondered whether Emma lived on the top two floors with Trung. He supposed she did, given that she was his consort.

"The suite will be complimentary, of course," Emma said. "The General would insist on it."

"I can pay my way," said Edge gruffly.

Edge swallowed thickly. His eyes burned. He was wired from the coffee, hopped up on the sugar. Edge could stay calm like a clam while fighting for his life underwater without oxygen. But right now each mention of Trung made it hard to breathe. Each time she called him *General* like he was some mythical figure made Edge's head throb. Each thought of Emma being touched by that massive monster made Edge's blood boil.

He was turning into someone he didn't recognize. Jealousy was alien to Edge. Possessiveness was weakness in his opinion. Every person owned his or her body and sexuality. Nobody had the right to claim *possession* of another person in that way.

At least that's what Edge had always believed.

Until suddenly he didn't believe it anymore.

Not when he wanted to possess Emma in the most dangerous way.

Not when he wanted to destroy anyone else who tried to dispute his claim.

Maybe he'd been punched in the head a couple times too many.

But he wasn't stepping out of this arena.

He was going to take this fight to the General.

Because he knew what he was fighting for.

Even though he couldn't explain why.

7

Why did he agree so easily, Emma wondered as she walked briskly with Edge towards the line of green-and-white taxicabs silently waiting in the hot Macau night.

Emma had arrived at the airport in one of the hotel limousines, but had sent it away, saying she'd call if she needed it. She wasn't certain how things with Edge would play out.

Zhu's instructions had been puzzling. She couldn't understand what game Trung was playing. Wasn't certain how Edge would react.

She'd decided it would be better if none of Trung's men were around. Violence tended to escalate quickly with some of Trung's foot-soldiers. Most of them did not have real military training. They were not disciplined like Trung and Zhu.

Emma had been enormously relieved when Zhu took the vial of poison from where it had been sitting ominously on her dark wood table near the red-curtained window of the suite she used as her private office. But then the relief had faded when Zhu relayed her new orders, direct from the General's mouth. Word for word, like Zhu always did it.

Return with Edgerton, or do not return at all.

The orders had been concise, but by no means clear. Zhu had refused to explain. It wasn't his place to interpret the General's instructions.

Emma had looked into Zhu's black-pearl eyes and nodded once, keeping her head slightly bowed but not all the way. She hadn't forgotten how Zhu had spat on her bare breasts that first day. For some reason that single act bothered her more than the times Trung had spat his seed on her lower back and raised butt.

Emma hadn't understood exactly why that was the case, but that wasn't the time for introspective contemplation about Freudian psychology. Her current problem was simple reading-comprehension, something she'd aced on the SATs.

Return with Edgerton. Or do not return at all.

Taking away the poison meant that Trung wanted Edgerton alive. That was clear enough. But the rest was disconcertingly open-ended.

Zhu had said the General wanted her to do it alone, by any means necessary. That meant no force or coercion, since Emma obviously couldn't forcibly do a darned thing to a former Navy SEAL with muscles like Zeus and a beard to match.

And Trung had never issued her a weapon of any kind. Certainly not a gun. Trung didn't trust anyone but Zhu to be armed within thirty feet of him.

Which meant that when Trung said "any means necessary," he meant what he had once described to Emma as a woman's most powerful weapon, if only she learned how to use it.

Extracting Emma

Emma felt a tingle between her legs as she bent her body forward to pull open the taxi door for Edge. Opening doors for men was just habit for her now.

But she got there too late. Her fingers closed on Edge's big hand. She drew back immediately, like the touch had shocked her.

"You're Trung's consort, not mine," he said somewhat gruffly. "I can get the door."

She nodded quickly, touching her hair and stepping back as Edge pulled open the door. She waited for him to get in, then felt that embarrassingly obvious blush come back to her cheeks when she saw him hold the door and gesture with his head for her to get in first.

"Thank you," she said softly, not sure why the gesture made her heart thump like that. Holding a car door open for a woman was still reasonably common in most of the Western world, even though Emma figured it was only a matter of time before someone passed a law cancelling any such oppressive, repressive, despicable behavior. "But you don't need to do that."

"Well, I *am* doing that," said Edge coolly. "So after you, Ma'am."

He stood holding the door with an almost theatrical air. Like a footman in some Victorian romance novel.

Except he was in military-style cargo pants and a tight black tee shirt with bulging muscles and crusted-over cuts and half-healed bruises and a beard that would make Bigfoot run for the hills.

"OK," she said, realizing that other passengers had already gotten into the next two taxis in line and the drivers were all getting impatient.

She got in butt-first, slid across the big back seat. Edge squeezed his big body in after her. The driver glanced back at him, eyebrows raised.

"Metropolitan Hotel," said Edge before Emma could say anything.

The driver nodded and screeched the tires in his hurry to let the other drivers behind him get moving. Edge reached his big hand out and lay it gently but firmly on the man's shoulders.

"Take it easy, OK?" he said with a calm authority that sent another tingle through Emma. "We're in no hurry."

The driver turned his head. He gave Edge a wide-eyed nod and a buck-toothed grin. Emma was pretty sure the driver didn't speak enough English to understand exactly what was said, but he certainly got the gist of it.

And so did Emma.

She stole another glance up at Edge's profile. It was past nine at night, and the streetlights cast Edge in a golden glow that highlighted the deep dark brown of his beard. His green eyes shone like emeralds pitted with gold. He was looking straight ahead, his gaze flicking between the driver and the road.

It took Emma a moment to understand, but then she got it and a warm buzz went through her body. He was making sure the driver knew what he was doing. Edge liked to be in control of things, even if someone else was behind the wheel.

Several moments passed, then Edge's shoulders relaxed almost imperceptibly.

"Is he driving to your satisfaction now?" she murmured as the taxi took a turn somewhat too fast, making Emma slide a little closer to Edge in the seat.

Edge glanced at her, then pointedly looked down at the space between them.

There wasn't any space between them after that fast turn.

"Yeah," Edge said as his gaze fell upon her in the dark back seat. "It's to my satisfaction."

Emma felt that thumper-rabbit behind her boobs. She sensed that tingle between her thighs.

She didn't understand either of them. They seemed like strong reactions towards a man she didn't know and probably would never get to know very well. After all, she wasn't going to need any of her "weapons" to bring Edge to Trung. Edge was going to get a room in the same building where the meeting was going to happen. She probably wouldn't even see Edge again after tonight.

But Emma didn't move away from him as the taxi ambled along like that Victorian carriage through the gold-specked cobblestone streets in what suddenly felt like a magical night.

There was something about his big warm body that made her feel safe by his side. There was also something about how Edge had taken care of those little details, attending to her comfort and safety in trivial ways that somehow made her feel weirdly special.

She stole a third glance at his proud profile. He was looking ahead at the road. His body was very still, like he'd learned how to control every twitch and tremor. She wondered how many hours Edge had spent sitting in silence and darkness in some forsaken part of the world, his mind on the mission, his thoughts on the target.

Emma's thoughts were pulled back to Trung's motives, and she shifted uncomfortably on the seat. Certainly Edge could handle himself, but he didn't know Trung like she did. Was it right to let him walk into that meeting which would likely lead to his death? Surely Trung had no other motive.

And don't forget *your* motive, Emma reminded herself as the bright lights of Macau's casino-hotels cast a red-yellow glow on the horizon beyond the endless highway. Don't lose track of your target, your mission, your reason for even being here.

Now Emma remembered the second part of Trung's instructions:

Return with Edgerton. Or do not return at all.

That last part bothered her. It was ambiguous. Not exactly a threat. Trung was clear about his threats usually. If he meant that she would end up as fish-food in the South China Sea, he would have said so.

So was Trung simply setting her free? Giving her the choice of whether to return or to keep going?

It was odd. Emma wasn't really a prisoner. Yes, she was expected to be available whenever the General demanded her presence. But Emma could mostly come and go as she pleased.

If Trung's guards accompanied her anywhere, it was just for routine protection. She expected that if she wanted to quit her position and decline the role of consort, she would probably be able to do it without fearing for her life. Sure, Emma had seen Trung beat that thug to death a few months ago, but the body was long gone and she had not directly witnessed any other murders.

Besides, Trung was mindful of his reputation. His consort could not suddenly just disappear without rumors spreading about her fate. Trung was capable of things much worse than murder, but Emma had entered this situation knowing full well what she might have to endure, and in truth none of it had been that bad. Trung trusted her reasonably well, his recent outburst notwithstanding. The only thing that would get her killed would be a betrayal of the General, and it appeared she had already passed that test.

So if she was a prisoner, it was only to her own mission.

And completing that mission required time. Patience. Discipline.

She needed to wait for that painfully slow DNA-cataloging to get far enough along. There was nothing she could do to speed it up. Nothing but stand her ground. Be still like a rock amidst the storm waves.

And it felt like there was indeed a storm coming, Emma thought as Edge glanced at her with those intense green eyes that seemed to see right through her. She still couldn't understand why he'd agreed so easily. But she didn't want to question it. She liked being near him. Being near him felt like . . . like being home.

"It's nice to talk to an American again," she said softly when she caught Edge glancing at her again silently, like he wanted to ask her more questions but was either being respectful of her privacy or didn't really want to know the answers. "Where's your home base?"

Edge's dark red lips eased into a smile. "Vegas, I guess. Though I don't have a place anywhere right now."

Emma blinked. Trung and Zhu had given her some basic information about Edge, but his connection to Las Vegas was news to her. She frowned when she thought back to that brief interchange about what she was to Trung. She'd expected to see a reaction of scorn or disgust, like many Americans showed when presented with the uncomfortable truth that some women rented out their private property without shame or guilt.

But Edge seemed completely unmoved, like it was no big deal to him, like it was clear that if a woman chose to do that without being forced, then it was her damn business.

"I spent some time in Vegas after UCLA," she said. "But you know that already, don't you?"

Edge blinked. He stayed quiet.

"You knew about me giving up my American passport," she reminded him. "Clearly you still know people in the system. You probably know more about me than my own mother did."

Edge stayed silent a moment longer. "So your mother's dead," he said.

Emma frowned. Then she realized she'd used the past tense. She nodded.

Now it was her turn to stay silent. She didn't want to talk about her mother. There was nothing to say.

"My mother's alive and well," Edge said after taking

Extracting Emma

a long look at her. "She works the slot machine areas at the Borgata and sometimes the MGM Grand."

Emma nodded, relieved to turn the conversation back to Edge. "Cocktail waitress?"

Edge shook his head, his eyes softening. "No," he said quietly, a gentle smile on his lips.

Emma blinked twice. She saw it in his eyes. There was affection there, but also regret.

She nodded, not sure if she should probe any deeper.

But she wanted to know more. She felt something tug at her from the inside.

Talk to him. Ask him. Tell him.

It was like a whisper from her heart. A yearning to connect with this man. A feeling that they were already connected, that the strange impulse she'd gotten that night at the arena to whisper into Trung's ear about that bearded beast looking up at her from the blood stained ring was more than just a random event.

It was like the universe had been operating through her at that moment. There was no thought or intention. It was pure instinct. Raw emotion. Like how animals operate in the wild.

She remembered that vivid rush of visceral energy. A mixture that she knew was dark and dangerous. That potent mix of sexual need and violent lust.

She'd had flashes of it over the years, seen it in some of the women she knew from red rooms everywhere. The women who accepted and used that energy were full of vigor, were overflowing with passion, lived their lives with joyful anticipation.

Emma hadn't completely understood it then.

But for some reason she was starting to understand it now.

She felt a sudden urge to kiss this man who was right up against her. The thought was vivid and violent. She blinked and swallowed and looked away from him, out the window.

She was very wet between her legs. It was unusual for her. So was the heat that burned up along her neck, made her cheeks flush with warm blood, made her ears roar like those storm-waves were coming close.

She didn't speak. They were quiet for a long time. Emma was very uncomfortable.

She wanted to get to the hotel and get away from this man. She was terrified that things were unraveling. She'd known this man for an hour and he was asking about her mother. Her thighs had brushed against his through two layers of cloth and she was wet like a virgin in a teenager's fantasy.

"This is a bad idea," she suddenly said, turning to him and looking at him wide-eyed. "You should just go. I don't have a good feeling about this. I don't think you understand what you're getting into."

Edge glanced down at her. There was no flinch in his gaze. "I understand it just fine," he said casually. Then he leaned forward in the seat. "Yoban Street. The warehouses along the waterfront. Past the old dockyards. You know what I mean," he said to the driver in Cantonese.

The driver shot a wide-eyed glance at Edge, then blinked twice and nodded. Emma could see him peering at her in the rearview mirror. Many locals knew who she was, but Emma rarely showed herself in jeans and with her hair open. Perhaps the driver wouldn't be certain it was her.

Not that it mattered too much. There were a hundred reasons why General Trung's consort might be seen with a strange man in Macau. It wasn't unheard of that a consort be offered to a business associate to sweeten the deal or even as a show of respect. Sort of like two Generals sharing a cup of wine to seal a peace treaty.

Or start a war.

"Yoban Street warehouses are the Russian fight arenas," Emma said softly as the driver took the next exit and circled beneath the expressway to take the frontage road along abandoned dockyards and rusted steel warehouses. "We cannot go there. I cannot be seen in Russian territory. It would be an act of war."

Edge lazily watched the dark water beyond the old dockyards.

"Thought you and Trung were done," he said. "That's what the tabloids say. They'll figure you're spreading your wings with someone new."

"You're crazy," Emma whispered urgently as the taxi driver's eyes darted between the road and the rearview mirror. "You might get us both killed. If the Russians don't do it, then Trung himself will do it when he hears of this."

Now Edge turned to her, narrowed his eyes. "You just called him Trung instead of the General. That's a good start."

"A good start to what?" Emma said, totally not understanding what was going on even though she could feel the excitement brewing in her breast, the wetness soaking into her satin, the heat burning in her cheeks.

"A good start to a war," said Edge. "Sun Tzu said *Never fight your enemy the way he wants you to fight him.*"

Emma stared at Edge like either he was insane or she was hallucinating. She considered popping open the car door and rolling herself out onto the bumpy road when the driver slowed down to take a turn.

She could also just tell the driver to turn around and head back to the hotel, but she guessed Edge would overrule her. The back and forth would make the driver even more interested in whatever was happening in his backseat.

So she stayed silent. Edge was silent by her side. The tension was so thick between them she could almost hear the air crackle with electricity.

She thought about what she'd learned over the years about the deepest drives in human nature. In the end sex and violence were what drove the pistons of the engine, created the current of the flow, guided the path of space and time. Chinese traditions of yin and yang talked about the polarities that made the universe do its dance. The dance of opposites that yearned to merge into one, then rip apart again. Back and forth. In and out. Up and down.

And wasn't that the core of both sex and violence?

Lovers yearned to lose themselves while possessing the other.

Wasn't it the same thing for two fighters?

Extracting Emma

A death-struggle to claim the essence of the other.
To claim your enemy's property.
To possess it.
Take it.
Own it.

8

He wanted to take her for his own.

The thought was clear in Edge's mind as he watched the old anchor chains on the dead dockyards drifting past the open taxi window. The air was warm, heavy with the sea, thick with the scent of old oil and stale sulfur.

He felt Emma shift on the seat beside him, but he didn't look at her. He was locked in place, his eyes focused to a single point of vision, like he was staring into the infinite vortex of a black hole that pulled everything into its gravitational center, bending space and time like plastic, rearranging events like some mystical blackjack dealer sliding the cards around the impossibly lush green felt of the universe's playground.

The realization had hit him suddenly, like he'd been ambushed and blindsided and sucker punched all at once. Edge had felt that possessive drive burn in him back at the airport, but now he understood it more clearly.

And he understood the game Trung was playing.

Understood why he'd sent Emma to receive Edge at the airport.

Extracting Emma

Why Trung was staying away for two days.

Edge had felt it in his dark heart when he realized his own need to possess Emma had spiraled upwards precisely when he imagined her with Trung. The arousal had burned harder when he felt the rage of jealousy. It was a sickening sensation that Edge felt deep in the pit of his gut, right behind that ganglion of nerves in his solar plexus.

There was no way he could say it out loud. No way Edge could admit to Emma that in his twisted mind he needed to own her, possess her, fight to have her, kill to claim her.

It was the dark underbelly of emotions he knew burned in every man's heart, and it sure as hell was burning in his damn heart right now.

The need came from an ancient place, from a time when men had to physically compete for the right to seed a woman. It was plain to see in the mating rituals of animals. But it was pushed to the shadows in human society. Nobody but so-called "savages" actually fought over a woman.

After all, a woman wasn't property to be claimed. She wasn't an object to be owned. She wasn't a piece of meat to be divided between hungry alpha beasts like Edge and Trung.

Except all that was just empty words compared to the animalistic surge that was consuming Edge, dominating him, possessing him like a demon or a drug.

He knew without a doubt that the only reason he'd gotten into this taxi was because of Emma.

He knew that every move he'd make from now on would be because of Emma.

He didn't know if he was losing his mind or if he'd already lost it.

All he knew was that he'd never been more certain of anything in his damn life. He'd been led to this moment in time. Led to this woman beside him.

But now it was time for him to lead.

For Edge to take control.

Direct the course of battle instead of being led to the slaughter.

Because Trung had already made the first move.

And now Edge had to make his counter-move.

The taxi moved through a sea of warehouses that had been fixed up and wired for lights. The abandoned dockyards had fallen behind them. Past the line of warehouses there was a rough unpainted concrete waterfront walkway with a high metal railing that was twisted and rusted, broken in some places. There was a large gravel parking lot up ahead. It was packed with cars.

Black Range Rover trucks and yellow Lamborghini Diablo's. Metallic blue McLarens and pearl-white Bugatis. There was a Rolls Royce Silver Ghost parked closest to the walkway. Three black Kawasaki Ninja motorcycles beside it, all leaning at the exact same angle like in a staged shot.

Chauffeurs and henchmen were smoking cigarettes as they strolled two and three together between the lines of cars. Edge could hear Russian and Turkish dialects mixed with the usual Cantonese and Mandarin.

Two chauffeurs in French cut black suits were speaking loudly in Swahili. Some henchman in one of the Range Rovers was yelling at someone on the phone in Arabic.

Edge smiled and cracked his knuckles. This was his kind of place.

He paid the driver in cash before Emma could get her fingers out of the front pocket of her fitted blue stretch jeans.

She had slumped down in the seat to get at her wallet. Edge glanced at her thick thighs spread on the seat. His gaze fell to the intersection at her fork. There was the slightest trace of an indentation down the middle. It was subtly darker than the rest of her denim.

He swallowed hard. He was bulging and bone-hard inside his cargo pants. He wanted to slide his fingers around the back of her neck, kiss her hard on the lips, push his tongue into her mouth, grind his knuckles against that forked space between those heavenly thighs, feel her dampness against his fingertips, get her sticky scent all over his beard.

Edge pushed open the door and got out before he did all of that. He hid his erection behind the door as he held it open for her.

Emma didn't come out. She opened the door on her side and got out.

Edge pushed his door shut. It slammed so hard the taxi rocked. Edge hadn't meant to slam it so hard. He was restless.

Too damn restless. Too much energy to work off. He needed to chill the hell out.

Edge wasn't planning on fighting here tonight. He just wanted to be seen in Russian territory with Emma. Wanted Trung to know that Edge understood what was happening here even though it wasn't something that could be spoken out loud.

The taxi drove off, its back tires scattering gravel on Edge's brown military-style boots.

He looked at Emma. She was standing and looking back at him across the empty space where the taxi had just been.

Edge felt an urgency in the air, even though everything about the parking lot was relaxed and calm. Nobody had even noticed them.

If you want her, just take her and go, Edge told himself as Emma walked across the gravel to where he stood. There's no way Trung will let you win at this game. Even if you win, he'll have you shot in the head and dumped in the sea. Then you can't help anyone, you dumbass.

Do you need help, Edge had asked Emma at the airport. He considered asking the question again, but reconsidered when she stood by his side and slipped her hand into the crook of his elbow.

"Trung is unpredictable," she said softly to him as they walked across the gravel towards the warehouse. "He's never sent me out like this before. To receive a man, I mean. It's very strange. That's what I meant when I said I have a bad feeling. The feeling wasn't about you. The bad feeling, I mean."

Edge's heart sped up as Emma's grip on his arm tightened for a moment. Again he was surprised at how Emma was secretive one moment, totally open the next.

Was it an act?

Sure didn't feel like it to Edge. But it was too surreal to be real either. Especially when he was feeling like this around her.

Nope. He couldn't figure her out. Not even close.

All he'd figured out was that he needed to stay close to her. That her refusal of his offer was real, but just because she didn't need help now didn't mean she wouldn't need his help in the future. Edge was certain she'd planned for years to get close to General Trung.

And he was certain she didn't plan to get out.

Well, that didn't work for him. He was going to stick around until Emma got what she was after.

And then Edge was going to get her out.

Take her home.

Make her his.

Now that restlessness settled down to a steady buzz in Edge's head. He glanced into her maple-brown eyes but stayed silent as he pondered the path he was heading down.

He glanced along the concrete path to the warehouse entrance. Edge saw two burly Russian doormen frown when they saw Emma.

Edge slowed down to a leisurely stroll.

"Isn't it a bit early in our relationship to be talking about our feelings?" Edge said as he cast another glance towards the Russian gatekeepers, then slowed down even more. "Especially bad feelings. Navy men are superstitious, you know. Premonitions and omens don't sit well with sailors."

"You're a SEAL, not a sailor," said Emma as they

strolled together like it wasn't the middle of the night and two Russian gargoyles weren't glowering at them. "And I don't believe in premonitions."

"Doesn't mean you can't have them," Edge pointed out.

Emma giggled. "You mean like a witch who doesn't believe in magic even though she turns toads into princes when she looks at them funny?"

"I think you're mixing up three different fairy tales, but yeah, something like that." Edge said.

Emma smiled up at him. Then her eyebrows knitted, her brow crinkled.

"I'm serious, Edge," she said. "Trung conducts these sort of paranoia-fueled tests of the people around him. It's hard to figure out the way his twisted games work sometimes. But they usually involve collateral damage." She glanced up at him. "It's not too late to just go on your way, Edge. There's no reason for you to get involved with any of this."

Edge stopped, slid his arm around her waist, pulled her around so her back was to the Russians. He placed his hands on her hips, leaned close like they were lovers whispering sweet nothings to each other in the park.

"Any of *what*?" he whispered. "What am I getting involved in, Emma? What are *you* involved in that's so damn important?"

Emma's eyelids fluttered rapidly. She tried to pull back away from him, but Edge dug his fingertips gently into her sides.

"You're making a mistake," Emma said, her voice wavering, her eyelids still moving like a butterfly trying desperately to break free of something. "Let's just go back to the hotel. They'll put you up in a nice room for two days. You can decide whether to wait for the General or just leave. I advise the latter. Just go home, Sailor. You're lost at sea here. Don't go down with this ship, you hear?"

Edge felt something blaze up in him. Something about her tone, her words, the way she wouldn't look at him.

For the first time tonight Emma was being dishonest, Edge thought. She didn't want him to leave. She didn't want him to go. She was just saying the words. Going through the motions. Reverting to her set course.

Then there was the way she reverted back to saying *General* instead of calling the bastard by his name.

It got Edge's blood boiling again. The fire of possession. The flame of jealousy.

It was immature and dangerous, but it was real. It was strong. It was unstoppable.

"You love him?" Edge muttered harshly as he dug his fingers harder into the softness above her wide hips.

"What?" she said, her gaze shooting up to his eyes, her smooth forehead crinkling for an instant. "What sort of question is that?"

"What sort of answer is that?" Edge rasped.

"Stop it," Emma whispered, turning her head sideways away from him. "You're creating a scene. You should go, Edge. Just go, OK? You mean well, but you can't help me. I don't need help. I'm not a prisoner. I'm not some captive sex slave. I don't need to be rescued. Just go. Please. You're going to mess things up. "

"Mess *what* up?" Edge growled, pulling her closer, so close he could smell her sweet shampoo mixing with the gentle aroma from her soft underarms.

He was dangerously hard. Maddeningly close. Sickeningly aroused.

"Let me go," Emma whispered without pulling away from him. "And you should go too."

"Say you love him and I'll go," Edge hissed through lips clamped tight so he wouldn't devour her whole like some sea monster with a mermaid in its vicious clutches. "Say it. Say you love him and I'll go."

Emma looked up into his eyes. Her face was expressionless, like the sea before a storm.

There was a moment of silence so heavy the air almost exploded with energy. Edge saw a darkness setting in behind those maple-brown eyes. A shadow like you see when a ship sinks beneath the waves or pulls away from the shore, heading for some lonely destination beyond the horizon or at the bottom of the ocean.

"I love him," she said through muted lips. "Now go."

Edge stared down at her as a chill rolled up his spine, then circled around his neck, gripped his throat from the inside like something was choking off the air, like he was dying as he looked into Emma's eyes, like she was pushing him away and he would suffocate if he let that happen.

Again Edge got that strange sensation like choices were being made, cards were being dealt, that invisible dealer in the sky was shuffling the deck and asking Edge to call the joker, place his bets, make his choice.

Was Edge going to fold and go home?

Or was he going to gamble on a feeling, double-down on a dream, and go all in on this woman.

He looked down at her pretty round face.

Shut down the part of his brain that said he was a damn fool.

And kissed her hard on those cold lonely lips.

He kissed her.

By God, he kissed her.

9

The heat of his kiss startled Emma back to her senses.

She'd felt like she'd been slipping into a dream. The kind of dream where you die in the snow, where you see your last hope at life slipping away and you just watch it go as you fade into numbness.

But now Edge's kiss yanked her back a world of crackling fires and smoldering heat. She gasped into his mouth as he devoured her lips with a hunger that made her sick with need. She tried to remember where she was, but the memory was not available to her frazzled mind.

Emma did remember a few things from before the kiss. She'd been saying things she didn't mean, telling Edge to go when she wanted to scream for him to stay, promising him she was all right on her own though now she understood that maybe she couldn't do it alone, didn't want to do it alone, never wanted to be alone again.

"Leave her alone," came a Russian voice through the cloud of heat shielding her senses from the real world. "This cannot happen here. Leave her alone, I say."

Emma felt Edge pull away and glance up. He swung Emma's body around so he could step in front of her.

Extracting Emma

She stumbled with the momentum of being turned like that, and bumped into something hard like a wall.

It was Edge's broad back. She stayed behind it, blinking furiously to clear her head. She was dizzy from being spun around, giddy from that violent kiss, panicked from the suddenness of it all.

She leaned out past Edge's muscled left triceps and saw the two Russian guards striding heavily down the concrete path like stormtroopers in black suits. One of them stopped a few paces away. The other was reaching into his jacket pocket as he marched over.

His hand emerged holding a gun. It was dull black metal. Not the kind Trung and Zhu liked to use. Theirs were silver and shiny and very futuristic looking. This gun had a speckled black tube attached to the end of the barrel. This gun would not be loud. It would spit bullets silent like a snake.

"Relax," said Edge coolly. "There's no problem here."

Edge kept his shoulders square like a shield. He reached his left arm back and pushed against her hip to make sure she stayed behind his body.

Emma stayed out of view. She wasn't certain what the Russian was all worked up about. She wasn't even certain if he knew who she was. After all, it was dark outside and Emma was dressed in western casual with her hair open. There were no photos of her with General Trung where she wasn't all painted up like a Chinese doll in a silk fitted gown down to her ankles and her gaze cast down in reverence.

"Russian hookers only in this place," barked the doorman with the gun. "No China whores. Only Russian girls. You buy Russian girls. No China whores allowed here, yah? This is high class place."

Emma felt Edge tense up. She placed her palm against his back. His muscles moved like a nest of snakes coming alive.

"She's not a whore," Edge said with a simmering coolness that Emma sensed concealed something dangerous underneath. "And if this is a high class place, what the hell are you and your ugly brother doing here?"

Emma heard the ominous click she recognized as the safety catch of a handgun being released. She felt Edge's back muscles move again. His muscular butt tensed up against the front of her jeans. She felt the fingers of his right hand slowly clench into a large fist that was about as big as her head.

"Let's go," she whispered from behind him. "Come on, Edge. Let's just go."

Edge didn't budge.

"Man calls you a whore, then points a gun at my face," Edge drawled. "That's two strikes. You play baseball, big guy?"

"I am not playing," said the Russian. "Take your whore and fuck off. Or I kill you both and throw you in the sea, yah?"

"Nah," said Edge. "Also, that's strike three."

Before Emma could take another breath Edge lunged forward and disarmed the Russian with shocking speed. The Russian blinked in bewilderment, looking at his own empty hand still pointed like there was a gun in it.

"Normally I would break all your fingers," Edge said calmly. "But I'm with a lady right now."

Emma exhaled behind Edge. She felt beads of relieved perspiration break on her forehead. She'd been certain that this was going to turn into a shootout that left a bunch of people dead, maybe even Edge and herself. She'd clearly underestimated Edge's ability to control the situation without losing his cool.

She'd also underestimated the effect Edge's words would have on her. Emma didn't give a damn about someone calling her a whore. But for some reason she did give a damn that Edge seemed to give a damn.

Sort of like Edge holding the taxi door open for her. Totally trivial gestures that felt oddly profound, like they were just ripples on the surface of a vast stillness, meaningless signs of something deeply meaningful.

The Russian grunted. He glanced at his commandeered gun in Edge's right hand. Edge was aiming it directly at the Russian's massive chest.

Emma felt the tension rise up in her again. Oh, please, she said silently to the Russian. Please don't say anything stupid.

The Russian grunted again. Then Emma heard him sigh. She felt Edge relax his shoulders slightly. She relaxed too.

Suddenly bright headlights swept across the scene from behind Emma. She turned and saw a large silver car pull smoothly up to the end of the concrete walkway. It had been parked off to the side of the gravelly lot earlier.

Now the warehouse door opened in front of them.

Two black-suited Russian bodyguards stepped out. A short, round, heavy silhouette appeared in the doorway behind them

It was a stocky man shaved smooth on his head and face. A large round gut but powerful shoulders and a thick neck. He wore a short-sleeved bush shirt of fine black silk. French, not Chinese. His forearms were thick with blond hair. The red glow of a cigar cherry moved as he puffed on it.

It was Grigory Parkov, one of the Russian bigshots in Macau's gambling and prostitution circles. He didn't typically make appearances at the fighting arenas, since those were illegal and the Russians took great pains not to implicate their leaders. It was bad luck that he was here tonight.

Not to mention very bad timing.

"What is this?" he barked when he saw Edge pointing a gun at one of his minions.

Then Parkov's gaze fell on Emma's face. He blinked twice, then stepped forward into the light and stared.

Instantly he snapped out orders in Russian. His two bodyguards drew their weapons. Black handguns but without silencers.

Three more Russians came charging out of the open warehouse door. Two of the new men were carrying automatic rifles.

"Shit," Edge muttered under his breath.

The Russian doorman grinned wide. He held out his big hand, palm facing up. Edge took a breath, exhaled slowly. Emma could tell Edge was evaluating the situation.

Extracting Emma

Edge was still pointing the black gun at the Russian doorman. Emma saw Edge move his arm slightly, like he was testing the weight of the gun.

It took her a couple of seconds to realize Edge was trying to estimate how many bullets were in the gun's magazine. He'd probably held enough guns that he could make a good guess just from the weight.

Now Edge lowered the weapon. "One bullet short," he murmured. "Plus, I don't know how more guys will pour out of that warehouse."

The humiliated Russian doorman snatched his gun back. Pointed it right at Edge's nose. Leaned in close but not too close.

"Now I break *your* fingers, yah?" he whispered. "And then I give your fat Chinese whore to the kitchen staff."

"She is not a whore," came Parkov's voice from behind the burly guard. "She is much more useful. Come. Bring them to the car. Miss Chang will sit with me. The hairy mongrel can ride in the trunk with the box of fish heads that my kitties are hungrily awaiting."

10

The stench of fish heads strong in the darkness reminded Edge of that mission in Yemen. It was just Fox and Edge on that one. They'd been dropped about a mile offshore, into the dark waters of the Arabian Sea. They'd timed the drop so the tide would take them towards the rocky beach on the Yemeni coast.

Unfortunately they hadn't timed the ISIS camp movements correctly, and so Fox and Edge had stayed wet and soggy for six hours behind a cluster of rocks in the shallows, waiting for thirty armed militants to clear the area so they could get ashore.

The cluster of rocks had sheltered a small pool of seawater. The dark pool was apparently a graveyard for warm-water ocean perch after the gulls had eaten their guts. There were about ten of them rotting on the flat parts of the wet rocks.

Edge and Fox had decided that the heads smelled the worst. Something about rotting brain that added a spicy tang to the putrid aroma. Probably why zombies like brain so much, Fox had suggested with that innocent wonder that made even his dumbest jokes seem profound.

But zombie jokes aside, that mission had been all

about bad timing. But in the end both Fox and Edge were still alive, and their three targets were rotting like those fish heads. So Edge didn't see the bad timing with the Russians as a premonition of looming disaster.

Or maybe it was because the disaster had already happened.

Edge rolled over onto his side, grunting as the car went over a bump and then took a hard left. The Silver Ghost was a beautiful classic car, but the suspension felt stiff—at least where Edge was riding.

He rolled all the way to the velvety back wall of the trunk. Ran his palms along the back. There was no panel that opened into the backseat. There was no latch to release the trunk from inside either. That must be a recent thing. Or maybe these old cars were designed for mobsters and their live cargo.

Edge pressed his ear to the back wall. Tried to hear what was happening inside the car. Couldn't hear a damn thing.

Edge lay on his back and relaxed his muscles, starting from his temples and scalp, moving down along his neck and shoulders, then focusing on each vertebra of his muscle-protected spine. Tense muscles burned more energy. He needed to preserve every ounce of strength. No telling when he'd get his chance to attack. He had to be ready to take it.

As Edge's muscles relaxed, so did his mind. He went over what he'd seen and heard back outside the warehouse.

The bald Russian was clearly a top dog. The car alone confirmed it. So did the man's decisiveness.

Grigory Parkov was his name. Edge had seen a mugshot of the guy in Benson's files. It was part of General Trung's dossier. Benson had helpfully included some background information on the Macau gang landscape.

Trung ran the Chinese gangs, even though the General wasn't technically a gangster. It was just that there were so many different Chinese gangs with connections to various provinces that the Ministry of State Security had placed Trung as the overall coordinator of Chinese gang activity in Macau. The General was a neutral party. Every gang hated and feared Trung equally, which made him a very good resolver of disputes.

The Chinese and Thai gangs were connected, which gave the General authority over both sets of thugs. But relations with the Russian gangs were more complicated. The Macau Russians paid tribute to the Bratva back in Moscow, and in return got financing, weaponry, and intelligence.

There had been brutal territorial wars between the Chinese and the Russian gangs in Macau. That was partly why the MSS had sent in General Trung. His reputation was intimidating enough to bring all parties to the negotiating table. His history was military, not mafia, and so everyone accepted that he was neutral in that sense.

Trung had brokered a peace, but it was an uneasy peace. Edge had learned early on that there was very little overlap between the Chinese and Russian operations.

They didn't share hotels or casinos or brothels. They sourced their own women. They ran their own fight circuits. Customers were allowed to go anywhere, but anyone else showing their faces outside their home territory would raise eyebrows at best, start a war at worst. Didn't matter if they were soldiers, fighters, hookers, or whatever the hell Edge and Emma were.

And what the hell *were* they, Edge wondered as he picked up her sweet taste on his rough lips. The memory of that kiss was vivid but also faroff and dreamlike. He wasn't certain if she'd kissed him back or been too stunned to react. *He* sure as hell had been stunned.

Either way, he was in it now. In every damn way.

He was locked in the trunk of a Russian mobster's Rolls Royce with a carton of fish-heads from a Chinese trawler. Emma had fresh air and a seatbelt, but she was clearly a prisoner too. Which meant Edge needed to get her out of this mess before he could worry about the General Trung situation.

So Edge turned his attention back to the here and now. Thought back to the rules about no crossover between territories. Emma had worried that showing up there could lead to an outright war. But she hadn't stopped him in the end.

Edge made a note of that. It mattered that she hadn't argued more forcefully.

Just like it mattered when Edge felt her palm flat against his back as he shielded her from that Russian gargoyle.

It had steadied Edge. Calmed him down like a horse-whisperer does with a raging stallion about to break through the gates.

Because Edge knew he'd been *this* fucking close to killing Gargoyle in front of that warehouse. Which of course would have been a disaster with a damn army of thugs carrying automatic rifles. Edge and Emma would have been exterminated like rats before Parkov even showed up in the door and recognized Emma.

Which meant it wasn't bad timing.

It was *good* timing.

So Edge smiled in the darkness and took a deep breath of fish juice. He directed his mind towards plotting his next move.

Right now Emma seemed safe. Parkov had called her Miss Chang. He'd treated her with some degree of respect. Didn't mean he wasn't planning to eventually kill her in some horrible way, but it did mean she was OK for now.

Edge figured he was probably OK for a little while too. No shots had been fired. Edge hadn't been clubbed or drugged or gagged. No real violence other than the violent stench of rotting fish in Edge's nostrils. Better than a broken nose. Or fingers.

Edge thrummed his fingers on his chest as he moved his focus down his tensed abdomen muscles, relaxing the ridges, smoothing the creases. Moved down to his quadriceps and shins. He'd just about gotten to wiggling his toes when the car hiccupped to a stop.

Doors opened and closed with muted thuds. Somewhere in the distance a dog yipped. Edge thought of Parkov's cats waiting for their fish-heads. He wondered if the bald Russian thug had a herd of those weird hairless cats that looked like aliens with their skinny bloodless bodies and big green eyes.

Edge's own green eyes went big as the trunk popped up and harsh electric light shone down. He dropped his eyelids down a half measure to block the white fluorescent beam. He knew it was a flashlight secured beneath the barrel of a Kalashnikov 74. The Russians had grudgingly stolen some of the design improvements of the U.S. Army's M-16 rifle for this upgrade.

Edge didn't like it pointed at him. He took it personally when someone put a gun in his face.

"What's your name, big guy?" he asked the Russian with the short spiky blonde hair and pale blue eyes and the Kalashnikov rifle with the flashlight attachment.

It was the same gatekeeper gargoyle who'd lost his gun and probably some of his dignity with that move which Edge had practiced a thousand times. Clearly Parkov had ordered him to come along. Edge filed away that snippet of data. It told him something about Parkov. He was not some dumb thug. He cared about discipline. He cared about the men working for him. He wanted to give this guy a chance to regain his dignity. Pay back the insult.

"My name is fuck you," said the Gargoyle. "Now get out. Slowly."

Edge considered getting out fast as hell, breaking Gargoyle's nose with the heel of his palm, then shoving that rifle so far down his gullet that the flashlight shone out of his bleeding asshole as he twitched and spasmed like those ocean perch who'd just had their guts eaten out.

The image was calming to Edge's gentle soul, and he wistfully indulged in the vision for a couple of seconds longer. But he could see a cluster of at least four armed guards near a door that probably led to the main house.

So Edge sighed, swung his legs out the trunk, and slowly extracted his long heavy body from the stinking velvet of the Rolls Royce's rear.

"Don't forget your fish-heads," Edge said. "If you rub them in your armpits, I think you'll smell better."

Gargoyle's face reddened. His fingers tightened around the wooden shaft lining the black metal barrel. If it were up to Gargoyle, Edge would have no head left right now. It occurred to Edge that maybe the long list of Navy and CIA complaints about insubordination weren't all bullshit. Perhaps a hint of truth in there. Just a smidgeon.

"I kill you soon," said Gargoyle. "Now lie on ground. Face down."

"Oh, baby," said Edge as he lazily did it like he wanted to, not because Gargoyle said so. "At least cuddle me before you do me that way."

The quip was beyond Gargoyle's comprehension, which was perhaps just as well. Edge lay on the ground, turned his head sideways, scanned his surroundings as Gargoyle patted him down even though they'd already taken his stuff before tossing him in the trunk.

They were in a garage the size of the Vegas Convention Center. There were rows of cars perfectly spaced and impeccably aligned. Dark luxury limousines in one row. Loud exotic sports cars in another. Motorcycles and ATVs in their own section.

The door at the far end was black painted metal. It looked thick enough to stop an anti-tank missile. Maybe even a tank itself.

It was closed. There were black metal cameras above it. Reinforced metal shielding. Bulletproof lens-covers. More cameras lining the floodlit walls.

This was not a low budget operation. There was Bratva money involved here.

Probably Bratva intelligence too. Parkov might be reading Edge's file right now.

Gargoyle kicked him in the side and told him to stand. Edge did it without comment. He wasn't in a joking mood any longer. Gargoyle would get Edge's undivided attention later, but right now Emma was what mattered.

Edge felt Gargoyle prod him between the shoulder blades with the rifle. He resisted the temptation to whip around and grab the barrel, wrench the rifle away and club Gargoyle to death.

It wasn't easy to stand down. SEALs were trained to take down multiple hostiles at close range within seconds. Edge could probably kill all five men in this garage with minimal risk of taking a fatal shot.

But the risk wasn't zero, and so Edge walked to where the four other guards stood. They opened a red metal door with an intricate spiral design around the border.

Edge stepped past the threshold. He was in a long enclosed corridor. It had hardwood floors and a red stucco finish on the walls and the curved ceiling. There were yellow lights behind frosted shades at regular intervals along the centerline of the red ceiling.

At the far end was another red metal door. It was closed. There was a camera above the door frame, centered perfectly.

Edge walked towards the door. It opened when he got close. Edge could see that it was a search station before the entrance to the main house.

Two guards stood inside. Russians with black suits. They searched him thoroughly. It was the third time he'd been searched.

They already had his passport and phone. They started up his phone and made him unlock it with his fingerprint. The messages from Benson had been automatically wiped clean after he'd read them. There was no call history or contact list. One of the Russians flipped the phone over and popped open the back cover.

Edge's breath caught. He imagined all sorts of tracking devices springing out like a mad inventor's jack-in-the-box. The Russian guy grunted. He seemed unimpressed. He tossed the phone battery into a hazardous waste receptacle like a responsible thug. Then he dropped the phone on the tiled floor and smashed it with the heel of his heavy black boot.

Edge stared at the broken pieces of the only connection to Benson, Darkwater, and any chance of backup. He blinked, then shrugged at the Russians like he didn't care about the phone.

They put his passport, cash, and cards in a metal tray on a high slim table against the wall. That was a good sign. It probably meant he wasn't going to be chopped up and fed to the fishies quite yet.

The Russians ran a metal detector all over. They made him pull off his boots and remove his socks. Then they asked him to strip naked. They checked every nook and cranny.

Nobody made any jokes. These guys weren't doormen like Gargoyle. They were hard men with serious tattoos that crawled up past their white collars. Their suits were tailored. The material around their arms were stretch fabric to give them full range of motion in hand-to-hand combat. They had German-made H&K machine guns slung across their broad backs. Bulges under their jackets indicating shoulder holsters. They were almost certainly carrying blades as well.

Edge felt a sliver of dread crawl up his spine. He'd already counted seven men. No doubt there were more in the main house, maybe a bunch more in staff quarters somewhere else on the estate. Sentries at the gate. This was not going to be a Hollywood style rescue-the-chick and ride off into the sunset type scenario. Edge was elite, but he wasn't invincible.

He walked silently towards where one of the black-suited guards gestured. It was an arched brick-lined doorway.

Edge walked through it and stopped. He was in a house the size of a football stadium. The ceiling was a high dome tiled with Russian porcelain mosaic. The floors were polished teakwood beams, smooth like dark packed sand after the tide went out. There were no windows. None at all.

"Ah, Mister Edgerton," came Parkov's voice from the far side of the vast room. "Come meet my kitties."

Edge walked into the center of the room and was immediately greeted by a powerful animal musk. He frowned and sniffed his armpits, then looked up when he heard a low growl that was sure as hell not human, definitely wasn't a dog, certainly wasn't a cat.

"What the hell?" Edge said when his gaze followed the scent all the way across to the left side of the room. "Are those . . . *tigers?*"

"Chinese White Tigers," said Parkov proudly as he strolled over from where he'd been sitting on a large leather recliner at the top point of the big circular room. "They like fish heads as a snack. Come closer. They don't bite."

"Tigers don't bite?" said Edge with a raised eyebrow as the stocky Parkov sauntered past him in bare feet. "Since when?"

Parkov turned his shiny bald head halfway and grinned over his shoulder. His teeth were very long and brilliantly white. His head gleamed like it had been polished. He was still in his black silk short-sleeved shirt and white linen trousers. Only the shoes had come off. His toes were splayed wide like he spent a lot of time barefoot.

Edge quickly swept his gaze across the perimeter of the room. There were twelve guards positioned strategically. Two at every door and the rest free-roaming.

Three of those hard-looking guards stayed within two feet of Edge. He had no chance of killing Parkov without a weapon and without getting himself killed in the process anyway.

"Where's Emma?" Edge asked as Parkov stopped near the large silver-barred cage and beckoned with his cigar to come closer to his kitties.

"Who is she to you?" Parkov replied, gesturing again with his head for Edge to come closer.

Edge strolled over. He glanced at the two large beasts in the spacious silver cage. They were beautiful animals.

Thick, lustrous white fur. Clean as fresh snow. Golden eyes that gleamed with intelligence and instinct. Paws bigger than Edge's face.

The male was longer, with heavy muscles around his shoulders and haunches. The female was shorter but larger. Quite a bit larger. Mostly in the belly area.

"She is pregnant," Parkov said as Edge got close enough that their scent was overwhelming though not unpleasant. "There will be cubs very soon. Twins. Doctor Wang did an ultrasound. She is due any day now, in fact."

"Where's Emma," Edge said again, this time lowering his voice to a smooth, deadly whisper.

He wasn't particularly impressed or intimidated by this showy bullshit with tigers in silver cages. Edge was from Vegas. Tigers in a rich asshole's living room was a reasonably normal thing.

"Who is she to you?" Parkov asked again, repeating his question just like Edge had repeated his own. Parkov grinned, shrugged his powerful shoulders, sauntered back towards his empty leather recliner. "I can do this all day, Mister Edgerton. You answer my question with a question. Then I ask my question again until you answer. Like ping pong. Back and forth as the clock ticks away. Tick tock. Bing bop."

Edge blinked, tried to figure out if this guy was making a real threat or bluffing. Was Emma hanging upside down over a shark tank, slowly being lowered on a winch by some cackling minion?

"Relax, Soldier," said Parkov, narrowing his dark blue eyes and smiling tightly like he'd seen something in Edge's expression.

Something that answered the question.

Who is she to you?

She's everything to me, came the thought as Edge glanced at the guards flanking him and then slowly made his way over to where Parkov had just planted his stocky self into the cushioned leather recliner. Parkov waved his left hand towards a leather couch across from the recliner.

Edge sat down and leaned back. Why was Emma anything to him, he wondered. There was nothing logical about his feelings. Nothing reasonable about his responses.

This was lust, pure and simple, Edge told himself. The kind of irrational sexual hunger that destroyed lives by the truckload in places like Vegas and Bangkok.

Women were kidnapped and stolen to satisfy that hunger. Families were bankrupted and broken to pay those pimps and procurers. Edge thought he was immune to the addiction because of where he'd come from. Maybe he'd thought wrong.

Then she walked into the room and Edge knew he wasn't wrong.

He couldn't be wrong.

Not when it felt like this.

Not when an hour felt like a lifetime.

When a kiss felt like forever.

11

"Women take forever in the bathroom and then come out looking the same," Parkov said as Emma was led to the seating area by the guard who'd stood outside the restroom.

Edge was sitting on the blue leather couch. His back was straight. His gaze was steady. He was looking at her. Only her.

Emma forced a smile and offered a little nod. Parkov had said very little to her on the way over. He'd been on the phone most of the ride. He'd been speaking Russian.

Emma didn't know much Russian. Just a few words here and there from brief interactions with some of the Russian and Ukrainian prostitutes. A few of them had showed up at one of the Chinese brothels asking for work. They'd heard that conditions in the Chinese hotels had improved since Emma started managing things. They wanted to work for Emma.

Of course, she had to explain that the agreements between the gangs were clear. No crossover. No poaching. Chinese women in Chinese brothels. Russians, Ukrainians, Slavs in the Russian red rooms.

"Sit," said Parkov without looking at her. He was frowning down at his phone. It was large and unwieldy, with a silver molded case. He was silent a moment, then his expression brightened. He tapped on the phone, then looked up and smiled. "Perfect. I have been given the go ahead from Moscow."

Parkov sat up in the recliner, leaned over to the round glass-topped table to his right, stubbed his thick cigar out carefully. He balanced the stub on the edge of the cut-glass ashtray, swept his dark blue gaze from Edge to Emma and back again to Edge.

"BCD for repeated insubordination culminating in assault on a superior officer," Parkov announced. "Tsk. Tsk. Bad SEAL."

Emma blinked, glanced down at her feet, then walked to the couch and sat beside Edge. She wasn't sure if that's what Parkov had intended when he told her to sit, but she didn't care. She wanted to be close to Edge. There was no point trying to understand exactly *why* she was so drawn to a man she'd met a few hours ago. Not when the draw was so strong. The pull so fierce.

Does he feel it too, she wondered as she looked down at her hands. They were palm-down on her thighs.

She sneaked a glance at the crotch of her jeans. In the restroom she'd been mortified to find her purple satin panties soaked beyond belief when she pulled them down to pee. Thankfully her wetness hadn't soaked through the denim.

Not noticeably, at least. Emma was relieved she wasn't shaved smooth down there like many of the Chinese prostitutes and virtually all the women who worked the Russian rooms. Trung had forbidden Emma to shave or wax herself down there. He'd told her pubic hair was nature's sign that a woman was no longer a girl.

That was perhaps the only positive thing Emma could say about Trung. He was a monster, but not *that* kind of monster.

In fact, Emma had heard from some of the older Chinese prostitutes that when the General took over in Macau, his first order of business was to empty all the underage brothels, deny entry to all child traffickers using Macau as a way-station or final destination. He'd enforced those rules on the Thai and Russian gangs too. In fact it was one of the reasons the early gang wars were so brutal and bloody. Men from all over the world paid high prices for bodies that were young and untouched.

"Does General Trung know that you have touched his property?" Parkov asked Edge as Emma blinked herself back to the moment. Before Edge could answer, Parkov whipped his gaze towards Emma. "Or perhaps you are not the General's property anymore. One of my men alerted me to a tabloid article from a few days ago. It suggested that perhaps there was trouble in paradise. Is it true, Miss Chang? Are your services now available on the open market?"

Emma felt Edge's straight-backed posture get tighter and straighter. She saw his steel-green gaze flick to the four guards that were standing at crosshair-points around the seating area.

She wanted to place her palm on his thigh, sort of like

she'd done when that Russian doorman pulled a gun on Edge. Emma had felt him relax when she'd touched him. It had given her a strange thrill. A secret pleasure that she had some effect on this muscled, bearded beast who killed bad men for a living and broke jaws and noses for sport.

"Relax, Soldier," said Parkov with a devilish grin, like he'd purposely phrased his question to get a rise from Edge. "Like I said before, I know Miss Chang is not a prostitute. I mean her services as an able manager of the women."

Emma blinked three times rapidly.

"Are you offering me a job?" she said after a moment's pause.

Parkov shrugged with his shoulders and his mouth. "I hear things from some of the Russian girls. They say the Chinese women are happier after the General put you in charge. Things are cleaner. Safer. You have a soft touch. You show them respect like some others cannot."

"Anyone is capable of showing respect to anyone else," Emma said firmly. "It is a choice. All your people have to do is make the choice to treat your women better. You don't need me for that. Anyway, I still work for the General. And there are strict rules in Macau. No poaching. General Trung has never hired a Russian solider or prostitute from your operation. Those are the rules. That was the treaty."

Parkov's eyes narrowed. They looked dark as midnight now. Vicious like a snow wolf.

"Does General Trung authorize his consort to remind

me of treaties and rules?" he whispered dangerously. "Remember your place, Miss Chang."

Emma blinked away her anger. She lowered her gaze reluctantly.

She felt Edge tighten again. Thankfully he stayed silent. Emma hadn't gotten a chance to warn Edge that Parkov could be amiable and even friendly, but he was every bit as ruthless as Trung and Zhu could be.

During the gang wars before the treaty, Parkov's men had done unspeakable things to the Chinese, each side one-upping the other with atrocities designed to instill fear and dread in every thug and certainly every working woman.

"And you must remember yours," said Parkov sharply to the silent Edge. "Now, listen. I know Miss Chang means something to you. Of course, I do not know *why* you see anything interesting enough in her to get involved defending her honor against armed men like some idiot cowboy. But I know what I saw in your expression earlier. And I know what I see in your expression now. Do not attempt anything heroic here, OK, big shot action hero? You understand? You will get your chance to be a hero shortly. To save your big-bosomed China doll. Allow me to finish."

Edge's eyes were like daggers, their points focused on Parkov. Slowly he nodded, keeping his gaze fixed on the Russian's face.

"So finish," Edge said in a deadly whisper.

Emma could tell there was more to that sentence. Thankfully Edge finished it in his mind.

Parkov held the visual standoff for a long unblinking moment. Then he grunted and flicked his gaze back towards Emma.

"There are two ways we can play this, Miss Chang," he said carefully. "See, you and this man showed up on Russian territory. You still work for General Trung, as you just confirmed. You were dressed in western clothes, with your hair open in a way atypical of you. It could be construed as a disguise." Parkov grinned. His teeth were too long and sharp for his round face. "And this man is a trained Special Forces killer who has been fighting the Chinese underground arenas. I could be forgiven for suspecting this to be a plot to undermine my fight operation." He did that slow, exaggerated shrug again. "Perhaps you bring your trained killer to my deathmatch arena and have him kill off my top fighters, ruin my business as spectators and gamblers go elsewhere. That is sabotage. General Trung will understand my predicament. He is known for his great paranoia, the state of mind that keeps one alive. So I could slit your throat right now, feed you to my tigers while you drown in your own blood. Trung will not go to war over that." He glanced at Edge now. "You see? I can kill her without fear of retaliation. You understand my bargaining power now, Mister Former SEAL Commander?"

"What do you want me to do," Edge said in a steeled monotone.

Parkov tapped the side of his head and nodded. He eased back on his recliner. Reached for his cigar stub and lit it with a silver lighter. He puffed out a thick cloud of smoke and nodded again like he was pleased Edge seemed to understand.

"I want you to get to General Trung," Parkov said softly. "Do what you are trained to do, SEAL. Both Trung and his man Zhu. Can you do it?"

Edge showed no expression. No hesitation either.

"Yes," he said.

No, Emma thought as panic gripped her from the inside. You can't kill Trung and Zhu. Not yet. I need them alive. Just a little bit longer. Please, Edge. Oh, please. Read my mind. Hear my heart. Oh, please, please, please.

She stayed motionless, cold and frozen like her life was being drained away.

Trung was expecting to meet Edge. Which meant Edge could get to Trung.

Edge could kill Trung. He could kill Zhu.

And that would kill everything she'd worked for, sacrificed for, lived for.

Survived for.

And maybe it would kill Edge too.

Or *only* kill Edge.

Now despair started to set in, and Emma's shoulders sagged. For one dark moment she wondered who she would choose if it were Edge or Trung.

She wanted Trung dead, but she needed him alive.

As for Edge . . . she just wanted him, pure and simple.

But was it just pure passion she wanted?

Was it just simple sex?

And was it going to destroy the mission that had given her life meaning thus far?

Emma thought of the kiss that had almost set her ablaze. She remembered her purple panties dark with her need. She felt that wetness still cool between her legs. She sensed Edge's presence warm by her side.

She wasn't sure what to do.

Wasn't sure what she wanted.

Wasn't sure who she was.

"You're insane," she said to Parkov. "Killing the General and Zhu will start an outright war."

Parkov shook his head. "Not if the American kills them. He is a disgraced former SEAL kicked out for impulsive violence. If he gets arrested or killed and it becomes public, American State Department will disavow him, release his violent record, shrug and say sometimes highly trained weapons misfire." Parkov grinned, nodding earnestly through the cloud of cigar smoke. "And if Edgerton makes it back here alive and undetected, then all the better! We will get the word out to the Chinese Ministry of State Security. They will immediately call their CIA counterparts through back channels. The CIA will assure them Edgerton is not some dark ops secret agent, that he is a disavowed renegade and the MSS can do with him as they please. If they catch him, of course." He turned his gleeful gaze towards Edge. "Which they will not, if you choose to work for me in return for protection from the Chinese." He winked at Edge. "And Miss Chang might be happy to see you too. After all, she will be working for me too, yah, Miss Chang?"

Emma stared at Parkov. She stayed quiet as she processed everything he'd just spouted. It wasn't the ramblings of a madman, she realized after considering how it might play out.

"You want me to keep the brothels running smoothly, both the Chinese and the Russian rooms," Emma said as she thought it through. "Without the General and Zhu, there'll be chaos with the Chinese gangs. There are over a dozen different gangs. They'd never be able to coordinate a sustained war against the Russians if you attack. They'd surrender to you immediately, hoping that the Chinese MSS will find someone else to take the General's role as a neutral peacekeeper who rules with an iron fist."

Parkov held up his hairy blond fist. He burst open the fingers and made a popping sound with his mouth. "And once the Chinese government sees that I have prevented a major gang war and all the brothels and hotels and casinos are running smoothly, they might decide that perhaps there is no hurry to replace the General with someone new. Better to leave well enough alone. It would not be so bad to have me in charge, so long as I keep the gamblers and whorers coming in, keep the tax revenue flowing back to the mainland. And China and Russia are buddy-buddy now in the real world, yah? Chinese MSS might even see it as a good thing. Yes, if the American kills Trung and Zhu, and I keep the peace, the Chinese will let me keep Macau. I am certain of it. My Bratva superiors believe it is worth the gamble. Go ahead and roll the dice, they say. Deal the cards and see what opens up."

Parkov puffed on his cigar and blew three perfect smoke rings into the still air of the large room. He watched them expand and rise, then finally break apart and dissipate into nothing.

"Guess I'll be on my way then," said Edge, his tone dead even, his gaze still on Parkov.

Emma watched Edge rise from the sofa. He didn't look at her.

Parkov gazed up at Edge thoughtfully.

"It has of course occurred to me that you could simply walk out of here and disappear," Parkov said with a shrug. "I have your passport and your money and your bank cards, but surely you can go to the American Embassy across the bridge and be identified via biometrics. They will get you temporary ID to travel back to the States. Or wherever else your travels take you, I suppose." He sighed and shrugged. "That is up to you, Soldier. I cannot send my men along to supervise you or even to spy on you. I cannot risk being associated with an attempt on General Trung's life. It is your choice. Miss Chang will have to die if you do not return, of course. But people die every day. Many have died by your hand, yah?"

Edge nodded like he'd already recognized that he could in fact simply agree to Parkov's deal and then skip town. That kiss aside, Emma was nothing to Edge. Their eyes had met less than a week ago. Their lips had met less than a day ago.

And Edge's life had gotten steadily worse ever since Emma had whispered into Trung's ear on a whim, an impulse, a random act of spontaneous insignificance.

He *should* skip town, Emma told herself while trying to keep her lips from trembling.

Extracting Emma

She'd already told him three times to just go, to leave, to save himself instead of going down with this ship, trying to bring this one home.

She wanted to tell him again. She tried to do it with her eyes, but Edge wouldn't look at her.

Emma wondered if he'd already made his choice. Already decided to cut his losses and sail off before the storm hit. Why in heaven's name would he dig himself deeper into the quicksand that Emma was already sinking into feet first. She was beyond saving anyway. He should just go.

Edge started walking towards the door that led to the corridor and out to the garage.

Emma stared at his back. She tried to be relieved that he was doing the logical thing and saving himself. At least his death wouldn't be on her conscience.

But the relief wouldn't come.

Instead she felt rage.

Inexplicable. Undeserved. Unjustified.

But it was there, pure and simple.

Just go, you asshole, came the vicious thought from someplace inside her that felt very much like a sulky indignant child.

Go ahead and leave me, you piece of shit.

Save yourself, you bearded bastard.

She hated the thoughts but couldn't stop them. She knew they were unfair but they kept coming. She felt her lips part to say something, but she clamped them shut because she wasn't sure what she'd say.

Please save me.

Please love me.

Please fuck me.

She almost choked on her tongue as those thoughts hammered her head from the inside like bullets. They came from some part of her she'd shut down long ago.

Some part of the girl she'd never allowed herself to grow out of.

Some part of the woman she'd never allowed herself to grow into.

Some part of the dream she'd never thought she deserved.

Emma watched Edge get to the door and wait for the guards to open it up. She willed him to look back but he didn't. She prayed for him to turn but he wouldn't. She tried to call out to him but she couldn't.

Despair and loneliness and hatred and fear all rose up in her at once, ravaged her like a gang of thieves stealing every secret in her throbbing heart. She'd been the picture of focused dedication her entire life, but right now she was coming apart at the seams, breaking at the borders, bleeding from wounds she didn't even know she had.

The guard started to pull the heavy red metal door open.

Then he stopped and turned.

Everyone stopped and turned.

Turned towards the source of that mournful, blood-curdling roar of confusion, that familiar cry of pain, the pain that comes when a new life is coming into this world.

"My kitty!" Parkov screamed as the female tiger flopped onto her side and raised her massive head and roared again. "Call Doctor Wang! Do it now!"

Emma stared at the lovely white tiger lying on her side and crying. There were specks of blood on the white fur of her hind legs, on her twitching tail, on the white painted wood floor of the cage.

The tiger was going into labor. She was about to give birth.

Emma leapt off the sofa and starting running across the huge room. In the background she could hear Parkov shouting something about Doctor Wang not being back from Beijing yet and how he was going to be shot when he did get back.

Then there was more yelling, mostly in Russian. Clearly none of Parkov's men wanted anything to do with a five-hundred pound tiger giving birth.

Emma got to the cage and slid down to her knees, her boobs bouncing as she panted from the run. She blinked wildly as her thoughts raced. She'd worked in brothels all over the world for over a decade. You learn a thing or do about midwifing and babies when you do that.

Of course, this was a tiger, but the basic machinery worked the same. The only real difference was this mama weighed about five hundred pounds.

Emma was going to need help.

She turned her head and looked towards that metal door.

Edge was already running over.

His green eyes were alive with energy.

His beard was flowing wild like a black sail in a stormwind.

And he was grinning just like she was.

Because he feels it just like I do, Emma realized as her heart thrummed and her spirit soared. He hears it just like I do.

The feeling of fate.

The call of destiny.

They opened the cage.

12

The cage was divided into two sections, so the male tiger was separated from the female by a wall of silver steel bars. That was probably a good thing, Edge thought as he tried to ignore the male tiger's massive maws pressed up against the bars as the big guy roared out of concern for his mate.

Emma had slid the deadbolt off the outside and pulled open the female tiger's cage, but Edge had yanked her back before letting her enter. It was only when he was sure that Mama wasn't concerned about anything other than whatever was fighting to come out of her, Edge nodded to Emma.

"Stay behind me as we enter," he warned her, glancing at Mama's big jaws and big paws and big claws. "Keep to the tail end of her, please."

"You hurt my kitty and you die," Parkov whispered from behind their shoulders. "But not before Doctor Wang dies for being in Beijing when I need the bastard."

"Nobody's going to die," Emma said with a firm confidence that made Edge almost believe that she'd delivered tiger cubs in a Russian mobster's living room before.

"Well, no tigers, at least. Can't speak for Doctor Wang's future." She glanced up at Edge. "Go over on that side and hold her tail up so I can see."

Edge stepped carefully over the tiger's body and crouched down near her back. Her tail was thick like an anchor rope. The fur felt like stiff bristles on a wire brush.

The tiger raised her big head and glared at Edge as he slowly pulled her tail away from her hind. Her eyes were big and orange like two suns of some distant planet. He looked into her eyes and smiled calmly. The tiger murmured something and licked her lips with a tongue bigger than a ham. Edge knew that tongue was a deadly weapon. Coarser than sandpaper, she could lick the hide off a wildebeest with that thing.

"We're good," said Emma after a careful look. "You can let go of her tail."

Edge nodded and let go. *Take the tiger by the tail* was an ancient Chinese proverb. It meant something equivalent to *Dance with the devil but don't get your feet stepped on.*

Or something like that. Edge wasn't certain. He only looked the part of a Warrior Monk. He hadn't spent too much time reading ancient texts in a frozen monastery in the mountains.

Edge settled down on his knees beside Emma. He stayed between her and the tiger's dangerous end. The tiger's head was raised and she was raising her hind paw. Papa tiger was staring, but he was quiet too now.

"What should we do?" said Edge, glancing at Emma.

She shook her head. "Nothing."

"Do something!" whimpered Parkov from outside the cage. "My kitty dies, then everyone in this house dies too."

Edge considered making the second part of that statement mostly true. In his peripheral vision he saw the guards standing far back from the open cage door. Edge could break Parkov's neck before they got a shot off.

Better still, Edge could hold the Russian in a headlock, use him like a shield, bargain their way out to the garage, steal one of those Range Rovers or maybe even the Silver Ghost.

Too risky, he decided. If he were alone he'd already be doing it, but with Emma it was different. One human shield for two people wasn't a good plan. Emma would take a head-shot from one of those rifle-carrying thugs who looked like they knew how to shoot.

"Relax," said Emma gently. Edge wasn't sure if she was talking to Parkov or to him or to the tigers. "She doesn't need help. She already knows what to do. Which is nothing but relax and trust her body, trust her instincts, trust the process. A process perfected over millions of years with thousands of species in jungles and forests and mountains and rivers." Emma shrugged. "Also huts and caves and farmhouses and basements."

As she spoke, the mama tiger tensed up, then shuddered. Edge stared in wonder as a slime-covered critter popped out of her. The tiger immediately turned and started licking her new cub furiously.

"She knows to get all that sticky stuff off her cub so it can start to breathe properly," Emma whispered. "There, see?"

Edge saw the little cub open its maws and cry out. Mama licked the hell out of it as it pawed at her face.

Then a second cub slid out of her, wet like a seal. Mama pulled her over in her jaws, licked her face clean, then went to work back and forth between the two squealing tiger cubs.

Edge and Emma watched in silence as the cubs were freed from the slime of the womb. Their fur was stained with blood, still wet and sticky, but they were white tigers too.

"At least you know they're yours, buddy," Edge whispered wickedly to the anxiously staring father. "Would've been awkward if they were orange like the mailman."

Emma giggled. She glanced up at him, then down at her chest. Her long black hair had fallen forward. She pulled it back, curled it around each ear, looked at Edge again.

He wanted to kiss her again. He wanted to take her away. He'd asked her if she needed help and she'd said no. They were already at the airport. General Trung's men weren't watching her. She'd said no, thank you, I'm fine, really, do *you* need help?

"You two get out of the way," said Parkov from behind them. "Go. Shoo."

Edge pushed himself off the floorboards of the cage, springing up light and quick. He reached out his hand to help Emma up. She took it and he pulled her up. She stumbled a little, her palm pressing against Edge's abdomen. He slid his arm around her waist and lower back.

She was facing him. Looking up into his eyes. They were so close.

Edge could smell her scent through the powerful musk of the tiger family. He wished they were alone in one of those jungles or forests or mountains or rivers. He'd settle for a hut or a cave or a farmhouse or even a damn Russian mobster's basement.

Parkov barked out something in Russian as Edge led Emma out of the cage. Edge saw a couple of the guards who'd been standing back step forward now.

Parkov gently shut the cage door, silently slid the deadbolt across, then pulled out his phone. He was going to take pictures, Edge realized with an internal eye-roll.

"Do not get any ideas, Miss Chang and Mister Edgerton," he said softly but with a sinister undertone as if to remind them that he only turned into a drooling, whimpering, sentimental fool when it came to his five-hundred pound kitties. "Relax and entertain yourselves while I record this moment to show my own children someday. Eat, drink, smoke, whatever. But remember where you are. Please do not disturb the peace by forcing my guards to pump you both full of bullets, yah?"

Edge grunted as he led Emma across the room towards where they'd been sitting earlier. When they got there Emma looked at her hands and made a face. She held her palms out towards him. They were sticky from the floor of the cage. Streaks of blood and other fluids.

Edge looked at his own hands. Sticky and streaked.

He glanced towards the door behind the seating area. Emma had emerged from there earlier.

There were two guards standing by the door, one on each side. They were not standing at attention like sentries. One was leaning against the wall and smoking a cigarette, dreamily gazing over towards his boss taking photographs and video of the tiger cubs. The other guard was on the phone, jabbering in Russian, pacing in tight circles. He was animated and grinning. Edge knew enough Russian to figure out he was calling home with the exciting discovery that little tigers came out of big tigers.

"Restroom's back there, right?" Edge called to the smoking guard.

The guy raised his head and narrowed his eyes through the cloud of smoke. Edge showed the guy his bloody, sticky palms. Emma did the same, except she smiled while doing it.

The guard grunted, stuck the cigarette between his teeth, pushed himself away from the wall, and unlocked the door for them.

"There is no back door, no side door, no windows, no ventilator shafts, no stairs, no escape," the guy informed Edge as the cigarette flapped between his lips. "Yes, you can try to swim away through the toilet. Of course, you will get stuck in the bowl and I will come shit on your head and then shoot you."

Edge grinned. "That's actually a pretty good one," he conceded. "May I use it sometime?"

"Sure, why not," said the Russian. He grinned back

at Edge. Then he gestured with his head towards Parkov coo-coo'ing his kitties. "Take your time," he said. "Boss will be a while."

Edge nodded, waited for Emma to walk up and go through the open door. He followed her. The door clanged shut behind them.

They were in a semi-circular corridor, like the ring of a donut with that big round tiger-room as the center. The walls were painted a dull but tasteful red, like sunburnt clay.

Edge strode along the pathway to each end and back. The guard was right. No windows or doors leading to the outside. The walls were reinforced concrete on the inside. Edge could tell just from thumping the base of his palm against it. This wasn't drywall he could punch through. This would be like punching the side of a cinderblock.

"Which one's the bathroom?" he asked, nodding when Emma pointed north along the semi-circle.

It was a wooden door, heavy teakwood from the forests of Myanmar. Edge opened it and looked inside.

The bathroom was enormous. Black marble and polished granite with heavy brass fixtures. The toilet was behind a walled enclosure with a full-measure door. There was no tub, but a large black-tiled shower area with a head the size of a sunflower.

Edge pulled the door closed and glanced up and down the hallway. The east wall had no doors other than the one leading back to the main room. On the west wall there were two more doors, both identical to the bathroom door.

Edge strode to the first door, knocked twice so he wouldn't get shot, then pushed it open. It was a gymnasium.

Two large complicated weight machines that looked like massive alien birds about to pull something apart with their claws. Three treadmills facing a mirrored wall. A rack of resin-cushioned hexagonal dumbbells that went all the way up to eighty pounds. The floor was stiff black synthetic resin, the kind they used in the Navy gyms. Everything was clean as a whistle and twice as shiny.

Edge closed the door and walked over to the last room. Emma had already washed her hands and was drying them with a white cloth hand-towel. She stood in the bathroom doorway and watched him.

"You're getting Parkov's doorknobs all sticky," she pointed out. "Here. Wipe them off."

She tossed him the towel. Edge caught it with his left hand. It was damp. It smelled like soap.

He wiped his hands dry and clean, then wiped off the doorknobs he'd touched. He tossed the towel back at Emma. It hit her boobs and fell to the floor. She glared at him, then used her feet to pull the towel into the bathroom. She got the toe of her cloth slip-on under the towel. With one flick of her foot, the towel sailed into a wicker basket against the bathroom wall.

Edge watched her all the way into her follow through. She had strong legs, thick thighs, and a butt that would fill his big hands just right. She was dynamite in those stretch jeans and black top tucked into the waistband.

He thought of that subtle dark line at the fork of her crotch earlier. He wanted to put his face in there, he decided. Inhale her scent. Taste her tang.

The thoughts were dangerously vivid. It was like his brain was already serving up sense data that completed the fantasy.

He could smell her, taste her, feel her. He blinked away an image of her spread wide for him. In the image he was outside his own body, looking down on him and her, watching his broad, muscled, scarred back move as his hairy face worked that space between her divine thighs.

Edge could feel himself thicken, sense his balls tighten. His throat constricted as his heart sped up, pounding erratically as he tried to push away the need to take her now, take her hard, take her home.

Except she wouldn't go with him. She'd already refused his help once. She wanted to stay with Trung. Maybe that was her home. Maybe that was her man. Maybe all this was just Edge's cock trying to run the damn show.

She was a taken woman. She'd said so herself. She'd said she loved the General.

Yeah, she was a taken woman, Edge thought. Maybe Emma was right. He didn't know what he was getting involved with here. And she didn't seem to want to tell him. So maybe he should just go.

Except he could tell she wanted him to stay.

He didn't know *how* he could tell, but he knew it.

He knew it because she'd been honest and forthright from the beginning, and he knew what that sounded like, what it looked like, what it felt like. So when she was bullshitting herself and bullshitting him, Edge could see it clear as the sun on a cloudless day.

She wanted him to stay with her.

She wanted him to save her.

She wanted him to . . .

"You should just go," Emma said from the bathroom doorway as Edge reached for the doorknob of the third room. "Parkov will probably just let me go too after a day or so if you don't come back and there's no disturbance at Trung's penthouse."

Edge glanced at her. "That's the third time you've told me to go. But it's not what you want."

Emma blinked and glanced down for a moment before looking up at him. "You were on your way out. Parkov isn't going to put any of his guys on you. They get seen by Trung and it's outright war. Parkov won't take the risk. He's a shrewd gambler. He sees a chance at stealing a victory with this plan, but he'll let it go if you just take off."

Edge didn't answer. He turned the doorknob to the third room. A blast of warmth hit him in the face. He peered into the room. The walls and ceiling were covered with rows of tiny round LED lights. There was a long wooden bench dead center in the room. There were switches on the wall beside the door. Edge flicked them on.

The room lit up red like a sunset. The LED lamps were infrared mixed with red spectrum light. The light spectrum replicated the redness of a sunrise or sunset.

It was a modern high-tech sauna that used infrared to generate gentle, non-burning heat. Clean heat that was good for the skin and penetrated muscle and even bone. The Navy had installed infrared panels in some of their facilities to speed up healing. Cuts and burns healed about ten times faster. So did broken bones and torn ligaments. It was like magic.

And maybe they could use a little magic right now.

Edge flicked on all the switches. Hundreds of red LED lamps fired up. The room was red like Mars at mid-day. Edge held the door open and gestured with his head.

"Are you saying I need a tan?" Emma asked, holding out her bare arms and looking at them.

She was very well tanned, Edge thought. He said nothing. Waited for her to step into the red room.

He went in after her and closed the door and sat down on the wooden bench. He patted the wooden slats by his side. Looked up at her, nodded, patted the bench again.

Emma blinked three times, then sat down by his side. The red lights were angled perfectly so they wouldn't shine directly into the eyes.

"Red light won't tan you or burn you," Edge said. "We should be OK here for a while. Recharge. Regroup. Rethink."

Emma nodded. She looked down at her hands. They were on her thighs. She looked over at him, then back down at her hands.

"What haven't you told me," Edge said softly.

It wasn't really a question. It was a tone he used sometimes when starting an interrogation. An undercurrent of seriousness that made it clear that this was the time to talk.

Emma shrugged. "Everything, I suppose. We met two hours ago, remember?"

"We first spoke two hours ago, yeah," said Edge. "But we met three days ago in that crowded arena. When you decided it would be cool to watch me get beaten to death."

Emma shot a glance at him. Her face flushed, then drained. She swallowed hard, then shrugged and offered a little smile. "Maybe I thought *you'd* win the fight. Beat the other guy to death."

Edge chuckled darkly. "Is that why you're with Trung? You get off on the violence?"

Emma's face showed a flash of indignation before she composed herself. "You're one to talk," she said somewhat sharply. "Your whole life is violence."

Edge shrugged. "So now you know about my whole life. Let's move on to yours. Why are you with Trung?"

Emma stared straight ahead. "That's my business."

"It became my business the moment you whispered into his ear in that arena. You pulled me into this, whether you meant to or not. And now I'm here, whether you like it or not. Everything about this is my business now, Emma."

Emma blinked, but kept staring straight ahead. The red lights made her glow like she was infused with the rays of sunset. She shook her head a little, moved her lips like she was talking to herself, muttering in her mind.

Edge looked at her, then grunted and stood up. He

looked at his wrist for the time, but then remembered that they'd taken his watch and phone and everything else before dumping him into the Rolls Royce's trunk. Edge was glad they hadn't found anything suspicious in the phone before smashing it. But he didn't like not being able to contact Benson.

Well, whatever. He'd cross that bridge when he came to it.

Right now he was at a different sort of crossroad.

He could still walk away from all this pretty clean. In fact he'd been considering doing just that when the female tiger went into labor and Parkov went to pieces.

Edge had considered the possibility that Parkov was bluffing, that he would eventually let Emma go if Edge just took off. Or maybe he'd even get her to work for him, negotiate some kind of non-violent transfer of assets between the General and the Russians.

Not a great chance, though. Edge knew how men like Parkov operated. The Russian mobster might be a pussycat with his kitties, but he was Bratva material, which meant he knew that every decision was a signal to anyone watching. If Parkov said Emma was dead if Edge bailed, then Emma would be dead.

Edge's temples throbbed as things started to split apart in his mind again, those crossroads of choices opening up before him like the forked tongue of some mystical snake.

Yeah, Edge could probably get to Trung and Zhu, maybe kill them both and get out alive. But once word got out to the Chinese and the Americans that an ex Navy SEAL had just assassinated a former Chinese Army

General who was an underground kingpin in Macau and probably supported by the covert Chinese MSS, things could unravel pretty damn fast.

Parkov's view on how it would play out was valid, but by no means guaranteed. China-U.S. relations were complex at many levels. There were a hundred different games being played between a hundred different agencies from each nation. Things could escalate in ways that could start some serious conflict between groups, maybe even all the way to the top. Hell, Edge could inadvertently get some active-duty American soldiers killed if things got out of hand and Special Ops on both sides got mobilized.

Edge couldn't take that chance. He had to stand down. There was no clean way to extract Emma from this situation. Hell, she didn't seem to want to be extracted anyway.

Which meant the right choice was clear.

He had to let Emma go.

Didn't matter how badly the man in him wanted to take care of the woman by his side.

Didn't matter how badly he wanted to kill General Trung.

Kill him not because he was a ruthless bastard with a list of victims longer than the Magna Carta and the Bill of Rights put together.

But because Trung had something he didn't deserve.

Something that Edge wanted for himself.

Something that Edge felt was his.

Now that jealous, possessive rage sparked again in

Edge's heart. He swallowed hard, then turned to Emma. That forked path opened up again in his mind with startling speed. Edge could feel himself losing his grip on logic and common sense. He was angry and jealous and wasn't thinking with a cool head, but he couldn't stop himself.

Maybe he didn't want to stop himself.

"Trung's expecting to see me tomorrow, isn't he?" Edge said, his eyes narrowing as he watched Emma's annoyingly peaceful expression as she stared straight ahead.

"Yes, but . . ." she said, hesitating and blinking as if she understood where this was going and she didn't want it to go there.

Which of course made Edge's blood heat up even more. Did she really love that guy? How could Edge feel drawn to a woman who chose to be with a damn monster? Was Edge cut from the same cloth as the General? Were they both destined to clash over this woman? Was Edge headed on a suicide mission because he was losing his mind over some whore?

Now Edge almost choked as the word echoed in his mind. He'd spent his early teenage years breaking noses and cracking jaws of the uppity assholes who called his mother a whore after they paid her for what they wanted. It always burned him that some dickheads thought they were paying for more than just sex, that their lousy hundred bucks gave them the right to treat Edge's mom and her friends like they weren't even human. Edge was good at using his fists, but he understood the power of words too.

Words could hurt. Words could burn. Maybe even kill.

And it had almost killed Edge to hear the words Pam Edgerton spat at him when she kicked him out of the house herself.

You're ruining my career, she'd screamed at him. Get the hell out and don't come back.

Edge had thought he was protecting his mother. Instead she hated him for it. Didn't want his damn protection. Didn't need him "taking care" of her delicate sensibilities.

Get the hell out and mind your own damn business, she'd told him before slamming the door on his face. It was the last image he had of his mother, angry and hateful, some asshole with a wedding ring on his finger and his dick hanging out in the background, his face all bloody from Edge's protective rage that was unwelcome and unwanted.

Edge blinked in shock now, astonished at the power of his anger, the viciousness of his thoughts.

What the hell, he thought with embarrassment that made his cheeks burn crimson in the red glow of a hundred lamps. Was he seriously sitting there and feeling grumpy about mommy yelling at him twenty fucking years ago? Hell, he should go out there and whimper like a fool alongside Parkov and his kitty cats.

"You all right?" came her voice through Edge's red haze.

Emma was looking at him with a weird smile. Like when she'd asked Edge earlier if *he* was the one who needed help.

"I can't let you kill him," she said slowly, like she was choosing her words carefully. "I need him alive. I can't let you kill him, Edge. There's nothing you can do to help me. Absolutely nothing. In fact you getting involved will mess things up. That's why I keep telling you to go, Edge." She blinked, looked down at her hands, then back up into his eyes. "Even though I want you to stay," she whispered. "Even though I want you to kill him. Even though I want you to . . ."

Her eyes widened for a flash and her cheeks reddened even though the whole room was red. She was quiet. Edge stared at her, not sure whether he could trust what he was feeling, what she was saying—or wasn't saying.

Edge tried not to finish her sentence, to speculate on what she hadn't said. Instead he focused on the words she *had* said.

They weren't the words of a woman in love.

They were the words of a woman with a plan.

A woman with a secret.

A woman on a mission.

13

Emma's mission was unraveling. It had taken years to get here, and now she was going to fail just as she got close enough to touch it, feel it, smell it.

The room was red like the two of them were inside a ruby. The lights weren't blinding or harsh. The heat didn't burn her skin. It was warm and soothing. It was wholesome and healing.

Just like being next to Edge felt strangely healing. Not just for her but for him as well.

Emma glanced up at him. He was looking directly at her. His green eyes looked purple-black in the red light. His beard was wild and red like some barbarian from a faroff planet. The whole scene was otherworldly and eerie, like they were in some alternate universe where perhaps nothing was as it seemed.

"Seems like maybe I should stop telling you to go," she said after Edge refused to take his penetrating gaze off her.

"Never been good at following orders, Ma'am," Edge said.

Emma smiled a little. "So if you're not going to go,

Extracting Emma

then maybe I should give you a reason to stay." Her eyes widened, heat rushing to her cheeks when Edge raised an eyebrow. "Ohmygod, that's not what I meant."

Edge grinned. His eyes danced wickedly. He stayed silent.

She looked at his dark red lips and thought of that kiss. Then she looked into his eyes and thought of what was at stake here.

She thought about that weird feeling of making a choice about which direction her life path was going to take. She wondered if she'd already made those choices. If Edge had made them too.

"I chose to be with General Trung," she said. "And I'm going to stay with him until I find what I'm looking for, Edge. You need to know that before you make decisions based on . . . on me, I guess."

Edge's face tightened. His cheekbones looked sharper, his eyes narrowed like arrowheads. He blinked, swallowed, then nodded for her to go on.

Emma shifted her butt on the smooth wooden bench. She patted down her hair at the back. Her thick black hair was straight as always. It was just the tiny colorless silky ones on the back of her neck that were all electrified.

"The Chinese took over Tibet decades ago," she said, blinking as she realized she was talking about things that she'd never spoken about, didn't even know about until her senior year at UCLA when she got the call that her mother had swallowed six 1mg capsules of Fentanyl and left Emma a sealed envelope and the house and a request to be cremated and her ashes cast into the Pacific Ocean. "My mother was ethnic Chinese, dad was Tibetan." She swallowed. "Do you know what happened back then when the Chinese took over?"

Edge's eyes lost the harshness that had burned in them when Emma had told him she was going to stay with Trung. He nodded. Set his jaw tight. Nodded again.

"Cleansing," he said. "There were rumors of orders to eliminate all traces of ethnic Tibetans. Make sure it was only ethnic Chinese left over. No chance of any future insurrection if there's nobody left to start a revolution. Clean and efficient."

Emma nodded. She swallowed as she remembered the letter her mother had left for her. Ma couldn't die without passing on that knowledge. But she couldn't live with it either. She'd survived long enough to see Emma through college and into the world. Then her petite, hollowed out, prematurely wrinkled Ma left her secrets behind in the harsh world and flew away to the birdhouse in the sky.

"She watched them stick my father with bayonets like he was a sack of potatoes," Emma said, looking directly into the comforting red glow of the wall. "They said she could go because she was Chinese." Emma swallowed, closed her eyes, held back tears that were not of sadness or rage or any emotion that had a name. It was too complex to be named. Too raw to be looked upon directly, just like the sun would burn your eyes off if you dared stare into it. "But they told her she had to leave her twin daughters behind. They were half Tibetan, after all."

Emma felt Edge stiffen beside her. He moved closer. She glanced up at him and forced a tight smile that said she was OK, that she wasn't the one who'd been hurt the most by what happened all those years ago. She was the lucky one. She was the chosen one.

She was the guilty one.

"Ma was pregnant with me," Emma whispered. "She wasn't showing, so they didn't know."

Edge exhaled hard. "They'd have killed her for it. Bastards."

Emma nodded. "Ma said she begged for her twin daughters' lives. Offered herself, to the death, she said. The soldiers laughed at her. Said she was too old and they had so many Tibetan girls that were going to be killed anyway, so nobody wanted some Chinese widow who was already stretched out from twins. They told her to go to hell. That she should be grateful they didn't hang her for bearing half Tibetan children."

Edge put his arm around her shoulders. It was heavy and warm. It felt very nice. Emma didn't tell him she was OK and didn't need to be comforted.

She *was* OK, of course. But she liked his arm there. She liked his body close.

"What were their names," Edge asked softly. "How old were they?"

"Five years old. Xie and Po," Emma said evenly. She looked at him, her gaze hardening. "They would be in their thirties now. And those still *are* their names."

Edge frowned. Then realization dawned on his bearded face. "Shit, you think they're alive," he whispered. "You're looking for them. You think they're . . . they're in Trung's brothels somewhere?"

Emma half shrugged, half nodded. "Ma said she was still on her knees begging when a young Chinese Army officer came to her. He told her he was in charge. He told her not to worry. He said Xie and Po were half Chinese, so they would not be killed. Instead they would learn what all women knew in their hearts was their natural duty, he told her with a very broad and brilliant white smile. They would learn to use their gifts in the service of others." She looked at Edge, her eyes narrowing as that unnamable emotion filled her throat and made it hard to speak. "He told my mother that everyone had roles to serve in life. Boys were soldiers and girls were whores, he'd said matter-of-factly to her. That was the natural order. He'd said his own mother had been a whore and his step-sisters too. There was no shame in it, no escaping it, no point fighting it. She saw his brass name plate when she looked up from where she'd been down on her knees. It said Captain Trung."

Edge took a breath, then let it out slowly. "Trung is a reasonably common name," he said quietly. "The Chinese Army is vast. Well over a million soldiers. Might not be the same Trung."

Emma shook her head stubbornly. "Ma wrote that she'd been searching online for years. She'd finally found a photograph of a man named General Trung. She recognized his dark yellow eyes. His unreadable smile. His square-jawed face. She wrote that it was him. Older and heavier. But it was Trung. She was sure of it."

"Wrote?" Edge asked with a puzzled expression. "You never spoke to her about it?"

Emma shook her head. "She kept it all to herself. Only when she gave up all hope of finding Xie and Po did she write everything down for me and allow herself to do what she'd wanted to for years. I was a senior in college. She wanted me to have a carefree, happy life in America with no baggage from the past. But at the same time she couldn't let the memory of Xie and Po die with her." Emma shrugged. "So here we are."

Edge was silent for a long moment. Then he nodded gently. "I'm sorry," he said. "Nobody deserves that. Not your Ma and not your sisters and sure as hell not you, Emma." He took a breath, his expression hardening again. "All right. So maybe it was Trung all those years ago. But what are the chances that . . ."

He trailed off. His question was clear.

Emma smiled. She blinked away something and looked down at her hands again.

"I've been running my DNA through all sorts of databases all over the Far East and South Asia," she said. "I've gone through all sorts of non-profits that can check DNA against DNA taken from criminal records. Murder victims. Accident victims. Anything."

Edge kept his arm around her shoulder, stroked his beard with his other hand. "There'd be a partial match, yeah. So you got a hit in Macao?"

Emma shook her head.

Edge grunted. Stayed silent.

Emma frowned up at him. "Why is that surprising?"

Edge shrugged. "Thought you'd have gotten a hit that

one of them was picked up on prostitution charges or something else in Macau. Some indication that they're alive and in the area. Why else would you put yourself in this position? Give yourself to Trung in some vague hope that . . . that what, you'll just *happen* to run into one of your sisters from two decades ago? That you'll just look into their eyes and know instantly that they're long lost sisters? Come on, Emma. That's just . . ."

"Just what? Stupid?" Emma snapped, her frown cutting deeper. "Is that what you think?"

Edge winced, shook his head, forced a smile. "Of course not. It's just . . . you know what, forget I said anything. It's none of my damn business."

Emma felt Edge take his arm off her shoulder. She blinked, her eyebrows knitting to a frowny V as she felt her anger rise.

She wondered if she was being defensive. After all, it *was* a pretty long shot that Xie and Po were alive and still working as thirty-something prostitutes somewhere in Macao, somehow still within Trung's domain.

But there was a non-zero chance. It was the best chance she had. And after hearing about Trung and Zhu's plan to get all the women's DNA into their system, Emma had started to believe there was such a thing as fate. That she was destined to find them.

She tried to understand why she was so worked up. She decided it was because Edge had suddenly gotten all worked up.

He'd taken his hand away from her shoulder. He was staring straight ahead like a sulky giant who wanted to stomp around and break things.

Now Emma went back over what Edge had said.

Extracting Emma

Why would you give yourself to Trung without more evidence.

Emma stole a glance at the big frowny grumpy SEAL. Was he . . . *jealous?*

Emma felt a rush of heat whip through her body. Her toes tingled in her cloth slip-on shoes. Those fine hairs on the back of her neck stood up like an invisible breath had whispered against them.

"I haven't *given* myself to him," she said softly. "I'm using him to get what I want."

Edge shrugged his grumpy shoulders. "Like I said, none of my business. If you need to fuck him to get what you want, that's your right."

"I'm not *fucking* him," Emma said somewhat defensively, not sure what she felt a need to defend.

Edge shrugged like he didn't care. Then he looked at her from the corner of his eye.

"Really?" he asked, eyebrow raised, curiosity in his gaze.

"Yeah, really," said Emma, sticking her tongue at him and rolling her eyes.

Edge grunted. Kept that sideways, raised-eyebrow, questioning look going.

Emma stayed quiet a moment, not sure whether to go on.

Edge shifted his big body on the wooden bench. Kept his inquiring gaze steady. Emma wasn't sure what was happening, but she knew something was happening.

The gently buzzing lights cast the room in a red halo that reminded Emma of red rooms she'd visited all over the world. Every culture had made the connection between red light and the world's oldest profession.

Red like flesh.
Red like blood.
Red like love.

"Trung has exotic tastes when it comes to violence," she said, gulping when she realized where her mind was going, where she felt Edge's mind was going too. "But pretty tame when it comes to sex. Thankfully," she added hurriedly, not sure if it came across as hurried.

Edge grunted once. It was slow and rumbling, almost a growl.

Emma felt a chill rise up her back. It wasn't the icy kind of the chill. It was the other kind.

"I . . . I can show you what he likes," she whispered, not meaning to whisper but unable to speak because of the shocking arousal surging through her. "If . . . if you want, I mean. If you want to see."

Edge took a long, slow, thundering breath. He gazed at her, blinked once slowly, then nodded once without shifting that deadly intense, seriously locked-in gaze that was making her very hot and very wet.

"I want to see," he said, his voice low and rumbly. "Show me."

Emma blinked wide-eyed as she felt the wetness burst into her panties like she'd just peed herself. Somehow she stood from the bench even though her legs were shaky and her lips were trembling.

She took small steps towards the wall of red lights. It was like walking onto one of those sex stages in Amsterdam. Red spotlights and crimson flares.

She could feel Edge's eyes on her behind. She could sense him stiffen on the bench. He was sitting upright and erect.

She didn't need to look to know that he was bulging like a beast, his green eyes riveted on her red-soaked figure, his attention completely on her in a way that gave Emma a thrill like she didn't think was possible for her.

She arrived at the wall. The rows of LED bulbs were beneath smooth glass. The bulbs were humming gently. The glass was warm but not hot. This was just enough heat to make her sweat a little in the armpits, wet a little between her legs.

Emma placed her palms flat on the warm glass like she did against Trung's penthouse window. She kept her legs together. Took a breath.

Then she slowly slid her hands down the glass, daintily shuffling her legs back and raising her bottom to the viewing angle Trung preferred. She kept her thighs together, her big round ass up on display.

The red room started to spin around her. She was dizzy with arousal. Giddy with desire. She wanted to be watched by him. She yearned to be touched by him.

The redness was hauntingly exhilarating. When she blinked she thought she saw herself wet and red and wide open like a flower in the rain. She understood why the lights were always red, everywhere in the world.

Maybe it was not for the men. Maybe it was for the women.

Now Emma felt a shadow fall over her arched body from behind.

Edge was standing behind her. He had not touched her. He was looking at her.

"Like this?" he asked, his voice thick with arousal. "Your thighs together like this?"

Emma nodded. Her hair fell forward over her face.

She tossed her head back to get it out of her eyes. As she turned her head sideways she caught a glimpse of Edge standing behind her.

His face was hard and peaked with arousal so vivid that Emma gasped under her breath. His arms were down by his side, both fists clenched, thick veins bulging around his forearms like vines on ancient tree trunks. Biceps rippling like a bull's haunches. Triceps thick like tires.

And he was monstrously erect in his black cargo pants.

Peaked like a pyramid.

Tented like the big-top.

"He makes you keep your clothes on?" Edge said, his voice low and dangerous.

Emma shook her head. She couldn't speak. She was so hot and so wet and the room was spinning so hard that it took everything to just keep her palms there and hold on for dear life like a girl on a possessed merry-go-round.

"Then take them off for me, Emma," Edge whispered, his voice oozing with authority, heavy with need. "Just like you do for him."

A tiny moan escaped Emma's trembling lips. When she was with Trung arousal wasn't even a consideration. But somehow Edge ordering her to show him what Trung liked was making her wet with the most furiously filthy need.

She couldn't move for a long moment. Then she stood upright again. She pried off each shoe with the opposite foot.

Then, with her back still to Edge, Emma slowly unbuttoned her jeans.

Extracting Emma

She unzipped carefully, her knuckles and fingertips grazing the front of her panties. She could feel the stickiness come through the satin and coat her fingertips. She could smell her scent rise up to her nostrils. It was very strong. It made her wetter.

Emma's breath came in short, shallow gasps. She stuck her thumbs on either side of her waistband, then slowly pushed her jeans down over her hips.

Edge groaned softly as Emma pushed her jeans down past the top of her ass. She kept going, her pussy throbbing as she peeled her jeans down her thick thighs.

She bent down and got one foot out, then the other. It wasn't the most graceful disrobing, but Edge groaned again when she straightened up, which made it quite clear that it was having an effect.

"Panties?" Edge asked in a growling whisper.

"He likes them on," she said hesitantly.

She thought a moment. Trung always made sure she wore thong underwear. The first time he'd made her change her underwear before he started doing his thing with himself.

If Edge wanted to know exactly what the General liked, then Emma should show him, she thought as that dark, sickening thrill raced up her bare thighs when she realized how twisted it was that the despicable General Trung was indirectly responsible for this filthy arousal that was raging through her body in this red room.

Emma took a breath, then ran her fingers along the back of her purple full-measure panties from behind. Slowly she pulled the back up until the satin wedged between her rear crack. She made sure it got all the way tight and deep. Then she placed her palms on the glass and arched her back down.

"Holy fuck," Edge muttered. "Damn, that bastard does not deserve this. I'm going to kill that motherfucker. I swear it, Emma."

Emma blinked and half turned her head. "Are you thinking about me or him right now?"

Edge was quiet behind her. He didn't answer. Emma could feel something building up in Edge. There was something dark and dangerous about this whole thing. Like Edge's knowledge that the General had been there first was enhancing his arousal in some sick way.

And maybe it was doing the same to Emma, she thought when she realized she was dripping like a tap through her totally saturated panties. She glanced down at herself and saw that the front of her panties looked black, they were so wet. The goosepimpled skin around the corners of her hidden V were shiny-red with wetness, the red lights making it look like it had just been raining blood.

"How does he touch you?" Edge whispered.

She could hear his voice move closer. Feel the heat of his body. Smell the thick masculine scent coming off his underarms.

"He doesn't," Emma said. "He . . . he just touches himself. Finishes on me from behind. It's very quick."

Edge came closer to her from behind.

He stopped right behind her raised bottom.

She yearned to feel his hands on her skin.

But his hands stayed by his side.

She listened for his belt buckle coming loose.

There was no clink of metal.

Then she heard the swish of cloth on skin.

A rush of Edge's warm aroma swept over her.

He'd taken off his shirt, she realized.

Then she heard two thuds on the wooden floor.

He'd kicked off his boots.

Now came the clink of metal. The sound of a zipper's sharp teeth.

The swish of thick canvas as his pants came off.

The scent of his sex thick and clean like the earth after a rainstorm.

"He doesn't touch you," Edge whispered, his breath hot on her bare lower back, so close to her skin she almost pushed back into his face.

"No," she whispered. "He doesn't touch me."

Edge grunted. "And he finishes *on* you?"

Emma nodded.

"Very quick, you said?" he whispered as she felt his beard graze her smooth ass and send a rash of goosepimples across her bare skin.

She managed to nod again.

"Well, Emma," Edge growled. "I *am* going to touch you. I'm going to finish *inside* you. And I'm going to take my own damn time doing it." He took a heavy, panting breath, exhaling hard like an animal in heat. "Because even though you're going back to him again, going to give yourself to him again, going to arch your back and raise your gorgeous ass for him again, right now you're mine, Emma. Right now you're mine, you hear? I'll get you back to him, help you get what you want. But first I'm going to take what I want. Claim what I want. Possess what I want. And what I want is you, Emma. Just you. All of you. You and only you."

14

You and only you.

Edge heard himself saying something but it all sounded faroff and faded, like trying to call to someone across the deck in the middle of a windstorm, while being lashed by rain big as bullets, pounded by waves hard as concrete.

Edge himself was harder than the cast iron masts of a Navy destroyer, and when he looked down he saw his hands planted firmly on Emma's round globes that were spread out before him like two red moons that only confirmed he was on some different planet which was red like blood, red like hell, red like her.

Edge groaned as he kneaded her buttcheeks forcefully, pressing his fingers deep into her flesh. He'd been stunned by how gorgeous she looked standing there in her black sleeveless blouse and her panties that were dark and damp. Now he was almost out of his gourd as Emma moaned and arched her lower back while pushing her ass into his palms.

Edge was bare-chested and his pants were gone. He kept his black briefs on, but they were tented obscenely and sticky from where his cockhead had been pushing against the cotton. The only thing holding him back was the knowledge that if he unleashed his cock, he wasn't going to be able to hold back at all. Not one damn minute. He'd be lucky to get himself inside her before exploding like a cannon.

No wonder Trung was very quick with his release.

Edge blinked away the sickening possessive rage that came from knowing that Emma had allowed the General access to what Edge believed was his own damn property. But it wasn't just jealous anger. There was a powerful arousal built into it as well.

Edge didn't understand it, but it was there and he couldn't deny it. He would have wanted Emma anyplace, anytime, anywhere, no matter who she was with or had been with. That wasn't the source of his mad arousal.

But it was driving some of the urgency, Edge realized. It made him want to take her *now*. Claim her before the General got his eyes on her taken ass again. Make sure Emma knew she belonged to him now, that when she went back over enemy lines, she'd be protected territory.

Protected by him.

Supported by him.

No matter how bad it ripped at Edge's insides.

Edge grasped the elastic sides of her panties and ripped them off her. He slid them out from between her thighs, then held them up to his face and sniffed them like some deranged dog.

Emma turned her heard and looked at Edge, and he

tossed her panties away and gripped her ass with both hands. Squeezed hard, then spread her rear cheeks, ran his thumb along her exposed crack until she shuddered.

Then Edge went down on his knees behind her, kissed her furiously all over her rump, reached his hand between her thighs and roughly rubbed her mound and lips with his open palm and fingers.

She shrieked and smacked her palms against the glass as a wave of wetness came down all over Edge's hand. He wasn't sure if she'd just come, but he was going to keep going until she collapsed or he died of a heart attack.

Edge's heart was pounding while his cock throbbed like it was drawing all the blood his heart could pump. Hold on, heart, he thought as he buried his face between Emma's luscious buttcheeks while he fingered her from beneath and thumbed her from behind until she was a thrashing mess slapping the glass like some animal in a showcase.

She came all over his hand like a waterfall, bucking her hips forward and then lurching back into his face. Edge grabbed her around the waist and whirled her around, holding her firmly as he dropped his body back from his kneeling stance.

She yelped in surprise, then gasped when Edge brought her down perfectly so she landed thighs-spread directly on his face. She was still gushing like a river in spring when Edge found her slit and rammed his tongue up it, keeping it extended all the way, stiff as he could make it.

"Oh, *Edge*," she wailed as he reached up under her

black blouse and clawed at her boobs while she rode his tongue, came all over his beard, down his cheeks, around his damn ears. "What are you doing to me? I'm . . . I'm losing my mind, Edge. I can't even . . oh, shit, I'm coming again."

Edge drank from her like a wolf at the waterfall. He swallowed her like he wanted to possess everything about her, hide it away inside him so nobody else could get to it. He pinched her nipples hard through her bra, then popped the underwire up over her globes and held her upright by her boobs as she finished all over his face.

Then he pulled her down onto him and kissed her on the mouth. Hungrily at first, then slowing down when he realized she was gasping for air from the fury of what had just happened.

He stroked her hair and kissed her lips gently as she caught her breath. She nuzzled into his neck, still panting against his skin. Her right leg was bent at the knee and crossed over his peaked briefs. She was looking down along his abdomen towards his bulge. She seemed fascinated.

He watched her looking at his erection trying to burst through the cloth. Then he grinned when she glanced up at him, her eyes shining red just like everything was shining red.

"You're so big and hard," she murmured, smiling like she was delighted. "Do you want me to . . . do something?"

Edge chuckled and shook his head. He was bigger than a house and harder than a hammer right now, but

Extracting Emma

he didn't want to rush it. He wanted the release to build in his balls until he exploded with every last drop of his thick seed.

He was shocked at how badly he wanted to come inside her. How deep he wanted to drive into her. How desperately he wanted to see her pussy overflowing with his semen.

"You're doing something to me too, Emma," he whispered as she moved her knee over his tortured cock, making it flex and throb like some trapped beast. "I'm imagining things that I never really thought about before. Not with anyone else. Not even in my fantasies."

"That's ambiguous and not very specific," she said. "Not fair. I was very specific and precise."

Edge saw red for a moment when he remembered how this thing had started. He considered telling her that he was fantasizing about filling her again and again until she overflowed like a flooded river. As far as fantasies went it was pretty damn tame, but there was something rippling beneath the surface of that need which made Edge stay silent.

He stroked her silky black hair, ran his knuckles along her pearl-smooth cheek, reached down along her sides and hips and around to her ass and down over her thigh. She was bare bottomed but her black blouse was still on.

Edge reached down with his fingers and pulled it up past her belly. He stroked her tummy and she giggled and shied away like she was ticklish.

Edge grinned and kissed her nose. He glanced down along her curves again, marveling at how well they fit against the ridges and grooves of his body. Again his gaze drifted to her belly. It was round and healthy. Edge wondered what it would look like heavy with his babies.

His cock almost exploded at the thought. He almost blacked out from the burst of arousal. This was new to him. This desperate urge to possess her and make her his the way animals do with their mates.

Of course, it was about as natural and primal as it got, but Edge still couldn't shake the feeling that there was a dark thrill of competition with Trung that was giving this need its razor-sharp point, making him so damn desperate to empty himself inside this gorgeous woman, like he had to get there first.

Edge pushed the thought away but it came back like a boomerang. Trung didn't touch her, Emma had said. He just released on her, then zipped up and went along with his day.

But now Trung had explicitly sent Emma over to Edge. He'd given Emma and Edge two days alone. What the fuck was going on in that General's head?

Was it the same thing going on in Edge's roiling mind?

Had the General suddenly felt the thrill of competition too?

Realized that Emma was a woman worth fighting for?

Shit, was the General throwing down the gauntlet?

Making Emma the battlefield?

"What was the fight about?" Edge said suddenly.

Emma looked up at him. She frowned.

"In the Hong Kong tabloids," Edge said impatiently. "Looked like Trung had pushed you around. Maybe even hit you."

Emma blinked. She shrugged against his body. "He said he'd lost his temper because Zhu had uncovered an assassination plot with one of the women. But it turned out the plot was one of Trung's own ruses to test how well his guards were searching the brothel rooms. So it couldn't have been that." She shrugged again, less convincingly this time. "Like I said, Trung is unpredictable. He tries to be unpredictable, in fact. Says it's an advantage in war."

Edge looked down at her. Unpredictability was indeed an advantage in war. Which meant Edge needed to get into Trung's head. Into his mind.

Into his woman.

"When was that photo taken?" Edge asked.

"Why does it matter?"

"Just answer me."

Emma blinked up at him. Edge realized his tone had sharpened. He exhaled, softened his gaze.

"Tell me," he said again. "When, Emma?"

"The same night," she said softly, not looking into his eyes.

Then she did look into his eyes, and Edge saw that she knew. She understood. She'd seen it. Maybe she'd even seen it before Edge did.

"After leaving that Hong Kong arena," Edge said as he stared up at the red lamps shining down on them from the ceiling, "He was jealous. He saw something in the way we looked at each other."

Emma snorted. "Trung doesn't get jealous. He offered me to Zhu the first day I arrived."

Edge's jaw tightened. "Zhu touched you?"

Emma shook her head. "I'm not his type."

Edge grunted. "He's still going to die. Slow and painful. Screaming and crying."

Emma giggled. "Were you always such a good sweet-talker?"

"That turn you on?" Edge whispered into her hair. "Imagining Zhu being slit open from the crotch all the way up to his neck?"

Emma made a disgusted sound against his neck. It wasn't real. Edge could tell she'd imagined worse. Or better.

"Both Zhu and Trung are off limits until all the women's DNA are in the General's computer databases," Emma reminded him.

"How long?" Edge said, feeling a constriction in his throat when he remembered he might have to let Emma go back to the General. That he'd promised to help her. Support her. Allow her.

Emma shrugged. "It's going slow," she said. "Zhu doesn't think it's worth the effort. He's still working on all the staff and soldiers. Could be months. Maybe longer."

"Why don't you take over?" Edge snapped. No way Edge would survive months knowing that the General's hellish hands and stinky semen was anywhere close to his woman. "Let me kill Zhu. Trung will give you the job. You can hire a hundred nurses to draw blood. Hell, you could hand out syringes and tubes and show the women how to do it themselves. We could be done in a week. A month tops."

Emma smiled up at him. "There is no *we*, Edge. I'm going back to Trung alone. I don't want you anywhere near him."

Edge felt that thickness in his throat again. "He asked you to bring me to him," he said through that thickening anger. "He's expecting me tomorrow, and I'm going to be there."

"No, you're not," Emma said sharply. "There's nothing good that can come out of you being in the same room as the General."

Edge blinked back the rising rage. "You called him the General, not Trung," he whispered. "There's a part of you that likes playing that role. Being his . . . his . . ."

"His whore?" Emma said, her eyes shining but not with anger. "You can say it, you know. I don't have the same hang-ups about the word. I don't mind it, in fact. It's an exciting word." She shrugged, those maple-brown eyes dark crimson under the red lamps. "I like it."

Edge's cock throbbed against Emma's thigh as he looked into her shining eyes. She moved her leg back and forth against his painfully erect cock, then reached down and gripped his shaft over his black underwear.

He groaned, his palm reaching for her ass, his grip tightening until he was clawing at her buttcheek while she slowly jerked him up and down while staring into his eyes with that shining crimson gaze.

"Fuck, Emma," he groaned as she kept her pace steady and slow even though her grip was tight around his thick shaft. "You're messing with my head. I'm so damn turned on and turned around being close to you. I want to possess you, Emma. Own you. Like you're my property, my domain."

"Well, you can't own a woman in today's politically correct society," Emma said with an innocent, wide-eyed shrug. Then those eyes narrowed again, that smile changed form, her tongue slid out for a flash. "But you can own a whore," she whispered. "You just have to pay the price."

Emma moved her hand faster now, and Edge almost choked as the arousal ripped through him like a knife through his guts. He was close to coming through his damn underwear, and he grabbed her wrist and yanked her hand away.

Emma tried to grab his cock again, but Edge twisted her wrist while rolling away from under her. She yelped in pain as he turned her around by the wrist. Then she yelped again when he raised her ass and spanked her twice on her right cheek, hard and fast, right on the meatiest part of her cushion.

He spanked her again, this time on the left buttcheek. His fingers marked her smooth skin like she'd been whipped. He kneaded her round buttocks as she whimpered, then smacked her again before clambering on top of her from behind and spreading himself over her body like a blanket.

Emma gasped as she went flat onto the warm wooden floor of the red room. Edge grabbed her wrists and spread her arms out wide. He pressed his face against her cheek. He was completely spread over her body. They were like two snow angels, face down, one on top of the other.

Edge's cock was pressed flat lengthwise along her rear crack. He ground his hips against her until he felt her open up and give him a nice groove for him to stay there. She tried to move, but Edge was heavy and Emma was pinned to the floor like this was the endgame in a wrestling match.

Extracting Emma

He smelled her hair and exhaled against her cheek. Her eyes were wide open, and she was breathing in shallow gasps. She was still in shock from being turned and spanked.

"Being unpredictable is an advantage in war," he whispered against her ear.

"Are we at war?" she whispered, still staring straight ahead, still breathing hard.

"That's how you capture territory," Edge growled. "You stake a claim to the property you want to possess. Plant your flag so everyone knows it's yours. Then you defend it to the death. Take on all comers. Beat them back if they dare breach your borders. Yeah, it's war. Damn right, it's war, Emma. And you're the prize and the battlefield and the damn weapon, all in one."

Emma tried to turn under him, but Edge kept his weight on her. She looked at him from the side of her eyes.

"You're crazy," she muttered. "You're both crazy."

Edge felt that competitive fire spark up again in him.

"So you saw it in Trung too, didn't you?" he growled. "You saw that he wants to compete over you."

Emma was quiet. She nodded best she could beneath his weight.

"He was never jealous, you said so yourself," Edge said, moving his hips over her bottom and grinding his suffocated cock lengthwise along her rear crease. "Until the night our eyes met in that arena. It was the thrill of competition, Emma. It's sick, twisted, maybe even unspeakably dark. But it's real, Emma. It's been real for millions of years. It's just been suppressed and silenced because it can't be spoken of in polite society. But there's something about a taken woman that makes a man want her even more. There's nothing like stealing something precious from a rival. Putting your seed in her. Deep in her. Every last drop. So he can't get there first."

Emma gasped, her eyes flicking from side to side as she listened.

"I mean Trung feels that way, not me," Edge said quickly. He swallowed hard. "We can use it, Emma."

Emma stayed silent. Edge wasn't sure if she was freaked out or insulted that she was being reduced to a vessel to carry a man's seed. Maybe she thought Edge wanted her because she was someone else's. Edge knew that wasn't true. But it wasn't completely un-true either.

There was a part of him that wanted to fight for this woman and win her in the most primal way, the only way that mattered to those base biological instincts that ultimately controlled all creatures great and small. And maybe that was useful too, in this situation.

After all, how else could Edge bring himself to let Emma walk back into the dragon's lair, let that evil beast taste her with his serpent tongue, claim her with his wicked claws?

Edge knew he had to use this savage, possessive part of himself, just like they needed to use it in Trung. Besides, Emma had already seen it in him, felt it in him, heard it from his own damn lips.

Hell, she understood more than anyone that everyone paid the price to get what they wanted. Everyone offered what they had to give to get what they wanted.

Emma had seen the same give-and-take arrangements that Edge had grown up around. She'd said the words herself, hadn't she?

You can own a whore. Just pay the price.

Now those words took on new meaning for Edge. Emma had told him she didn't find the word offensive in the right context. She found it exciting. She wasn't baiting him into insulting her. She was speaking her truth.

If you want me, then you need to pay the price, she was saying. *And that price is to let me go back to him until I get what I want. Then get me out of there and take me home. Make me your private whore. For always and forever.*

Now Edge's mind spun down from its manic tornado-like swirling. He gazed down at the silent Emma, a red snow-angel beneath his big broad body.

He thought of how she'd told him to leave her and go. She'd said it with a strange resignation in those maple-brown eyes. He considered how she'd made her way all the way to Trung's inner circle with just the power of her will, pure dedication, one step after the next.

Suddenly Edge was certain Emma would find her sisters. What seemed at first to be a stretch at best was now almost a certainty in Edge's opinion.

Single-minded focus like that always got results. Edge had seen it again and again in the field. Improbable events could be made certain just by the power of will. She was close, he decided.

And that's why Edge had been drawn into her universe.

He was her way out.

He was her way home.

"You never truly expected to survive this mission, did you?" Edge asked quietly. "You wanted to find your sisters just to know they're alive. That they survived. That was the goal. You wanted to know they were alive. Then you were going to kill Trung and Zhu. Probably die in the process. This was about revenge more than anything. That's part of the reason you gave up your American citizenship, isn't it? Not just to prove yourself to Trung, but also to make sure you didn't create a political mess in case you did manage to kill a Chinese General with ties to their MSS intelligence organization. You weren't sure you would even contact your sisters if you found them."

Emma's eyes flicked side to side again, floor to ceiling as she breathed beneath him.

"What would I say to my sisters?" she whispered. "There's nothing I can say. Nothing that won't just cause them pain. They probably don't even remember our mother. If they do, they hate her for abandoning them." She shrugged beneath him, blinked away a tear. "And they'd hate me for being the lucky one, Edge. Maybe they'd even blame me for being the reason my mother left them. Maybe if she wasn't pregnant, she'd have fought harder to save them instead of becoming a refugee and running away to the safety of America."

Edge stroked her hair, listened to her voice, dug his elbows into the floorboards and eased up his weight so she could turn beneath him.

Emma wriggled her body around and looked up into his eyes. "A part of me suspects I'll never find them," she whispered. "Maybe even *hopes* I'll never find them.

Extracting Emma

But I can't stop looking. I'm terrified that if I give up looking, a bigger part of me will die. Just like it did for Ma." She shrugged again. "I know I want to kill him, Edge. But when Trung dies, the last hope of finding out what happened to them also dies. That's why I'm stuck in this place, Edge. Can't turn back. Can't move forward. Not heaven and not quite hell. I . . . I don't know what to do, Edge. I thought I did, but after meeting you I don't know anymore." She blinked. Her eyes were bright with tears. She wasn't sobbing. Just gently crying. "Now there's a part of me that wants you to take me away from all this. Just get me out of this hole I've dug myself into. But . . . but how can I turn my back on this? It would be like turning my back on my own history, my own family, my own duty. I can't do that."

"You can't and you won't," he said softly but firmly. "I understand duty, and my duty is clear, Emma. I'm going to help you finish this. I'm going to get you out. I'm going to take you home." He nodded, his jaw tight, eyes focused and clear, just like his future seemed focused and clear. "You *are* going to find them. You *are* going to end this cycle of inherited trauma. And it ends with your sisters alive and Trung dead. With the two of us together. It's pretty damn simple. You just have to allow yourself to dream that ending, Emma."

Emma shook her head. She smiled through her tears. Looked up into his eyes.

"How do we get there from here, Edge?" she whispered. "We can't just walk out of Parkov's bunker. And if you kill Trung, the Macau Chinese gangs will splinter apart. There could be infighting, gangs trying to steal each other's territory until the Chinese MSS install somebody else to keep the peace. They might not even do it, just decide to let the gangs sort it out. Maybe the Russians will muscle in, like Parkov said. Either way, that would probably be the end of any coordinated effort to get all the women's DNA. So you can't kill Trung for months, maybe years. And Parkov wants you to kill Trung tomorrow. It's well and good to dream of some happy ending someday, but right now we're trapped, Edge. It's hopeless. We're back to the same place we started. Your best option is to walk out of here. Maybe you can help me from the outside."

Edge shook his head. "If I leave here, it's to kill Trung and Zhu, just like Parkov wants. I'm not gambling with your damn life, Emma." He closed his eyes for a moment. "There is another way this works, though. If we can find another way to track your sisters down, then I can kill Trung and Zhu tomorrow. Give Parkov what he wants. We can stick around in Macau for a bit so you can settle down the women like Parkov wants, then we'll find a way to abandon ship. That won't be a problem."

Emma's eyes brightened with hope. "How will we find my sisters without Trung and Zhu? Even *I* don't know exactly how far Trung's empire stretches in all the hotels and back-rooms and alleyways of Macao. He's starting to expand in Hong Kong too. Might also have brothels on the China Mainland coast, for all I know. I've only been working with his operation for a few months. I don't have access to all his records, just the ones for the main red-light hotels. Besides Trung and Zhu, who else could get to that kind of information? Unless you know someone connected to Chinese Intelligence or some super-shadowy group of super-shadowy people in trench coats and hats and dark sunglasses," she added with a chuckle. Then the hope came back to her eyes. "Do you?"

Edge rolled off Emma with a groan. He lay on his back and stared up at the ceiling. Glanced down at his tented underwear. Then he groaned again and let out a long, annoyed sigh.

Damn you, Benson, he said to himself. You suck at timing.

Then Edge remembered that the Russians had smashed his phone.

15

"About time you traced that phone," Benson barked into the black plastic desk telephone in his Hong Kong hotel room. "I was about to send in a squadron of drones to blow your bedroom windows apart and wake your lazy ass up."

The CIA tech guy who still owed Benson a fistful of favors muttered something. Benson nodded, grunted, then hung up without saying goodbye or thank you.

This wasn't the damn time for politeness. Benson was anxious. Edge was new to him, new to the game, all alone out there. Benson had nudged the guy along with instructions to "feel out the situation" with Emma. But he'd forgotten that Edge wasn't like Ax and Bruiser and the other Darkwater guys.

Yeah, Edge was different. More impulsive. More reckless.

More dangerous.

Benson stood from the solitary white wooden chair. Thoughts started flooding his mind. He worried that maybe he was the reckless one, creating dangerous situations with this obsessive drive to test out his theories about space and time, fate and destiny, the secrets of the universe. Just because it *seemed* to have worked with those four SEALs and their women didn't mean it would work every time.

Was Benson falling prey to the gambler's fallacy? That insatiable need to spin the wheel one more time, again and again, going for broke until everything really did break?

"Too late to fall apart now, old man," Benson muttered out loud as he started to pace the carpeted floor of the hotel room. "Get your damn head in the game. Figure out how you can help them instead of going all paranoid like some newbie agent on his first real mission."

Benson took one more round of the room and then strode back to the desk. His laptop was open. The tech guy had sent over the map of Macau tracing the path of Edge's phone. The phone's signal was lost a couple of hours ago. Last known location was the estate of Grigory Parkov. The tech guy suggested that Parkov's garage and mansion were reinforced with steel and concrete to block any signals. Or the phone had been smashed.

Either way, it meant Edge was trapped in Parkov's fortress.

Not what Benson expected.

"What the hell were you doing on the Russian side of town," Benson muttered, his silver-gray eyes following the path from Parkov's estate back to Macau's Warehouse District near the old dockyards. "Were you with Emma? Or did you go there to blow off some steam in the arena?"

The Darkwater phone was equipped to record sound and video and transmit it to Benson's laptop, but the phone needed to be turned on for that. Edge hadn't turned it back on after landing at Macau airport.

Benson wished he'd given Edge the fancier model which worked even when it was turned off. Still, it was better this way. The other model had a bunch of tiny circuit boards beneath the battery that would look very suspicious if the Russians popped open the back cover. This model was pretty standard. And Benson had remotely wiped all the messages after Edge read them on the way to the Hong Kong airport. So even if the Russians forced Edge to unlock it, they'd find nothing suspicious.

The downside was that Benson was flying blind here. He didn't even know if Emma and Edge had connected. Hell, maybe Edge had gotten the phone stolen at the arena when he left it with one of the handlers during a fight. Maybe Edge had decided not to bother with Emma at all.

He might have just tossed the phone in the trash. Some Russian grunt could have picked it up. It could have gotten carried back to Parkov's place. Edge might not be there at all.

"Well, you don't have the authority to call in a strike or a rescue or even get a damn surveillance drone down there," Benson muttered as he sat down hard on the chair. "Edge isn't SEALs anymore. And I'm not CIA anymore."

Benson considered calling CIA Director Martin Kaiser, but decided against it. Kaiser was an old friend, but he'd still tell Benson to fuck off. Especially without any clear evidence that Edge was in trouble and needed help.

"How can you help them," Benson wondered out loud, tapping the edge of his laptop feverishly. "What can you do right here, right now, to help them?"

Benson thought back to the directive he'd given Edge.

Find out why she's doing this, Benson had suggested. *What are Emma's motives?*

Now Benson leaned forward, excitement surging through his battered old body. He went online, logged into the National Security Agency databases with the credentials Kaiser had secretly passed on to him for Darkwater. The NSA, bless their tender hearts, had used the Patriot Act to justify recording every single email message, phone call, and internet keystroke made by every American.

Benson reached for the half empty cup of now-cold black coffee. He drained the dregs and wiped his mouth with his shirtsleeve. He settled his fingers on the keyboard, then pulled up Emma Chang's NSA records.

The raw data was too much to digest, but the NSA had pre-programmed reports that used Artificial Intelligence to find patterns, notable events, things that stood out.

He scrolled, clicked, poked, and prodded. Squinted, sighed, groaned, and grunted.

Nothing out of the ordinary all the way through high school and most of her time at UCLA.

Then something changed in Emma's senior year.

Her mother killed herself, which Benson already knew from Emma's basic file.

But Mama had left her daughter a note.

A note that Emma had scanned and uploaded to her private cloud account.

A private account protected by a password and all sorts of fancy promises about encryption and privacy.

To which the NSA just shrugged, smirked, and gave each other super-secret high-fives.

Benson sat up straight, riveted as he read Emma's family secrets, her private drama, her heartbreaking duty. He sighed, slumped down in his chair, rubbed the bridge of his nose, considered his next actions carefully.

He was still flying blind, but that familiar buzzing in his brain told him he was on the right track. That Emma was being driven by something deep and powerful, emotions that were dense and dark, concentrated energy that was creating a vortex just like Benson had marveled at during the Dogg and Diana mission.

Which meant Emma had indeed drawn Edge into her universe.

Into her drama.

Into her mission.

"So if they're together, what does Edge want to do," Benson wondered aloud. Then he chuckled, shook his head, grinned wide. "Yeah. He wants to kill the bastard. Break the good General's neck. Probably that guy Zhu as well."

But Benson lost the smile as he thought through how it might be playing out. Emma was clearly looking for her sisters. She clearly believed Trung was her only hope of finding them.

Which meant she wasn't going to let Edge kill Trung yet. Which meant Edge was desperate for another way to find Emma's sisters so he could kill Trung and take his woman home.

Benson had seen the DNA searches Emma had been running with every organization she could think of in the Far East and South Asia. There'd been zero partial matches in law enforcement and death records all over China, Macao, Hong Kong, and most of the outlying territories. The trusty NSA had captured Emma's own DNA sample, and so Benson ran it against the CIA databases.

NO MATCHES.

He sighed, thought a moment. China's intelligence agency was the Ministry of State Security—MSS. They were like a combination of the CIA, NSA, DHS, and maybe even the FBI. They were serious people. And China's level of surveillance made the NSA look like paragons of privacy and non-intrusiveness.

So Benson sighed, rubbed the bridge of his nose again, then picked up one of his three cell phones. He tapped, scrolled, then tapped again. It rang three times before a familiar voice answered in a familiar tired tone.

"What do you want now?" came Martin Kaiser's voice. "I just got done cleaning up that mess with Dogg and Diana."

"That *mess* saved your ass along with the entire State Department," snapped Benson. "Anyway, this should be straightforward. You know anyone who can run a DNA sample through MSS?"

Kaiser was silent for a moment. "Chinese State Security? That's a big ask, John."

"Well, I'm asking," said Benson without missing a beat. "Just sent you the DNA on email. Looking for partial matches. Siblings. I'll hold."

Kaiser muttered something about Benson running out of favors. Benson leaned back in his chair and sighed. The two of them owed each other so many favors it was too hopelessly entangled to sort out. Like it or not, their own destinies were inextricably linked. Perhaps one day they'd laugh about in the afterlife. Benson was relishing telling the skeptical old bastard *I told you so, Martin.*

"All right, hold on," Kaiser finally said.

Benson heard him clacking on his computer keyboards. Then Kaiser got on another phone. Benson heard him speak quietly to the other guy. Calling in a favor. Give and take. You suck mine, I tickle yours.

Benson scratched his nose and waited. He looked at his watch, that battered old Fossil Chrono from his Navy days. Stretched his arms out wide. His shoulders had been tensed up. Benson wasn't used to being left out of the game.

Benson rubbed the back of his aching neck as he heard more clackety-clacking from Kaiser's end. This was only the beginning of Benson's problems. If Martin's guy came through with a match, then Benson still needed to get the message to Edge that Trung and Zhu were wide open for the taking, that they weren't needed any longer, that he could go in hot and come out clean.

Except that might be difficult if Edge was being tortured and beaten in Parkov's fortress. Maybe even dead, just like his phone.

Let's handle one problem at a time, Benson reminded himself as Kaiser hung up with the other guy and came back on the line.

"He's running a search. He'll send you the results directly via anonymous encrypted email. Now stop using me as your secretary, John. I'm the Director of the CIA, for fuck's sake."

He hung up. Benson stared at his phone. Counted the seconds. Then minutes.

Suddenly the email icon lit up. Benson tapped it open. That tension in his shoulder came back hard. That pain in the bridge of his nose made him wince.

"Shit," Benson muttered, reading the report and then slumping back down in his chair.

He absentmindedly turned the coffee cup around, then glanced into the sludge at the bottom like he was hoping to see some gypsy signs of good fortune.

Benson thought hard and fast. He thrummed his fingers on the glass-topped desk. Tapped his brown leather brogues on the rough carpeted floor. Ran his fingers through his gray hair. Then he grunted, shrugged, and stood up.

"I should probably pack," he muttered. "Before this turns into a real mess."

16

"This guy Benson could create a big mess," Emma said anxiously. "He could have tracked your phone here, right? So he'll know you're here. He might send in some kind of team to get you out. And if Parkov gets killed, there'll be ripples through the entire Macau scene. Zhu wouldn't let anyone within a mile of the General until things got sorted out. The whole DNA thing would come to a standstill for who knows how long. Shit. Shit. Shit."

Emma pushed herself to her feet, then went around the red-lit room picking up shoes and underwear and jeans. She put on one shoe before realizing she hadn't put her jeans on yet. She cursed in Cantonese and then started over.

"Benson's not going to send in a team," Edge said, raising his head off the floor and cradling it with the interlocked fingers of both palms. "I'm not Navy anymore. He isn't CIA anymore. He won't risk creating a massive international incident by storming a Russian Bratva guy's fortress in Macau. Hell, it would be a three-way international incident."

Emma frowned at his choice of words. Her gaze fell upon his mostly naked body. He was lit up by the red blaze.

She took a moment to admire his ridges of hard muscle, massive pectorals that were lean and cut like slabs of granite. He was huge and bulging in his black underwear, and Emma felt a stab of both arousal and guilt when she saw it flex as he smiled lazily up at her.

"All I said was that Benson might be able to get your DNA run through Chinese Intelligence," Edge said with a sigh as Emma got her jeans up past her thighs and started the tough climb around her hips. "But my phone is gone, so there's no way to contact him."

"You said he found you in Egypt and then Hong Kong," Emma said as she struggled to get her jeans all the way closed. She frowned down at her belly. Then she sucked in some air and pulled the button closed. "He might send someone here. We have to get out of here, Edge. Break out. Fight our way out."

Edge propped himself up on an elbow. He stroked his beard thoughtfully, then nodded and popped up to his feet with the grace of an elite athlete. His package also looked elite, all peaked and glistening at its apex. Emma blinked away a thought that made her blush.

"Oh, Edge," she whispered as he stood and faced her, stretched his arms out wide, twisted his body at the waist to open up the kinks. He was beautiful, she thought. She wanted to make him feel good now. She felt like she'd broken her end of the bargain. Had there been a bargain? Oh, she didn't know. She was anxious now. Worried that things were falling apart. That if Trung closed the door on her, she'd never get back inside. "I want to . . . you know I want to, right?"

Edge grunted, shrugged, then swiped at the air.

"I fight better with a loaded weapon," he said, forcing a wink and a sideways grin.

He turned and started to gather his stuff. He began to dress, still facing away from her.

Emma watched him pull his black tee shirt down over his broad, sinewy back. She looked down at herself. Her feet were tight together. Habit.

She blinked in shock when she remembered who'd forced the habit onto her. She felt a strange ripple of something she didn't want to believe was real pass through her insides.

She realized she was excited to go back to the General.

Not because she wanted to be with Trung.

But because she was excited by the effect it was having on Edge.

Thrilled by that possessive beast she'd seen behind the SEAL's burning eyes.

He'd called her his property. His patch of land. His piece of meat.

He wanted to plant his flag in her. Stake his claim. Seed her garden.

Edge turned back to her as the thoughts made her hot again, wet again, whole again, a whore again. She kept her feet tight together and looked at him. She saw his big Adam's apple move as he swallowed. She sensed that bulge at his front expand again.

And she knew that some dark part of Edge was secretly pleased that phone had been smashed.

That there was no option but to send her back to General Trung.

Pick up the gauntlet the General had tossed at Edge's feet.

Answer the challenge that called two warriors to the arena.

One good. The other evil.

One her guardian angel. The other her tormentor demon.

One a promise of a dreamlike future. The other a reminder of the brutal past.

There was no way out, Emma realized. No way out without going back in.

"Parkov will send someone back to look for us soon enough," Edge said. "Let's wait in the gymnasium. Those eighty-pound dumbbells will work real nice. If I can snag one of those H&K machine guns, we've got a chance of getting out of here."

"We can't kill Parkov," Emma reminded him as he walked to the door and opened it carefully.

Edge glanced back at her. "Any other villain you don't want killed? I feel like my talents are being wasted here."

Emma smiled. Edge grinned back. He winked. This time the wink wasn't forced.

Edge glanced up and down the curved corridor. He reached his hand back for hers. She shuffled her cloth shoes along the smooth wooden floor and slid her hand into his. He pulled her out into the hallway.

Seconds later they were inside the gymnasium. The lights were bright overhead. They were fluorescent lamps beneath criss-crossed ceramic grills on the ceiling. One wall was all mirror. The other three walls were blue. Everything looked far too blue, even with the walls. It was because they'd been in a red room for so long, she figured. It would sort itself out soon.

Emma saw herself in the wall of mirrors. She looked very red in the face, but with a blue tint because of the screwed-up rods and cones. Edge looked about twice her size in every direction in the mirror. She giggled and pointed at them.

Edge raised an eyebrow at himself, then strode over to the steel rack with the dumbbells. He picked up an eighty pound weight in one hand and practiced swinging it like a club, then a sword, then a baton.

She was shocked by his strength. She wondered if Edge could twirl her around by her waist and toss her up in the air like those dainty UCLA cheerleaders.

She was about to ask him when there was a sound outside in the corridor. Edge put his finger to his lips, then directed her towards where she'd be in plain view of anyone opening the gymnasium door.

She nodded and hurried silently across the stiff black floor mats in her rope-soled cloth shoes. She sat on a freestanding exercise bench. It had firm blue cushioning on it. She kept her thighs together and her back straight.

She glanced at Edge. He was standing against the blue wall by the closed door. It would open over him, hiding him from immediate view. The guard's attention would be drawn to Emma. All she had to do was draw him far enough into the room that Edge could swing his eighty-pound baton-club.

Emma listened as a door opened in the corridor, then closed after a couple of moments.

The next door opened, then closed when the guard found it empty. Now heavy footsteps came to their door and stopped outside.

The door opened a crack. Edge pressed against the wall, holding his breath. The door stayed open just a crack. The guard was smart enough to think about which room might have something that could be used as a weapon. He wasn't going to come barging blind into a room with eighty-pound clubs available to an ex-Special Forces guy who'd been kicked out of the SEALs for excessive violence.

A waft of cigarette smoke entered the gymnasium through the cracked door. Emma frowned when she saw Edge relax and exhale the breath he was holding in, then lower his club and saunter out from his ambush spot.

"You got me," Edge said as he walked around to where the guard peering through the cracked door could see him. "Come on in, buddy. Just don't shit on my head, OK?"

The door swung open all the way. It was the Russian guard who'd been manning the outside door. Emma had seen Edge and him grin at each other like they'd been sharing a joke earlier. She figured the don't-poop-on-my-head comment was their inside joke. At least she hoped so.

The Russian guy walked in with his machine gun slung low and pointed at the floor. The cigarette was hanging from his lips. His right eyebrow rose as he eyed Edge's caveman club.

"You are lucky it was me," he said somewhat disapprovingly. "And that I am not dumb enough to walk into a room full of dumbbells without checking first." He took a drag from his cigarette, blew out a puff of smoke, then waved the burning butt in Edge's direction. "Do not be stupid, SEAL. Grigory is not a pussycat even though he does cootchie-coo with those damn beasts that stink like my ballsack in the summer. There are men all over the place. Too many, even for a Navy SEAL. Many of us were Russian Special Forces. You can try, I suppose. But you will just get killed and she will die too. Grigory is not amateur, OK? And not everyone is forgiving like me." He glanced at the club, then gave Edge a hard look dead-on.

Edge didn't flinch. The guard held the hard look for a long moment, then broke a grin.

"Grigory is still occupied with his mangy kitty-cats," he said in his thick Russian accent. "I came to make sure you are not planning anything like what you were just planning."

Edge did a bicep curl with the dumbbell. "Don't know what you're talking about," he said innocently. "Just showing off my muscles to the little lady here, see?"

The Russian glanced at Emma, then snorted and shook his head. He turned and walked out the door, still shaking his head. Emma heard his boots thump down the corridor to the main door leading back to the tiger-den. The big door opened and then closed. A metal deadbolt slid noisily over it.

Emma started to exhale slowly. Then she huffed out the air when Edge did another bicep curl and posed for her viewing pleasure. He held the pose for a bit, then grinned and let his arm drop to his side. He strolled over to the rack and put the dumbbell back in its slot.

"Looks like we're stuck here," he said, opening and closing his right fist. He strolled to the door. The guard had left it open. Edge kicked it shut with a suddenness that made Emma jump. "Little lady," he added with an eyebrow raise as he slid the deadbolt across the door.

Emma stayed seated on her blue-cushioned workout bench. She kept her knees and feet together. Edge looked very large from her angle down on the low bench. She felt like a little lady in this position.

She liked the feeling. It didn't come to her often. She wondered if she'd always feel that way around Edge.

Then she felt a flash of fear when she realized she might not always *be* around Edge. They weren't in danger right now. But there was danger all around them. Danger in their future. Maybe too much danger for them to even *have* a future.

She glanced up into his eyes, then blinked and looked down. As her gaze moved down, she caught a glimpse at the front of his pants. She felt her breath catch.

"Relax," Edge said as he walked up to her and sat down on the bench beside her.

Emma touched the back of her neck. "I am relaxed."

Edge glanced at her. "You look tense."

Emma shrugged her shoulders. Arched her neck back. It was very stiff.

"Not at all," she said stiffly.

They were silent for a long minute. Emma thought the lights were still very blue. She blinked three times, then touched her neck again.

"You need a neck rub?" Edge said somewhat awkwardly. Maybe hopefully. Perhaps wickedly.

Emma shook her head. She looked at him. Shook her head again.

Another tense moment of silence thicker than the concrete walls, heavier than the eighty-pound dumbbells staring in quiet amusement from their rack by the mirrored wall.

Edge cleared his throat loudly and pointedly.

"Well, if you need a neck rub, let me know," he said gruffly, looking around like a bear searching the trees for honey.

Emma stifled a giggle. She sighed loudly, to counter Edge's throat-clearing.

"Well, I don't *need* one," she said softly, looking around wide-eyed like a she-bear trying to help her growly mate find that darn honeypot.

Edge let out a growly grunt. He inhaled deep, then exhaled slow.

Emma felt her thighs tighten even though they were already tight together. She wondered if her pussy was pulling her thighs together as it clenched like the hungry little creature it felt like right now.

Extracting Emma

Then slowly Emma parted her thighs. She turned on her ass, then swung one leg over the bench until she was facing away from Edge, straddling the long blue-cushioned exercise bench.

She waited silently. There was no movement behind her.

She held her breath.

Then let it rush out when she felt Edge move behind her.

Two big hands grasped her shoulders from behind.

Two thick thumbs pressed into the stiff spots beneath her neck.

Emma let out a groan as the tension evaporated. The relaxation came so fast she slumped back against Edge's hard body. It was like hitting a moss-covered wall. She leaned her head back and looked at him upside down like a cat.

Edge leaned forward and kissed her on the lips. It was strange to kiss upside down. She giggled as he licked her nose.

Then she gasped as he pushed her head forward, lifted her hair off her neck and whipped it forward so it came down like a jet black mop over her face.

He pressed those big thumbs against the base of her neck from behind. Then slowly brought the fingers of each palm around the sides of her bare neck.

Edge massaged her with his thumbs as his fingers stayed firm around the sides of her neck. His hands were huge, and she knew he could extend his fingers and circle her entire neck with a two-handed grip.

He made no such move, and there was no pressure on the front of her throat. But the knowledge that Edge could do that make Emma shudder.

"Edge," she muttered as he pushed those golf-ball sized thumb-tips against the base of her neck.

She didn't say anything more. Didn't ask him to bring his fingers all the way around. Didn't admit she wanted the feeling of being totally in his grip, in his control, at his mercy.

Edge's body shifted behind her. He came closer, kissed the back of her neck.

His fingers stretched out, his grip widening until those big hands were circling her throat. Zero pressure as he stroked her smooth neck from the front and rolled his tongue around her ears from the back.

Emma was hunched forward and moaning softly. Her hair was in front of her eyes like a curtain of black rope. Her nipples were hard beneath her bra. Her cunt was warm beneath her hopelessly soaked and mostly ripped underwear that she'd somehow tied up so it would stay on.

Edge moved his right hand up under her chin, then slid two big fingers into her mouth. They felt big like chubs of sausage.

Emma gasped, then started to suck them. Delicately at first, then hungrily as Edge reached his other hand around, pulled her hair off her face, then gripped her locks firmly by the roots from behind.

Emma's head was locked in place. Her roots burned as Edge fisted her hair and fucked her mouth with his fingers. She felt her wetness start to soak through her jeans onto the synthetic cushion beneath her parted thighs. She could smell herself in the closed room. She could taste herself on Edge's fingers.

"This needs to come off," Edge growled against her neck. He slid his fingers out of her mouth, then grasped the bottom of her blouse and pulled it off past her head. Then he examined her bra. "Hell, this bra is more secure than Fort Knox. I'm gonna hunt down the designers and pluck out their eyeballs."

Emma giggled as Edge snapped off her admittedly overly complicated bra.

"What is it about eyeballs with you guys? That's what the General wanted me to do to you before he changed his mind," she said without thinking as she hunched her shoulders forward to shrug her bra off.

Now she realized what she'd just said. She wondered if it registered with Edge. She wasn't sure if she wanted it to register or not.

Edge was silent as her bra dropped to the floor. He pulled her against his body, then reached around with those big hands. His palms cradled her breasts from below, raising them up as his thumbs stroked her nipples until they pebbled and pricked up.

Then Edge pinched her nipples hard. So hard she yelped and jerked against his body.

"The General ordered you to kill me?" he whispered against her throat from behind as he held her nipples tight. "How?"

He pinched her big areolas again when she didn't answer. Then one hand moved back up to her throat. He cupped his palm around the front of her neck. No pressure. Just firm enough to make her wet herself like a girl scared of the dark.

Or maybe like a woman afraid of the darkness.

The darkness in her need.

The danger in his touch.

The desire in his voice.

"Poison," she whispered, her eyelids fluttering as Edge stroked her throat and plucked on her nipple. She thought a moment, then went on. "He told me to use my gifts to get close to you. Do whatever I needed. Whatever I wanted. Whatever was necessary."

"I see," growled Edge as he licked her cheek from behind, squeezed her throat slightly before easing up. "Are you disappointed he changed his mind?"

Emma giggled, then gasped when Edge let go of her nipple and slid his hand down the front of her jeans and right past the waistband of her panties.

Suddenly his fingers were pressed lengthwise against her naked slit, and her eyelids flicked wide when his thumb ground against her sensitive hood.

Emma gasped again, then let out a slow moan as Edge curled those sausage-sized fingers into her vagina and held them there.

Now with one hand around her throat, the other curled up her cunt, Emma felt herself completely locked in place. Edge was calm and still, but she could feel the arousal running through him like a deadly current far beneath the surface.

"Maybe he didn't change his mind," Edge whispered

into her ear as he stroked her throat, dragged his fingertips against the top wall of her vagina. "Maybe you're just doing whatever it takes. Whatever you need to do." He paused, licked the side of her neck. "Whatever I want you to do."

Emma could barely see through the waves of ecstasy raging through her mind and body. Her wetness was pouring over Edge's fingers, seeping through her panties and jeans. She thought of how he'd fucked her with his tongue and then his fingers. She wanted to feel the rest of him inside her. All of him. Like she wanted to devour him. Possess him. Claim him just like he said he was going to claim her.

Edge stroked her throat one last time, then dragged his open palm down past her collarbone and grasped her left breast. He lifted and squeezed, pinched her nipple hard, pulled and plucked at it before doing the same with her right breast.

Then he slid his wet hand out of her jeans, caressing her smooth round belly with both palms, squeezing and compressing, pressing and rubbing.

Emma sighed and stretched back against his body. She looked down at Edge's big hands rubbing her belly like she was a little she-Buddha.

She blinked away a vision of herself bigger and rounder down there, bursting with new life, about to pop like a champagne cork. She thought of that mama tiger pushing out her babies so smooth and easy, with natural grace. She wondered if she'd ever get the chance to experience that miracle.

Then again fear rose up in her. The real world was

trying to get back inside her frazzled mind. She tried to push it away, but it grabbed her by the throat and tried to shake her back to her damn senses.

But the fear couldn't chase away the arousal. She was moaning and writhing, groaning and gasping, reveling in Edge's rough hands all over her naked breasts and bare belly. She could feel his erection big and upright against her lower back even through two sets of clothes.

Edge most certainly wasn't losing his arousal. Telling him the General had sent her to poison him had only gotten him harder.

She moaned again as that thick, twisted sensation of dark ecstasy slithered through her, using the fear to drag her higher, pull her deeper, remind her that she was the prize, the weapon, the battlefield all in one.

Emma's eyelids were fluttering. The light came through in splintered strobes. She was aware of little more than Edge's big warm body behind her, his rough hands clawing and caressing, his hot tongue licking and lapping.

For a moment it felt like more than one man was there, and she let out a gasping moan at the thought. She kept her eyes closed and let the fantasy flow through her.

It was Edge and his mirror-opposite both taking her at once. Then it was more. Countless more. Lines of them. Every man who'd touched her sisters. Every nameless, faceless, soulless beast who'd tasted their innocence, savored their skin, stolen their souls.

A hundred hands exploring her.

A thousand fingers claiming her.

A million men sharing her.

Then suddenly it was one man again. She was turned around on the bench and Edge was kissing her on the lips. His mouth was big and his kisses were hungry. His tongue was thick in her mouth. He rolled it around and then licked her lips, her cheeks, her nose. He sucked her chin, dragged his tongue down her neck.

Then he pushed her down onto her back, leaned over, started to suck her nipples, back and forth between them, his eyes ferociously focused with mad lust, his beard wet and matted from when she'd come all over his face like a waterfall in the spring.

"I need to have you," Edge growled as he shoved his bearded face between her breasts, reached between her legs and started to unbutton and unzip her. "All of you, Emma. Get these off before I eat them off you."

"Don't eat my clothes," Emma mumbled as she fumbled for her zipper. She wasn't sure what she was saying. She wasn't sure if Edge knew what he was saying. Either way, it seemed reasonable that he not eat her clothes.

Edge stood up off the bench and pulled off his tee shirt and kicked off his boots and yanked down his cargo pants and pulled off his underwear. Emma was still flat on her back lengthwise on the bench, one foot planted on the rubber mats on either side. She was bare chested and her jeans were unbuttoned and mostly unzipped. She stared up at Edge naked above her.

He was a wall of dark, rippling muscle. His hair was wild and his chest was expanding and contracting hard as he breathed in and out like he was either building up power or trying to push back some alien beast about to smash through his rib cage and leap at her to seed her womb.

"I warned you," Edge growled as his gaze flicked to her unzipped jeans. "Now I'm going to eat your damn underwear."

Emma squealed as Edge licked his lips and came at her like he was already that hungry alien beast that had arisen from the South China Sea in search of panties. She rolled off the bench and landed hard on the cushioned mats. Edge grabbed her ankles, but she kicked his hands away and crawled away like the world's fastest baby.

"Wait, I'm taking them off," she pleaded as Edge grabbed the waistband of her jeans and yanked her back to him. "You'll tear them."

"That's the damn point," Edge said with a wicked gleam in his eyes. "Your clothes are too complicated. I bet the General doesn't let you wear impossibly tight jeans and bras designed by nuns."

"I only wear dresses for the General," Emma said, hurrying to get her jeans down past her hips before Edge tore them to shreds and made the rest of her day very inconvenient.

But Edge had stopped. Emma looked up at him. Then she blinked in shock when she saw how Edge's cock was curved upwards in a way it wasn't before.

Edge's face was tight. His thick neck was strained. His eyes narrowed to green points.

He was upright on his knees on the mats. She was on her butt, legs out in front of her, staring at his monstrously thick erection. It was like a tree-trunk around the base, with bulging veins circling the dark shaft that was glistening with pre-cum oozing from the bulbous red tip.

Emma wondered what he was seeing behind that shadowy gaze.

What he was picturing. Imagining. Fantasizing.

She kept looking into his eyes as she got her jeans off, then rolled her panties down her bare thighs and past her toes.

Edge's gaze dropped to the space between her legs. Emma felt heat rush up her neck. Her cheeks were burning as she watched Edge move closer to her on his knees, his thick cock gently bouncing up and down as he approached.

"You've got me turned inside out, Emma," he whispered as he got close enough that his cock was stretched out over the fork between her spread out thighs. "I'm seeing things in my head that are driving me insane with need. I want you in a way I've never imagined with anyone, Emma."

"Me too, Edge," she said softly as she watched a long thick trail of pre-cum drip onto a spot just above the top of her dark triangle. "I can't even tell you what's been going through my mind just now."

She gasped as Edge reached between her legs and ran his middle finger up along her slit lengthwise, parting her lips with his fingertip.

"I don't want you to tell me a damn thing," he said, his voice thick with arousal as he dragged his finger back down along her wickedly wet slit. "Hell, I'm not going to tell you what's got me turned around and messed up, got me wild with this need to fill you until you overflow, fuck you until you don't remember anyone else's touch. It's not something that can be spoken about. It comes from a place in us that doesn't understand words. It just knows how something feels."

Emma nodded as Edge pushed her onto her back, then leaned over her and kissed her mouth, lined up his cockhead against her slit, kissed her lips one more time.

She tried to say something but no words came.

She was in that place which didn't understand words.

That place where nothing had names.

That place which was eternal and unchanging but somehow always in motion, never the same.

And then Edge started to go into her. Past her threshold. Into her body. Merging with her. Collapsing the infinite possibilities into one singular event that would spin out a new set of infinite possibilities, spin them both out onto the universe's dance floor as the band played on, fate screaming through the violins, destiny pounding on the drums.

Edge drove all the way into her as Emma's vision split into a million colors and shapes like a kaleidoscope. Her wet red lips parted, as above, so below, both sets of lips mouthing a word that was beyond the reaches of sound, like the first word that created the universe with its power, shattering the dark void into a burst of color, a cosmic flower opening its petals, creating infinite variety from infinite nothingness, birds and bees, snakes and trees, angels and demons, man and woman.

It was only then that Emma realized she was already coming.

17

Edge felt her come all over his shaft, down to his balls. He looked down at her grimace of ecstasy, kissed her quivering lips as she muttered something under her breath, held himself deep inside her and let the violent orgasm work its way through her shuddering body.

Then he started to move in her again. He pushed her hair back so he could look at her face. He went slow at first, savoring the sublime sensation of opening her up and then feeling her warm folds close as he withdrew. It was like a flower taking long deep breaths as he opened and closed her with each stroke.

Edge felt the blood throb behind his ears as he dragged his cockhead against the upper wall of her vagina. His hips moved with slow, steady, rhythmic power. His vision was a haze of moving color. She felt so warm and smooth, he thought. So perfect. So his.

Now an image of Emma in a gown fluttered through Edge's mind. He saw her with her back to him, her feet together just like she'd shown him in that red room next door.

Edge's next stroke was harder. Emma gasped. Her eyelids flicked open all the way.

He forced a smile and kissed her lips. She murmured and smiled back. Wrapped her arms around his neck.

Then she raised her legs and locked her ankles around Edge's waist. Her eyes were wide open. She was looking at him directly.

"It's all right," she whispered. "It's OK."

Edge blinked as his cock flexed. She didn't say anything more.

No words.

Just feeling.

Edge blinked again. That image popped back into his mind. He saw her in that gown again. This time he knew the gown was dark red. There was a golden dragon emblazoned along the back. Its tongue was out. Its teeth were sharp and shiny. Its eyes were bloody and bulging.

The dragon was Trung. Its claws were all over his woman's body. It was tearing her apart. Eating her alive. Fucking her from the inside out.

Edge's jaw clenched. He pumped harder. He was fighting the dragon. Trying to get it away from his property.

He needed to get longer and thicker. He needed to go deeper and harder. He was grunting with the effort. Dizzy from the arousal.

He realized he was ramming into Emma. She was letting out tiny yelps each time Edge drove into her. Her head was jerking back as he pounded his hips against hers.

He slowed down. Then he felt her pull him into her. Hard.

Edge could feel her ankles locked tight behind his back. Her thighs were flexing, pulling him back into her in perfect rhythm as he began to thrust again.

Soon she was bringing him in even harder. Her fingernails were ripping his back to shreds, tearing through skin and digging into flesh.

It was the dragon fighting back. Edge fucked her harder, as hard as he dared, as hard as she pulled.

She was calling out his name as Edge moved with delirious fury. She was saying please and yes and fuck and shit and hell and damn. She was saying it in many different languages. She was telling Trung to die. She was spitting into the air and cursing Trung to hell. She was laughing and gasping. Writhing and thrashing. Raising her legs and ramming her heels into his back like she was trying to pound him into her.

Edge could smell his own blood from where she'd torn his back up. He inhaled deep, licked her face, pulled back and then growled in pleasure as her strong thighs dragged him back into her cunt.

Her eyes were shut tight. Her face was a beautiful mask of pure ecstasy. She was digging her heels into his lower back, urging him on like she needed him to fight harder, dig deeper, fuck the dragon out of her and free her from its claws, save her from its maws, rip her from its jaws.

Edge's jaw was so tight his head pounded from the pressure. He realized he was yelling like a some deranged animal in its death throes.

He was incredibly hard. Monstrously thick. His balls felt heavy like those eighty-pound dumbbells. They slapped wetly against her underside as he went all the way into her with each thrust.

Two more thrusts and Edge felt his balls start to seize up. A massive build up that felt like slow motion footage of a star starting to explode in outer space.

Edge's entire body was shaking. He could feel the thick river of semen thundering up his shaft like a million marching soldiers, rifles loaded, bayonets sharpened, boots pounding the fleshy battlefield as they marched towards their final stand, fully committed to fight to the last proud man.

Edge arched his neck back and roared as he came. Emma screamed at the same time.

Edge swore he heard the mirrored wall shatter from their combined cries. Felt the ground open up so all the demons of hell could marvel at the sight. Saw the skies split open for the angels to look down in delight.

The explosion felt like the death of one world and the creation of another. Edge was blind with ecstasy, his climax thundering like a hundred cannons firing at once, shooting fiery rockets deep into the earth, high towards the heavens.

Edge felt Emma squirt past his shaft as she came violently under him. His body was convulsing as he poured himself into her like a star shooting its molten core out into the universe. He was completely out of his damn mind, nowhere near anything resembling the real world, no sense of space or time, up or down, inside or outside.

It was only when he heard the pounding on the outside of the door that Edge blinked himself back to reality. He raised his head in panic. Looked around, then down.

He was on his back on the mat-covered floor. Emma was breathing gently against his chest, curled up against him, naked like a baby, thick semen oozing from between her legs onto the black rubber mats.

She was sound asleep. A smile on her pretty face. She looked like an angel.

Edge frowned. He had no damn idea when he'd collapsed on top of her, when he'd rolled off her, when he'd pulled her against his body and cradled her like she was his to protect, his to cherish, his to take home forever.

He raised his head and stared at the door. It was still closed. The deadbolt was still across it. Edge wondered if he'd been hearing things.

Then someone pounded on the door again.

"When I said take your time, I did not mean forever," came the Russian's voice. Edge could smell the cigarette smoke from beneath the door. "Grigory wants to see you both. Five minutes."

18

Seven minutes later, they were sipping black Russian tea with Grigory Parkov. Edge's Russian buddy was back at his post near the door. Edge had glanced at him after emerging with Emma four minutes after the knocking. The guy had said nothing. There'd been no nudging or winking.

Which meant Edge had blacked out during that orgasm. Emma seemed to have too. She remembered nothing after the climax that shattered them to pieces. She'd woken up in his arms, a smile on her face. He'd explained that they weren't in a dream.

She'd taken a good thirty seconds to understand that they were still in Parkov's fortress. That they hadn't died and been reborn in some happy world where all dreams came true and everyone held hands and danced in circles like weirdoes on a Utah commune.

Just as well, Edge thought as he remembered that Emma's panties were rolled up in his left cargo flap. He liked this world better. He wanted to fight for his happy ending. He wanted to kill the dragon and save his princess. Hooyah, baby.

"The babies are suckling," said Parkov, putting down his blue-and-white porcelain teacup and picking up his half-smoked cigar. "We can finish our business. Now, what have we decided?"

Edge glanced at Emma. She looked at him and blinked. They hadn't decided a damn thing. Not about that, at least. They'd come to some other conclusions, of course.

One of which was that Edge wasn't going to walk away.

Not today.

Not ever.

Edge smoothed out his fuzzy beard as he considered his next move. Thankfully, Parkov's phone buzzed just then. Parkov glanced at the screen, then grunted and answered.

"Doctor Wang," Parkov said with deadly politeness. "How nice of you to return my call. Perhaps I will leave one of your eyeballs in its socket after I am done with you." He listened for a few seconds, then sighed. "All right. Tomorrow. You can give them their shots."

He hung up and tossed the phone onto his recliner's matching footstool. He returned to his cigar, then returned to the business at hand.

"As I recall," said Parkov to Edge. "You were on your way out when we were interrupted." He glanced at Emma. "Thank you for helping my kitty, by the way. But it changes nothing. The only concession I will offer is a quick death if that is where we end up." He scratched the blonde fuzzy hair on his forearms, then waved his smoky cigar at Edge. "And where we end up is up to you, SEAL."

Edge nodded. He wasn't sure what he was going to do, but it was clear that his next move was to get out of here. He wasn't going to run, of course. But he couldn't do much from inside here.

Besides, Emma would be safe for a day in here. Enough time to make a rescue plan.

Hell, maybe he could find Benson. Maybe the guy would come through with a hit on Emma's sisters. Then Edge could go right into the dragon's lair and clean house. Kill Trung and Zhu, not necessarily in that order. Maybe involving eyeballs, maybe not. Either way, Parkov would get what he wanted.

And after that it would be a fairly easy extraction. Couple of weeks, maybe a month, then he and Emma could disappear. Maybe to that commune in Utah with the circle-dancers in homemade shoes.

He glanced at Parkov. "I'll need a weapon to kill Trung and Zhu."

Parkov snorted. "Zhu does not even allow Trung's own soldiers to carry weapons within thirty feet of the General. They will search your body cavities deeper than you have depth." He scratched his bald pate. "Your first problem is how you will even get close to Trung."

"Trung is expecting Edge at the Metropolitan penthouse suite tomorrow evening," Emma said, much to Edge's surprise. She frowned. "What time is it?" she asked no one in particular.

"Just past sunrise," said Parkov. "So you mean today evening, yes?"

Emma nodded. She glanced at Edge. "Trung and Zhu

both carry handguns. I don't know what kind. They're silver metal. Those will be the only weapons. There will be nothing else in the meeting area of the suite. No pens or pencils. No forks or knives. The wine cups are designed to shatter into little rounded squares like auto glass. Trung and Zhu don't even use chopsticks in the suite."

Edge nodded. He studied Emma's face. Was she telling him this for Parkov's benefit or for Edge's? Had she changed her mind about wanting Trung alive? Was she ready to let go of her past and walk into a future with Edge?

No, he realized when he looked into her eyes. She was simply trusting Edge to make the decision.

She had given herself to him. She was his. She was telling him that he could decide what to do about Trung. She'd made her own preferences clear, but she understood that Edge needed the freedom to do what he did best. Violence was Edge's domain.

"What else?" Edge said, looking directly at Emma.

He watched her eyes carefully. She blinked, glanced away, then looked back at him.

"There might be something you can use," she said softly. "Zhu took the vial of poison back from my office beneath the penthouse. He went directly to the General's suite after that. He may have left the vial in the suite."

Edge noticed she called Trung *General* again. He felt something stir in that place where emotions were raw and nameless, where drives were ancient and primal. He took one long last look into Emma's eyes.

Then he stood and walked towards the metal door

leading to the garage. The guards at the door looked past him towards Parkov. Edge stood with his back to Emma as Parkov said let him out in Russian.

The metal door opened. Edge stepped through. It clanged shut behind him.

He walked down the enclosed corridor. The guards who'd searched him earlier handed him his passport and cards and cash. Edge grunted and took them. He shoved them into his left cargo flap.

Then he blinked twice as the scent of Emma's pussy rose up to his nostrils. Her panties were in that cargo flap. They were wet like sin. She didn't want to put them back on. Edge had shoved them into his pocket without thinking.

Now he thought about them.

And the thought sent him spinning down a path that made him dizzy.

He knew what he was going to do.

19

What was he going to do, Emma wondered as she sipped her black tea and watched Parkov crouch by the tiger cage across the open room. What did she *want* him to do?

Emma shifted on the leather sofa as she finished the tea. It was bitter and strong. She was wide awake now. Borderline jittery. But she wasn't worried about her safety.

She was worried about her sanity.

Worried that she was spiraling off into some kind of madness that was unique to her twisted little mind. She had vivid memories of what she'd seen in her head as Edge fucked her. She remembered things she'd screamed as she hammered her heels into Edge's back as he drove so deep into her she could feel him in her throat.

She'd seen visions of a dragon with the eyes of the General. She'd seen that dragon in Edge's eyes as he came inside her like a hundred volcanoes erupting all at once. She'd wondered if the dragon in his eyes was a reflection of her own eyes. She'd wondered if he'd killed the dragon or simply woken it up.

Emma leaned forward and placed the empty teacup on the low wooden table. As she did it she got a whiff of

Edge's semen from her sex. She thought of that strange moment when she'd woken up against his chest. Her face hurt from smiling as she slept. Her head ached from the strain of the sex.

But her body had buzzed from the feeling of his thick seed deep inside her. She'd blacked out during that climax, but the memory of his hot jets blasting against the back wall of her vagina was imprinted in her mind, recorded in her archives, sealed in her chambers.

She blinked away the memory and sat back in the sofa. She crossed one leg over the other knee. She stole a quick sniff from her armpits, smoothed out her hair.

Then she glanced at the door leading to the back. There was a bathroom with hot water and lush towels. She could clean herself up. She could pee, like they say you should do after sex.

But Emma stayed right where she was. She didn't want to clean Edge's semen out of her. Didn't want to do away with the aroma of their passion.

Edge was on his way to fight for their future. She wasn't certain how it would play out, but she was sure she could trust his heart, trust his choices, trust his instincts. And so she also had to trust her own instincts.

The instinct that told her to sit tight.

To be ready for her role in this fight.

20

Benson was ready and waiting. He watched through his scope as the black Range Rover slowed to a stop along the side of the long straight road. The back door opened and Edge stepped out. The Range Rover took a U-turn and headed back in the direction of Parkov's estate.

Benson glanced at the sun, then at his watch. Not bad. He'd been here about two hours, staking out the coastal road connecting Parkov's estate to the main expressway that led to Macau Central.

Benson had called Kaiser back and badgered him into giving up a contact with Russian Intelligence to see if Grigory Parkov had made any recent calls to his Bratva bosses back in Moscow.

Indeed Parkov had done just that. The call was encrypted, and since the Bratva and Russian Intelligence often did business together, Benson was not given access to the contents of the call.

But Benson's mind was well conditioned to sniff out conspiracies and make educated guesses about how an ambitious mobster with an ex-SEAL at his disposal might think. Then Benson had gotten Nancy Sullivan to run through the flight plans out of Hong Kong to see when Trung's private plane was heading back to Macau.

After some calculated guessing, Benson decided that it might be worth staking out this road just in case he'd guessed correctly and Edge would be sprung by the Russians in time for the arrival of the Chinese.

Benson had been prepared to wait all day. It was barely past sunrise. Hell, they could get a free buffet breakfast at the MGM East and then play dice or mahjong all afternoon.

So Benson hopped into his white Toyota Land Cruiser rental and gunned the engine. The heavy-duty SUV bumped its way down the hillside above the road. Benson's teeth were rattling in his head by the time he got down to the road and pointed the truck towards the tall, bearded hitchhiker in black.

Edge stopped walking when Benson was a hundred meters away. It was too far to see clearly. Edge must have good instincts, Benson thought. A good feel for how things played out. A natural talent for how the game unfolded.

But when Benson screeched to a stop, put down his window, prepared to flash a wily coyote style grin, a chill ripped through his body.

Because one look into the SEAL's mad green eyes made it clear that this game was wildly different from anything Benson had ever played.

Beyond anything Benson ever wanted to play, would ever *dare* play.

Which meant Benson needed to try and shut this

game down now. Before it got out of hand. So far out of hand even Benson might not be able to reel it back in, bring it back home, give them a shot at their forever.

"It's over, Edge," Benson said calmly through the open window. "Come on, kid. Get in. Let me buy you some breakfast while I explain it to you."

21

Edge did most of the explaining, much to his annoyance.

Benson ate a western omelet and listened carefully. He nodded a couple of times, shrugged about a dozen times, wiped his mouth with the MGM East's monogrammed black napkins far more than seemed necessary.

Benson put down his fork just as Edge finished catching him up on the broad strokes of events. No details. Certainly not the kind of details that couldn't be put into words. Edge gave Benson the facts. He kept the feelings to himself.

But Edge had an odd sense that Benson understood what was simmering beneath the surface here. He'd seen it back on the road when Benson had lost the grin the moment he looked into Edge's eyes.

Something had clicked for Benson. Something that made the strange old CIA man want to shut this thing down. Get Edge to stand down from walking into the dragon's lair to fight for the right to carry his princess away into the clouds of destiny. Or something like that.

Benson wiped his mouth again with the napkin. He waited patiently as a waitress in a black pantsuit cleared the table and asked if they wanted more Malaysian coffee or Mandarin orange juice or Singapore fried rice. Or perhaps the gentlemen would like to see the women in the red rooms upstairs? They had all shapes and sizes, she assured them.

Edge declined everything with a hand wave. He'd grabbed a dozen spring rolls from the buffet line and wolfed them down like a starving shipwrecked sailor. Broiled eel, shredded cucumber, thin strands of radish. Wrapped in sheer soft shells with orange-pepper dipping sauce. He could probably have eaten a dozen more. He might do it if whatever Benson had to say didn't give him indigestion.

The waitress left and Benson looked across the two person table on the mezzanine. They were sitting against the railing looking down at a sea of mahjong tables with their colorful tiles. The main floor was packed with tourists from every Asian country and a good helping of Europeans too. The noise was a thick steady sound, so many people chattering at once that it just felt like an undifferentiated buzz.

"Oh, by the way, we got a partial match on Emma's DNA," Benson said merrily through a bite of a dim-sum sweet bun that seemed like an odd choice to go with a western omelet.

Edge stared at the sweet bun as Benson's words didn't quite register in his brain. Maybe it was something about the nonchalance with which he'd said it. Like it was no big thing. Like Emma's entire quest of a lifetime could have been solved by Benson while chewing on a dim-sum bun and sipping orange juice.

Extracting Emma

But Edge listened with mounting excitement as Benson told him that CIA Director Martin Kaiser had called in a favor with someone deep in some shadowy corner of Chinese Intelligence or something like that.

"Almost certainly one of Emma's lost sisters," Benson explained. "From there, Emma should be able to piece together what happened to the other sister too. Maybe even meet them." He shrugged. "If she *wants* to meet them, of course."

Edge blinked in surprise at the shrewd insight. Benson was good. He'd gotten into Emma's head without even meeting her in person. Yeah, he was good. Maybe Edge should listen to what he had to say.

"So now Emma doesn't ever need to go back to Trung's operation," Benson said. "You don't need Trung at all. Besides, the DNA sample gathering that Zhu is doing with the prostitutes will take months, maybe years. And what's the chance Emma's thirty-something sisters are still part of Trung's operation? Maybe they never were. Maybe he sold them years ago. Maybe they retired. Maybe they—"

"All right, I get it, Benson," Edge snapped. He blinked and swallowed. He wasn't sure why his temper had flared. Everything Benson had just said was correct. Edge had said the same thing to Emma himself. "That's . . . that's great, I mean. Really, Emma will be thrilled. Thank you for doing that." He paused, took a breath. "But I still need to kill Trung to free Emma from Parkov's clutches. Then Parkov can do whatever the hell he wants with his takeover attempt. Maybe Emma and I stick around for a bit. Just until I find a safe way to get us out."

Benson shook his head. "You can't kill Trung. You know that."

Edge frowned. "Is that an order?"

Benson chuckled darkly. "It's just a fact. I don't mean you couldn't kill him in a fair fight. I just mean you won't get a chance to kill him. He's a survivor, Edge. He's got that preternatural sense that you Special Forces guys have. The instinct that knows when there's a bullet headed his way. You'll never sneak a weapon into his penthouse. You step into that penthouse with murder on your mind and he'll smell it on you like you just rolled in a barrel of fish oil."

"I told you about the poison," Edge reminded him.

Benson shrugged. "I guess there's a chance. But you won't use it."

Edge cocked his head and blinked. How the hell did Benson know that?

Benson's well-lined face settled into a knowing smile. "You won't kill Trung with poison. Trung would consider poison a woman's weapon. He'd consider that cheating. So would you."

Edge made a scoffing sound that was strangely unconvincing. "This isn't a game, Benson."

"No?" whispered Benson as his gray eyes shone with some light that seemed to come from inside him. "Don't underestimate me, kid. You think I haven't gotten into Trung's twisted head? Seen what's going on in your dark mind? Emma's too? You think I didn't spend a lot of time wondering why a man like General Trung even gives a shit about a washed up SEAL out on his ass? Why he sent Emma to invite you to a meeting in his locked-down lair high above the clouds?"

Edge reached for his water glass to cool down whatever was rising in him. He couldn't look into Benson's eyes. He drank slowly from the glass, careful not to shatter it in his grip.

"Maybe Trung wants to offer me a job," Edge said. "Maybe he wants me to assassinate Parkov. Wouldn't that be a fun twist."

Benson sighed. "All right. I'll humor you. Go on. So you get to Trung's penthouse without being skinned alive by Zhu. Great. You have no weapons. What happens next?"

"Right," said Edge, looking past Benson as he tried to fight his way past this crafty old dragon to get to the final boss dragon. "I'll get to the poison. Smash the vial against his face. Watch the guy convulse to death like an eel."

"Great plan," said Benson with taunting earnestness. "I'm sure Zhu will let you blow right past him and get to the man he's successfully protected for thirty years. And obviously neither of these two seasoned army men will even *consider* drawing their H&K 9mm machine pistols and put more holes in your face than there are holes in your bullshit story."

Edge bristled inside, but stayed silent. He hadn't been expecting a professional interrogation by one of the best who'd ever lived.

"It's a dynamic plan," Edge said with a casual shrug. "I'll improvise once I get to that penthouse, get the lay of the land."

Benson sighed again. "Listen, kid. You've got fire in your blood. You can do a lot of good for the world with Darkwater. But you need to learn how to play the game. Control that fire. Direct that energy instead of letting it flail wildly between sex and violence like a garden hose gone wild," said Benson with gentleness in his voice but sharpness in his eyes. "Let me tell you how it is, Edge. You're being pulled into a battle triggered by the deepest, darkest drives of man and woman. They served their purpose in evolutionary history, but they're too twisted to survive on the surface of today's society. You, Emma, and Trung are all getting wrapped up in this dark spiral of a very intense emotional mixture of sex and violence. It's not for everyone, kid. Most don't get through something like this without losing themselves in the process." He sighed again, rubbed his eyes, then took a slow breath and looked directly at Edge. "Let Trung go," he said evenly. "Focus on getting Emma out. I can help with that. Guy like Parkov will always make a deal. He's not married to this plan. He just saw his chance and decided to roll the dice. He'll talk to me if I offer him something good. Kaiser will help, even though he'll complain about it for the next three years."

Edge shook his head. "Can't take the chance that Parkov says no. Because then Parkov knows I talked to you, that I'm connected to CIA or dark ops or something. He'll kill Emma and nobody will ever find her body.

He'll figure she isn't important enough for anyone to go to war over." He took a slow, rumbling breath. His jaw tightened. "But she's important enough for *me* to go to war over, Benson. I won't give up control over this situation to anyone else. Not even you, Benson." He chuckled darkly, shook his head slowly, keeping his gaze rock steady on Benson. "I understand what you're saying about this spiral of dark emotion that's spinning us into it like a tornado. But we're in it now. Yeah, maybe Emma and I risk losing ourselves in the process. But if we walk away now, we're lost anyway. Trung has to die for us to walk away clean. We have to go in deeper if we want to find our way out. That's how it is, Benson. You don't like it, then tough shit. You try to stop me, I'll kill you myself."

Benson took a long breath, puffed it out like he was blowing smoke. He stayed silent for a long time. Three minutes, according to Edge's mental clock.

"All right," Benson said finally. "Just keep in mind that General Trung being murdered by an ex-Navy SEAL could create an international incident. Teams could get mobilized across borders. Soldiers could get killed." His eyes narrowed. "You know that better than anyone, Edge."

Edge nodded grimly. Hell yeah, he knew it better than anybody. He was living it. The CIA asshole with a broken jaw had done just what Benson was warning Edge about. The guy had mobilized Special Forces because some spook on some shadowy job fucked up and created an incident because of some personal bullshit.

Then SEALs got killed. And CIA assholes got their faces messed up by men like Edge.

Circle of life. Cause and effect. Give and take.

"Take this," Benson said softly. He slid a piece of paper across the table. It had a phone number written down. "Memorize it. Call me if you two make it out. There's a place in Team Darkwater for you both. The others would love to have you and Emma."

He paused, glanced away, scratched the bridge of his nose, then looked back at Edge. His gray eyes were shining again. Silver like a wolf's under a full moon.

Edge wondered if Benson had been testing him. Then Edge wondered if he'd passed the test.

"I'd love it too," Benson said softly. He stood from the chair, slid a hundred dollar bill beneath his empty coffee cup. Then he winked at Edge, rapped his wedding ring on the tabletop, flashed that wily coyote grin. "So go fight your dragon. Save your princess. Bring her home in your arms. Just like the story goes, kid. The only story ever written."

22

Edge had his story straight before he stepped into the Metropolitan Hotel's lavishly gaudy lobby.

Everything was wood and gold. Walls, furniture, even the ceiling. The chandeliers were real crystal. They looked big enough to crush an entire football team. The reception desk was solid wood with gold trim and about a hundred receptionists in high-collared tunics that were military-crisp and royalty-grand.

The gold-framed glass doors swished closed behind Edge. He walked to the reception and leaned across the wide desk. He gave his name to the sharp-looking young Chinese man who'd hurried over to serve Edge.

The man blinked twice, glanced up at an ominous one-eyed camera, then told Edge to wait. After that no receptionist made eye contact with him.

Edge waited for almost an hour. He didn't budge from his spot near the front desk. He had no problem staying in one place for hours, even days. He and Fox had spent three days buried in mud on one filthy mission. They'd watched crabs crawl slowly across their chests. The crabs had figured Fox and Edge for rocks. It was only when

Fox gave in to his hunger and cracked one open for a slimy midnight snack that they scurried off in panic.

Edge glanced up at that one-eyed camera. It had been staring at him for the entire hour. Edge stared back. He was expressionless. Unreadable. He assumed he was looking directly into Zhu's or even Trung's eyes.

It was another full hour before someone came for him.

It was Zhu. Edge recognized him from the photograph in Benson's files. He was tall and wiry, with a long face and a deep black goatee sharpened to a point. He had lines across his brow and around his eyes like his face was a map of the Yangtze river system with all its tributaries and branches. His eyes were shiny like black pearls. They were focused directly on Edge's face. Unwavering and unblinking.

Edge kept his own gaze straight ahead, past Zhu. He wasn't going to get into a staring contest with Zhu. Edge didn't back down from a staring contest, and it appeared Zhu might take it as an affront or a direct challenge.

Yeah, Zhu was going to die too. But Edge's mission was Trung. The big dragon was the prize. Zhu was merely a lizard to be stepped on when Edge got a free moment.

"Where is Emma?" Zhu asked crisply.

He stood directly in front of Edge, that pearl-black gaze fixed on a spot between Edge's eyes. Zhu was almost as tall as Edge. Long arms and lanky legs. Wiry, lean muscle all over. Still a lizard, Edge told himself. Squish. Done.

"Where's Trung?" Edge said. He flicked his eyes suddenly to meet Zhu's gaze.

Zhu flinched instinctively, then immediately brought his gaze back on track. But it was too late. Edge had made him look away. The eye contact game was a one-shot thing. No do-overs.

"The General is not available," Zhu said sharply. There was a flash of hesitation in his eyes. "You may go."

Edge thought fast. Two hours was a long time to make him wait. Sure, part of it was to let Edge stew, see if he lost his patience, see what kind of a man Edge might be. But that wasn't the whole story.

Edge remembered what Benson had said about Zhu. The guy had successfully protected General Trung for thirty years. Zhu was probably a hundred times more paranoid than the General.

Which meant Zhu didn't want Edge anywhere near the General. They must have been arguing about it up there. Clearly Trung had won the argument, but it had been a battle. It meant Trung had been in two minds. Had perhaps understood that he was being reckless. Hell, maybe Trung even agreed that Edge should be sent away, that it was best to retreat from a battle that might prove to be a strategic mistake.

But Zhu had asked about Emma.

Which meant the General had asked about Emma.

Which meant Edge was still in the game.

"OK," Edge said with a shrug. "I'll go."

He turned and started to walk towards the gold-framed glass sliding doors. He was close enough that they swished open before Zhu cracked.

"Come," came Zhu's sharp voice from behind Edge. "This way."

Edge kept his back to Zhu long enough to hide the smile. Then he turned and shrugged again like it didn't really matter either way. That wasn't the game Edge would play when he was facing Trung, but it was the right move with Zhu. The lizard was the gatekeeper to the dragon's lair, after all.

"After you," said Zhu, stopping near a solitary elevator between two wood-paneled pillars.

The elevator doors were thick steel plated with gold. They were bulletproof and blastproof. There was no call button, just a keyhole in the metal doorframe.

Zhu reached down the front of his black silk shirt and pulled out a small golden key attached to a steel chain looped around his neck. He inserted the key and turned it twice to the right, once to the left, twice to the right again. It was a combination. The doors slid open.

Edge stepped inside. Zhu did not follow him. He turned the key again. Maybe a different combination. Edge couldn't tell.

The doors closed. The lights went dead. The elevator stayed where it was.

Edge blinked as a thread of dread ran down his spine. Was he about to be gassed to death or crushed like a walnut as the walls closed in on him.

There was a whirring sound in the ceiling. Lights came

on. They weren't the soft golden lights around the sides of the elevator. These were strange red-and-blue lights that moved along the dark glass walls and ceiling. Like how the lights move on a flatbed scanner. Back and forth as they captured an image.

Edge relaxed and stood very still. The whirring stopped. The regular lights came on. The elevator doors slid open.

Zhu was standing there looking at his phone. He tapped it and nodded at Edge. Got into the elevator and drew the weapon bulging beneath the loose red silk jacket. It was a German H&K machine pistol. He kept it pointed at Edge, but didn't seem too concerned. Clearly he knew Edge was unarmed. He'd seen the images on his phone.

"Magnetic imaging tech," Edge said as the elevator gathered speed on its way up to the dragon's lair. "Find anything interesting?"

Zhu grunted. "Passport, cards, cash, all of which you will leave with the guards at the sixtieth floor waystation before we proceed to the penthouse. Steel reinforced boots, which you will also leave behind." He grunted again. "You may keep the three titanium screws in your left ankle."

Edge grunted back. Not a bad joke for a humorless lizard.

"Stomped a little too hard on some bad guy's head a few years ago," Edge said with a shrug. "Messed up my ankle, but you should have seen the mess I made of that bad guy's skull."

Zhu was unmoved. "Perhaps to him, *you* were the bad guy, yes?"

Edge grinned. "I sure hope so."

Zhu offered his own version of a grin. It showed two rows of misaligned yellowing teeth that were raggedly sharp, like a shark that had been chewing on Florida license plates.

The elevator whined as it slowed to a stop. It was the sixtieth floor. The doors opened and two black-uniformed guards armed with H&K machine pistols took his passport and cash and cards. They waited silently for Edge to take off his boots. He kicked them past the elevator door. The guards did not touch his boots. Edge didn't really blame them.

The elevator doors closed again. Twelve seconds later they opened on the top floor penthouse of the seventy-two story skyscraper.

"After you, I guess," Edge said to Zhu as the tall black-eyed lizard stepped quickly out the door, holding his arm out for Edge to wait.

Edge stayed put. There was a dark red granite wall in front of the open elevator doors. There were dull yellow patterns in the dark red granite. They were intricate and tendril-like threads. Edge didn't care for it much. He preferred blocks of simple primary colors.

Zhu beckoned for Edge to step out of the elevator. There were eight uniformed guards, four on either side, standing at ease with their hands on belted H&K machine pistols.

Edge nodded at them as Zhu led him past the four

guards on the left. They turned and followed as Edge and Zhu walked towards the main room. The remaining four guards followed exactly ten feet behind the first line. The first line marched ten feet behind Edge and Zhu.

Edge wasn't particularly concerned. He wasn't going to fight his way through eight armed guards. He wasn't going to be fighting at all.

Not here, at least.

Edge was a hot-head at times, but he'd never been an idiot. He was deadly aware of the risks of fighting on someone's else's territory, where the enemy had an overwhelming advantage.

Never fight your enemy the way he wants you to fight him.

Edge had always known he needed to get Trung out of his penthouse if there was going to be any chance of taking him down. You don't fight the dragon in his dark lair.

You draw the beast out into the sunlight.

You lure him to neutral ground.

You take away his advantage.

But how do you do that?

How do you tempt a dragon to step out of his cave?

Edge smiled as the General's massive figure loomed against the darkening sky. The General was cast in shadow from the lights of the city coming through the floor-to-ceiling windows behind him.

Trung looked bigger and broader than the height and weight numbers from Benson's reports. His hair was thick and full, cut savagely straight across the top like it had been slashed by a razor-sharp blade. Edge thought of the beheadings ordered by Trung in the Tibetan highlands. He wondered if Zhu had given the General this haircut with that deadly sideways slice.

The eight guards moved back as the General came closer. Edge remembered Emma telling him that Zhu didn't allow armed men within thirty feet of the General.

It was a good precaution, Edge thought as he eyed the holstered machine pistol on the thick black belt which was buckled over Trung's gold-buttoned red tunic. The H&K was accurate up to a hundred feet, but a man's aim got exponentially worse after about ten. Plus, even if all the guards were loyal, a shootout too close to the General would be risky.

Zhu was a good tactician, Edge reminded himself. He would immediately see through Edge's plan. The lizard would not allow the dragon to step out from the safety of his lair.

Not unless the dragon could not resist the temptation.

Could not ignore the challenge.

Could not defeat the beast that lived inside every man's dark dirty heart.

Now Edge let his hand drop down by his side. He could feel the clump of soft satiny cloth in his cargo flap. It wouldn't have looked like anything on the scan.

But it sure as hell meant something.

After all, there was a reason that powerful men, from politicians to professors, police chiefs to presidents, paid high prices for a woman's used panties.

Same filthy reason a hound dog runs around sniffing every crotch in the pack until he finds one that tickles his fancy.

Prickles his pricklies.

Curls his curlies.

Tempts the dragon out of his lair.

The filthy fabric calling him to his fate.

The dank dampness drawing him to his destiny.

Edge reached inside the cargo flap and pulled out Emma's panties. In one quick move he tossed them at the General's feet, then held his arms out wide so he wouldn't get shot.

The General stepped forward into the light. His head was large like a boulder. His jaw was smooth and square. He had lines on his forehead that were straight and deep. Lean jowls that were slanted slashes on either side of his mouth. Eyes shining yellow, bright like suns.

Trung lazily glanced down at the crumpled purple satin. Made no move to pick it up. Looked back into Edge's eyes.

Not a word from the General, but his eyes were shining brighter. A glint of something that told Edge this just might work.

It had to work.

This was for all the marbles.

If Trung just laughed and snapped his fingers, Edge was a dead man and Emma was fish food.

Edge swallowed hard. He thought about that strange feeling he'd gotten from Benson. Like Benson had been testing him.

So had Edge passed the test?

Only one way to find out.

Edge had picked up the gauntlet thrown down by Trung.

Now Edge was tossing it back at the General's feet.

Daring him to pick it up.

"Parkov has her," Edge said. "I need your help to get her back. Just the two of us. You and me, General. We go and get Emma together."

23

You and me together. We get Emma together.

General Trung stared at the SEAL's shining green eyes, then glanced back at the crumpled purple satin on the red-gold carpet between the two men. His first thought was to laugh heartily, shake his head, then order Zhu to get rid of Edgerton. The man was a fool to think that Trung would be so stupid as to go anywhere alone with an ex-SEAL with murder in his green eyes.

But Trung stayed silent. The laughter would not come. Zhu was saying something to the General, but Trung waved him away. The General could not hear anything, so it did not matter.

No, Trung could neither hear nor see. He was only vaguely aware of the cool air conditioning against his thick warm neck. The acidic taste of the rice-wine was no longer discernible on his tongue.

No sight.

No sound.

No touch.

No taste.

Just scent.

Just *her* scent.

But a particular kind of scent. Unmistakably hers, but yet something that Trung had never smelled on Emma before.

It was not urine or sweat.

It was not blood or tears.

Trung knew what all those smelled like on Emma. This was none of those things. This was something else.

Something that could not be faked.

Something that could not be forced.

Something that could only be coaxed out of a woman.

Drawn out by passion, not pain.

Trust, not torture.

Sex, but without the taint of violence.

Emma has given herself to him, Trung thought with boiling red rage as her unmistakable scent rose to his large gaping nostrils, flared like a bull preparing to defend its turf.

Now I must take her back, came the next manic thought as Trung felt himself harden beneath his long red tunic.

And I must take her back soon, fill her with my seed before my rival's soldiers can plant their filthy flag on my property, came the final wild impulse as Trung felt something start to unwind in his military-precise brain, like some ancient need in his body was taking over, ripping away any thought of caution or care.

Of course, Trung knew it was the same reckless, senseless, mindless need that had set this whole thing into motion. But he had not expected it to twist its way around and suck him in like this, tempt him to do something he knew was madness beyond measure, reckless beyond reason.

Zhu tried to reason with Trung again. This time Trung could hear his faithful old companion's wise words of caution and care. Zhu could be trusted as a countermeasure to Trung's willfulness. Zhu had saved the General many times over the years.

"I am ending this nonsense," Zhu said to Trung in Mandarin Chinese. "Edgerton is already dead. Consider him gone. As for Emma, the Russians can dispose of her. She is not worth starting a war over. Parkov's estate is a walled fortress. It would take a hundred soldiers to even get past the front gate."

Zhu glanced down at Emma's panties. He snorted in disbelief, then noisily gathered a mouthful of saliva to show his disdain for this ridiculous game.

But before he could spit, Trung yanked Zhu away by the arm, hurling him across the room. Trung had used more strength than he'd intended, and the wiry Zhu went stumbling against the wooden table with the wine cups.

The cups fell onto the carpet with soft thuds. Zhu cursed out loud, then hurriedly regained his composure. He shot a dark look at the General, then muttered out an apology for cursing in his superior's direction. He leaned his long lanky body over to pick up the cups.

The General took a moment to regain his own composure after the momentary loss of control. He stroked his smooth jaw and swallowed hard

Zhu was obviously right. Edgerton should be shot and

Emma should be cut loose. It would be easy enough to dispose of Edgerton's body. Emma's body was the Russian's problem. It would be inconvenient to lose her skills with the women, but Zhu was correct that she was not worth going to war with the Russians over.

Edgerton stood silent like a specter. He was tall and broad, all in black, beard heavy and wild like some animal. Trung himself felt like an animal as he breathed in heavily, yearning to catch a whiff of that seductive aroma from the carpet.

Trung's eyes misted over as the scent of a woman in heat took over his senses again. He dreamily thought back over his life. Those early years watching his step-sisters please the soldiers in their little two-room hut. His step-sisters would often get pleasure themselves, he'd noticed. Often with the same few men. Their favorites. Their special ones.

They smelled like this with their special ones, Trung thought as he wondered if any woman had wetted herself like that at his own touch. He had never concerned himself with such matters before. They had seemed trivial and fleeting.

Now they seemed monumental and eternal.

Trung paced the carpeted room as he considered his move. He knew that scent was a powerful part of old memories, old traumas, old desires. But there had been none of that when Trung put the wheel in spin, started this strange game that felt like a fated fight, a destined dance, some ancient spiral pattern that had brought the three of them together in a cosmic plot that could

Extracting Emma

not be sidestepped, could not be avoided, could not be thwarted.

Sometimes there was no option but to meet your enemy directly on a mutually chosen battlefield, Trung thought as he paced past the long windows overlooking the city whose underworld he ruled.

But the underworld of a man's heart was not as easy to rule, Trung considered as he saw the silent SEAL's dark reflection in the window. Sex and violence were the currents that ran deep in the oceans of a man's psyche, the seas of a man's soul. And this SEAL was offering Trung a chance to ride those dangerous currents like a dragon rides through the burning sky.

Now Trung gazed at his own reflection in the dark mirror, with the bearded SEAL in the background. For a moment Trung saw himself as a boy pretending to be a soldier, all dressed up in his red tunic and smart black pants, big leather belt and fully loaded gun.

But when was the last time Trung had actually stormed into battle like that boy had always dreamed of doing? When would Trung ever get that chance again?

Especially with stakes like this.

An opponent like this.

A feeling like this.

And now the feeling rose up in him like a dragon spreading its wings for the first time, maybe the last time, maybe the only time.

The General suddenly knew there was no turning away from this. If he retreated from this battle, he would live his remaining days as a hollowed out shell of a soldier, a scarecrow of a man, a boy with fancy clothes and a loaded gun that had not been used when the battle cry sounded.

Perhaps he was mad, but then so was Edgerton.

Fuck it, the General thought as excitement roared up his spine like that dragon coming alive. Or like the Navy SEALs liked to say, Hooyah. It meant the same thing, yes?

So Trung walked over to the symbolic satin gauntlet on the blood-red carpeted floor.

He picked it up.

Stood up straight and tall.

Faced Edgerton and nodded.

"How will we get past the gates?" Trung asked softly.

24

Edge stared in disbelief as General Trung held the purple panties up to his face and breathed deep of Emma's scent. He watched in stunned silence as Trung brushed away another verbal assault by the panicked Zhu. Then Edge almost choked on his own damn tongue as both dread and rage rose up in his throat at the sickening truth of what was happening.

For a moment Edge almost blacked out from the thought that Benson had offered him a way out. But instead of trusting the old CIA man who'd made deals with demons a hundred times worse than Parkov, Edge had politely declined.

I need to control the situation, Edge had told Benson with cool confidence.

Except now Edge felt wildly out of control. The same loss of control he saw in General Trung's shining yellow eyes. At least if it was madness, then they were both mad.

"You are both mad," shouted Zhu in Mandarin simple enough that Edge could understand. "General, you must listen to me. He will kill you the first chance he gets. And that is only if you both survive the Russians. Which you cannot. Not without armed support. And armed support would start a war." Zhu's black eyes widened. He opened his yellow-fanged mouth like a surprised piranha. "A war over a whore! Are you mad, General? Is your brain broken? Are you to push me to mutiny? Force me to relieve you of your command?"

Trung leaned his head back and laughed. "Stop acting like a scared housewife and help us strategize, Zhu," Trung said in English. "If you are so concerned about my safety, then contribute something useful instead of whining like a woman."

The General laughed again. It was a throaty, open-mouthed laugh that showed off two rows of perfectly aligned brilliant white teeth.

It made Edge think of those tigers. He blinked as the thought led to another.

"I can get us past the gates undetected," Edge said calmly. "Get us all the way into the garage. Those garage doors are heavy enough to stop a tank. Once they're closed, nobody will hear us shooting."

"Cameras everywhere," said Zhu somewhat condescendingly. He was reluctant to help, but Edge could see Zhu's mind slowly getting into tactical mode. Zhu thought a moment, then nodded. "But there is a chance if you get to the house. All camera feeds will be viewable from inside the house. But the guard station at the gate does not see inside the main house. Privacy reasons."

Edge raised an eyebrow. "So the cameras in the garage

Extracting Emma

and house will not broadcast to the guards at the gate?"

Zhu nodded. "The Russians use different men inside the house and outside. Trusted men inside. Disposable men outside."

Edge thought a moment. He remembered Gargoyle, who was a dimwitted street thug compared to the no-nonsense hard men who'd searched him at Parkov's house. Made sense. Parkov didn't want a hundred men watching live video feeds of the inside of his house all the time. After all, he wasn't living in a chaotic war zone.

This was doable. This might work.

"So once we're inside the garage, we can use guns, contain the action to the house itself," Edge said, nodding and glancing at the General. "I counted sixteen guards inside the house. But maybe there'll be fewer now. They may have brought in a couple of extra in my honor."

Zhu grunted, but the General agreed. He walked to where Zhu had knocked over the wine cups. The wine was in a short screw-top glass bottle. It hadn't spilled.

The General poured himself a cup of rice-wine. He didn't offer Edge any. He drained the cup, smacked his lips, then placed it back on the table. There was still some debris on the carpet. Trung looked at it, then shot a sharp glance towards Zhu.

Zhu blinked and went wide-eyed. He hurried over to the mess on the carpet. Bent down and picked up something. Dark glass. A vial of black liquid.

The poison Emma had told Edge about. Zhu must

have just seen it and realized he'd left it in here. Edge watched Zhu slip the vial into the right pocket of his loose red jacket.

Then Edge winced when Zhu suddenly glanced up and caught Edge watching.

Zhu shook his head, muttered something, then took the vial out of the jacket pocket and zipped it into a small cargo flap just above the left knee of his black utility pants.

Edge was annoyed at himself. It would have been easy to pick Zhu's pocket from that loose jacket. Not that Edge wanted to give up the pleasure of beating these two bastards to death with his fists, but it was always good to have a backup plan.

"Floor plan of the mansion," said the General to Zhu. "Satellite images of the estate. Now, please."

Zhu pulled out his phone and did some tapping, scrolling, pinching, and dragging. He held the phone up, screen slanted so all of them could see.

The house floorplan was igloo-shaped, with the long enclosed corridor connecting the garage to a mansion built on a circular foundation. The roof was dome shaped. Edge wasn't sure if it was for aesthetic reasons or precautionary. Tough to rappel down from a dome. Not that there were any windows to smash through, of course.

"What's that area?" Edge asked with a frown. He pointed at a rectangular section attached to the main circle of the house. "Looks like it might be an open area. Maybe for the tigers. They must have access to the outdoors. That cage didn't smell like tiger piss."

Zhu shook his head. He flipped the image and brought up the satellite photos. "It is an outdoor area with grass and plants. But covered with a steel-framed canopy. No way through from above. The bars are crisscrossed. Like a waffle. But very small squares. Not enough room for even a squirrel to get through. No hatch or trapdoor in the top."

Edge exhaled. "An outside extension of the tiger cage. Must be a back door in the wall behind the inside cage. But no use to us, sounds like."

The place was a bunker. A fortress. One way in. Same way out.

"OK, so how do we get out?" said the General.

"Same way we get in," said Edge.

Zhu frowned at Edge. "You never told us how we get in," he said gruffly.

The General nodded. He crossed his arms over his massive chest and looked at Edge expectantly. He was still the General. He didn't waste energy repeating questions.

Edge cleared his throat. He thought of that tiger-mama and her cubs. Remembered that phone call Parkov had gotten just before Edge got sprung.

"Doctor Wang," Edge said like it was obvious. He waited a moment, but clearly Trung and Zhu were not familiar with the good doctor. "He's due at Parkov's place tomorrow. He'll have a truck big enough to hide us beneath the floorboards in the back. He's a regular visitor. Trusted and verified. The gate guards won't strip down his truck to the frame. They'll glance in the back, search Wang head-to-toe, then send him into the garage." Edge glanced at Zhu. "I trust you can persuade Doctor Wang to drive us in and out without giving the game away?"

Zhu nodded curtly. His eyes were up and to the left. He was thinking of something else.

Zhu's eyes snapped back front and center. He turned to the General.

"One more thing," Zhu said. "I go with you. That is non negotiable, General. If you deny my request, then I will order the guards to break their thirty-foot perimeter. I will inform them you have been relieved of your command pending medical and psychiatric evaluation. I will order them to execute Edgerton immediately." Zhu gulped, stood up straight, raised his head proudly. "If you decline, then go ahead and order the guards to execute me immediately. Else I will attempt to disarm you myself, General." He clicked his heels together smartly, saluted with a practiced elegance. "I await your decision, General."

Edge glanced sharply at the General, dread rising as he felt his chance slipping away. Again Edge wondered if he'd made a fatal mistake by declining Benson's offer. Zhu was a combat veteran. He would absolutely stay behind Edge at all times, never letting Edge slip out of view. It would be very hard to kill both Zhu and Trung if they were on either side of Edge.

Yeah, Zhu coming along might very well be fatal for Edge.

But it might not be fatal for Emma, Edge thought as a strange calmness fell over him when he saw the hint of dark stained purple satin peeking out the top of Trung's tunic pocket. Even if Zhu put a bullet in the back of

Edge's head after they rescued Emma, at least she would still have a shot at a future, a chance to survive, maybe even thrive someday.

So Edge stayed calm and nodded when the General sighed and agreed. Zhu bowed his head, the relief showing on his gaunt, lined face. He shot a sly look at Edge from the side of those pearly black eyes. Then he got back to the phone, presumably to look up the good Doctor Wang.

There was a moment of tense silence as the General and Edge stood facing each other. There was six feet of unobstructed carpet between them. Edge kept his gaze steady on the General's clean shaved face, but his peripheral vision was taking in the button-flap on Trung's belt holster.

Edge knew a dozen different ways of disarming someone in less than a second. An H&K machine pistol with an extended clip could take out everyone in the room in less than four seconds. The eight guards were thirty feet away. No problem mowing them down like yesterday's weeds. Maybe Edge would get hit, but almost certainty not fatally.

Zhu was a different matter. He was on the phone, but warily eyeing Edge. Still, Zhu was nine feet away from the General. He would have to drop his phone to draw. Plus Zhu's holster was on his shoulder, under his jacket. Edge had a reasonable shot at ending this whole thing in less than four seconds.

Now he saw a slight twist on the General's dark red lips. Trung's eyes were steady, but his mind was moving fast. He'd clearly been watching Edge very carefully.

Trung was testing Edge. Seeing if the SEAL was going to lose his nerve and try and finish the game before it got too hot for him.

It reminded Edge about what Benson had said about the poison. About how Edge wouldn't use it because it would be cheating. That Trung would see it that way too.

So Edge relaxed his gaze. Broke a deadly grin at his opponent. Nodded to acknowledge what they'd both silently understood.

That there was nothing but the game.

That it was all about the game.

The game of man and woman.

The only game in town.

25

"Shall we play a game while we wait, Miss Chang?"

Emma glanced up from her spot on the blue leather sofa. She'd barely moved from the spot in hours. Just the restroom once and then back again.

It was a quick visit. She couldn't stand to see herself in the mirror. There were dark circles forming under her eyes. Her silk blouse was horribly creased at the bottom. The dark stain around the crotch of her jeans was unmistakable. Her armpits smelled atrocious.

Parkov had offered her fresh clothes and the use of the shower, but Emma had politely declined. She wasn't sure why. Perhaps it was a sign that she'd given up. They said that happened to people nearing the end of their lives. They just let everything go to hell. Stopped bathing. Didn't care about looking good or smelling nice.

"No, thank you," Emma said sullenly to Parkov. "I don't play games."

Parkov snorted from his spot on the recliner. He'd changed into black Adidas athletic shorts that showed off a powerlifter's thick quadriceps and muscular calves. The synthetic material made the shorts ride up past his knees and gather around his heavy crotch. He'd matched the shorts with a silver synthetic tee shirt with a Nike logo across the front. Emma guessed he'd been in the gym.

"Sure you play games," said Parkov softly. His dark blue eyes flashed. "You started as a nobody in this town. Within a year General Trung takes you as his official consort. There are even rumors he might marry you."

Emma blinked and looked away. "The tabloids say all sorts of things. They mean nothing."

Parkov shook his head. "Not from tabloid. Real source." He paused, rubbed the blonde hair on his forearms like he was smoothing it out. He glanced over towards the guards. They were far across the room. "One of my men likes the Chinese whores," Parkov said quietly like it was sacrilege. "The one he fucked last week had just been visited by General Trung himself."

Emma felt her neck stiffen. She thought of the woman that Trung had gotten killed as part of his purity-tests and loyalty-checks. Letting her get killed was a bit extreme even for Trung, but it was not unheard of. Still, Emma now wondered if there was something more to it.

"The General visits the women often," Emma said carefully. "That is no secret."

"Ah, but this whore learned a secret," said Parkov with some relish. "She told my guy that the General never touches the women when he uses them. Just finishes on their backs or sometimes on the floor."

Emma crossed her leg over the opposite knee. She plucked an imaginary thread from her jeans. Looked up at him and shrugged.

Parkov's gaze fell to her breasts, then back up to her eyes. "This China girl tells my man that the General did something surprising. He put his cock inside her, she says. Just for an instant. Then he pulled out and exploded all over her arse and up along her back. Violent explosion." Parkov paused a moment, his gaze flicking back down to her bosom, then lower down. He blinked, then looked back into her eyes. "She says the General called out your name. But not just Emma. He used the honorific prefix. Consort-Wife."

Emma almost gasped out loud at the word. Somehow she kept her composure. Then she shook her head and smiled pleasantly. "It must have been a miscommunication somewhere along the line. Russian man. Chinese prostitute. She may not even have heard the General correctly. Who knows what things a man mutters in that moment?"

"The truth, Miss Chang," said Parkov with a chuckle. "In that moment, a man speaks the truth in his heart. That is the dastardly trick of nature. A man cannot lie in the moment of release." He wagged his finger at her again. "Wife-Consort means the General was considering you for the highest position by his side. You might bear his children. Continue his line." Parkov sighed and leaned back in the recliner. He rested his bald head on his big blistered hands. "It might have been a fantasy, yes. But it was still a thought in the General's mind." Parkov sighed noisily again, then placed his hand over his heart. "And then the big bearded American comes along and steals you away. Takes the General's consort-wife away and makes her his." Now his blue eyes turned dark. His playful mockery was gone. "So do not pretend like Emma Chang does not play games, you hear me?"

Emma gulped back what felt like something thick in her throat. She said nothing. The revelation about Trung shocked her, but not in the way she expected. She wondered what she would have said if Trung asked her to be his Wife-Consort.

That would open the door to his entire operation, Emma realized. She might be able to take over the DNA sampling effort from Zhu, speed it along. She'd get access to all the brothels and red rooms that were currently off limits to her. She might find her sisters in months, weeks, maybe even days.

Emma's eyelids fluttered as that thickness returned to her throat. She couldn't swallow. She could barely breathe. She wondered if she was broken inside. Damaged by years of single-minded focus, everything in her life revolving around General Trung.

Was she terrified of losing that single point of focus?

Scared to walk away from the hatred that had given her life meaning?

Was there a part of her that was desperately holding on to the General even though she hated him, wanted him to suffer, wanted him to die for who he was, for what he'd done to her family, to thousands of families across China?

Then Emma almost lurched forward as the sickness rose up in her like something trying to escape. She saw herself in a world where Edge had never looked up at her from that dusty arena.

And she knew in that instant that Edge had saved her not from the General but from herself, from the path she was heading down, a death spiral that would have taken her past the point of no return, dragged her down into the dark swirling sea, sucked her into the General's twisted world.

And she would have stayed in that world.

Telling herself that she was searching for her sisters.

Knowing deep down that she was losing herself in the process.

Trading herself for the memory of her sisters.

Offering her own future as penance for someone else's past.

Trying in some insane way to undo the choice her mother made.

"You saved me, Edge," she whispered under her breath as another feeling rose up in her breast. This felt warm and comforting. It felt bright and beautiful. It felt rich and real. It felt like home. "Now come take me home, Edge. I want to go home now. Please take me home."

"This is your home now," came Parkov's voice, cutting through the rising hope in Emma's heart. He looked at his big metal watch. "The SEAL's meeting with Trung was twelve hours ago. There is no sign of anything eventful occurring at the Metropolitan. No word on the street about violence. Nothing from my contacts in the police. Either the SEAL never went to Trung or he was killed without much fuss." He shrugged those powerlifter's shoulders, wiggled his hairy toes. "So it appears I will not be taking over General Trung's empire." His gaze settled comfortably on her face. "But perhaps I will still get something that once belonged to the General, yes?"

Emma blinked rapidly, looked down and frowned. Then she looked up and shook her head. "You know I can't start working for you in the Russian brothels. The General might take it as a betrayal. I will disappear within days of the news becoming public."

Parkov's gaze stayed easy and relaxed, but not in a way that made Emma relax.

"That had indeed occurred to me," he said. "With Trung alive, it could be tricky to poach you from his operation like this. That is why I said there was no good alternative but to kill you quietly and feed you to the fishes. Plausible deniability. The General will not need to save face, because nobody will ever see your face again. It is how powerful men like us play the game, Emma." He rubbed his forearms again. The fuzz was like blonde Velcro. "But now that I have spent a few hours in your presence, I am wondering if maybe there is some other arrangement that can be made. A private arrangement. After all, if you never leave this house again, that it is not so different as you being dead. Either way you are gone to the outside world. Which brings me back to my original question, Miss Chang. Shall we play a game? A test run?"

Emma shifted uncomfortably on her bottom. She was dry underneath her jeans, but the smell of sex was unmistakable on her. Emma shifted again when Parkov's gaze moved down along her curves. He took his time taking her in. There was no attempt to hide what was going on behind those dark blue eyes, under those grotesquely bunched up athletic shorts.

Now Emma thought back to the gym where Edge had taken her to some place she didn't even know existed in her body and mind. She'd blacked out when he came in her, woken up hours later in his arms. She remembered feeling Edge's thick semen oozing out of her slit when she opened her eyes and moved her thighs. She remembered the wonderfully warm smell of it on her skin.

Then the Russian guard had hammered on the door. Edge and Emma had scrambled to cover up. Perhaps they hadn't cleaned up behind them. Maybe Parkov had seen the signs, then smelled the scent on her.

Men were supposed to be visual creatures when it came to sex, but scent was a powerful stimulant. It was the dominant point of sexual attraction in other mammals. Perhaps with the glut of online porn freely available, everyone was getting desensitized to images. Maybe scent was becoming more dominant. Maybe as civilization progressed, men and women were regressing, reclaiming their savage roots, heightening their primal desires.

Scent couldn't be transmitted over the internet. And the real scent of a woman's arousal couldn't be faked. Couldn't be bottled like a perfume. It was unforgeable truth. It couldn't be tricked or tampered with.

Because a man had to draw it out of a woman. He couldn't force it out of her. He couldn't beat it out of her, blackmail it out of her, beg it out of her.

A man roared out his truth in the violence of his release. But a woman whispered her truth with her silent secretion, her secret scent, her private promise.

Emma wondered if that was why so many prostitutes these days were running little side businesses selling their panties to perverts all over the world. She imagined millions of lonely men sniffing the scent of unknown women. It sounded sad and lonely but felt strangely beautiful. It reminded Emma of the old saying that men wanted a virgin princess in the ballroom, but a well-fucked whore in the bedroom. What was sad was that women felt they needed to be one or the other.

The truth was they could be both.

They wanted to be both.

The princess and the prostitute.

The virgin and the whore.

So maybe Parkov just wanted what millions of men paid prostitutes for every night in red rooms around the world. Just like they had in the early days of civilization thousands of years ago. Women had been bought with chariot wheels and gold coins and sea shells and glass beads and sacks of rice and herds of oxen and dollars and pounds and yuan and rupees. They were bought with power and promises and blackmail and lies.

And so what was Parkov offering, Emma wondered as a shard of despair cut through her heart, a curtain of gloom descended over her soul. She'd been sitting stiffly on the sofa all night, trying to avoid thinking about what Parkov had just forced her to face.

It had been fourteen hours since the General had been back in Macau.

Twelve hours since Edge had been due at the Metropolitan's Penthouse Suite.

She'd tried to remind herself that she'd trusted Edge to use his judgment. She'd wondered if Edge had connected with that guy Benson. She'd feared that Benson had talked some sense into Edge and told him there was no way to win and it was time to walk away. That Emma was a Chinese national and she wasn't worth starting a gang war in Macau or a real war in the South China Sea over. That Edge should stop thinking with his cock and balls, that he should get a haircut and shave his beard and return to the world of men instead of acting like a feral beast driven wild by the scent of his mate.

The thought brought out a little smile on Emma's lips. She covered her mouth and looked away. She closed her eyes and thought of waking up snuggled against that feral beast of a man.

Then she opened her eyes and looked directly at Parkov with a confidence that had no grounding in the real world.

"Edge isn't dead," she said softly. "He'll come through. Don't play out your hand yet, Parkov. Don't do something you can't take back."

Parkov snorted viciously. "You don't tell me what to do. What, you think that American piece of dogshit gives a damn about you?"

Emma gazed coolly at Parkov. "Yes, I do. And you think so too. You thought there was at least a chance Edge would walk into Trung's headquarters and try to assassinate the most protected man in Macao to save me. You still think there's a chance."

"No chance," Parkov said stubbornly. He crossed his thick arms over his chest, frumped his round face, shook his bald head. "He would be crazy to try. Crazy and dead.

It is just you and me now, Miss Chang. You are out of options. You know I can never let you leave this house so long as General Trung still breathes. You will go back to him, tell him of this, and he might decide to retaliate. Zhu would not let him start an outright war with the Russians, but Trung might be able to get to me, make me disappear without a trace. Plausible deniability." He shook his head again. "No more options, Miss Chang. Just one card for you to play. The only card any woman truly has to play in this game."

Emma's gaze narrowed at Parkov. She wasn't afraid of him. She knew full well that Parkov could take what he wanted. But he hadn't made a move to do so. Not even an outright threat. It made Emma feel strangely safe, but also weirdly worried. She took her time to consider her next move. She decided her best option was just that: Time.

She needed to buy time.

No matter what she had to sell to get it.

Because there was just one reason Emma was still alive twelve hours after Edge was probably dead. The oldest reason in the book.

Parkov slid off the smooth leather recliner. His dark blue eyes were locked on her. His shorts straightened out as he stood. The bulge that had been hidden by the bunched-up cloth could no longer be plausibly denied.

"There is something about a woman who is desired so violently by many others," Parkov whispered as he took slow steps towards her. His bare feet looked large like paws on the carpet. "Something about knowing that she is full of another man's seed. It strikes up a powerful competitive fire in some men. Men who are used to winning. Men who live to take from others. To defeat other men in battle." He came closer as Emma tensed up on the sofa. She turned her head to the side as Parkov reached out and stroked her cheek with the back of his rough calloused hand. "It is why even wealthy, powerful men pay high prices not just for the virgin princess but the well-fucked whore. There is some ancient need in us alpha beasts to claim victory over other alphas in the only battlefield that matters to nature."

Emma trembled as he caressed her cheek with the knuckles of one hand, rubbed his bulge with the grip of the other. Emma thought she might vomit. She choked back the sick feeling in her throat.

She could barely come to terms with what was happening. A part of her understood the darkly animalistic truth of what Parkov was saying. That same part of her recognized that somehow this strange ancient craving in these alpha men was keeping her alive, keeping her in the game, maybe even keeping her in control of the game.

Parkov's touch moved down to her lips, then her neck. He stroked the front of her throat with his thumb. Gazed down into her eyes.

It was only when she looked into his eyes that she understood why he hadn't just knocked her senseless and taken what he craved.

Parkov wanted Emma to give herself to him. He wanted the part of her that she'd given to Edge. The part of her that Edge had drawn from her depths.

He wanted to see it, hear it, feel it, smell it.

The unmistakable scent of assent.

The undeniable whisper of welcome.

All right then, Emma thought as she fluttered her eyelids and offered the hint of a smile. She could play this game all night. She'd been training for it all her life.

She could buy time with her body.

Play her role in their fight.

After all, boys were soldiers.

And girls were whores.

Emma felt a strange rush go through her body as Parkov groaned just from the feel of his hand on her skin. It wasn't the sensation of arousal but the thrill of the game.

A game she'd watched play out in red rooms all over the world

In bedrooms all over the globe.

The same game that played out in classrooms and boardrooms, on wedding nights and in barroom fights, in village huts and within palace walls.

The game of man and woman.

A man who'd risk his body to save her life.

A woman who'd risk her body to be his wife.

26

She will be my wife.

General Trung watched the SEAL check the fully loaded H&K 9mm machine pistol. Zhu had his own weapon drawn. It was pointed at Edgerton's head.

Zhu was taking no chances. Trung was glad of it. He recognized now that he was vulnerable. Not just physically but in a deeper way. A way the General had not believed was possible.

"You sit in front," Zhu told Edgerton as the sleek black BMW limousine pulled up to where the elevator opened in the private garage far below the Metropolitan's lobby. "If your head turns or your arms move I will put twelve bullets into your skull."

Edgerton shrugged and did what he was told. Trung was not worried about the SEAL attempting anything during the car ride to where they were to meet Doctor Wang. The SEAL cared about Emma. He would not be able to rescue her without help. Edgerton knew it and Trung knew it too.

Which meant the game would truly start only when Emma was safe. And that was what worried Trung. It would be the moment of truth. He would be stepping onto a different sort of battlefield. A battlefield the General had avoided all his life.

Dodging the bullets of fate.

Sidestepping the spears of destiny.

Shielding his heart from the stab of the only weapon that could pierce his armor.

A woman who would someday bring forth that ancient battle cry.

She will be my wife.

The General thought back to the words he'd uttered during that moment of weakness with the whore who had thankfully died with that shameful secret. The words had broken free of his lips without even forming thoughts in his mind. It was like his body had bypassed his brain, spoken a truth directly from the heart, no consultation with the faculties of reason and logic.

Trung pushed aside that dangerously raw wound that had been ripped open by the scent of Emma's submission to Edgerton. He marveled at the mysteries of a man's heart, his animal drives, his primal passions.

A week ago the General could have offered Emma a seat by his side, given her the honor of being a Wife-Consort. But he had not even acknowledged the thought, let alone considered following through on it. The utterance at climax was the only hint of the truthful desire buried in his heart.

He'd let it go when it was his to take.

Now he was risking death to get it back.

The General leaned back against the black leather

seat as the limousine cruised up the ramp and merged silently into the light morning traffic. He felt the cold calmness of his military-precise mind return as he gazed through the tinted bulletproof glass and stared directly into the dark red morning sun.

Slowly Trung felt the warm rawness of that stab-wound inflicted by Emma's submission to another recede. He took a slow breath, closed his eyes, visualized a cold, hard, callous forming over the wound.

The callous would protect the wound. But the cut would only heal when the General took back what he now admitted was precious property. When the General's enemy was dead at his feet.

But of course Edgerton must be made to feel his loss before he died, Trung reminded himself as he saw Zhu's finger on the trigger of his ready weapon. The SEAL would have to see that the General had defeated him. See it in the flesh. Feel it in the spirit.

Yes., Edgerton would have to witness the General taking back what was his.

Watch the General plant his flag on disputed territory.

Stake his own claim on precious property.

Make the SEAL taste the bitterness of his own defeat.

Force him to smell the sweetness of the General's victory.

27

"Sweet," said Edge as the black BMW limousine entered a covered parking garage that had been cleared out beforehand. "There'll be plenty of room beneath the floorboards in the back of that thing. That's a two-tiger truck, minimum."

Doctor Wang's tiger-ambulance was a light-duty Mercedes truck-cab attached to a shiny aluminum-topped wagon with a steel frame, wood plank floor, and heavy-duty wheels. The curved aluminum shell was painted orange and black. Tiger stripes.

A skinny, short man with round glasses and a nervous hunch to his shoulders stood by the truck. He raised his hand and let it drop. He was not exhibiting positive body language. Edge wondered about Zhu's persuasion methods. It was unlikely Zhu had simply asked nicely. Bribery, perhaps. Threats, more likely.

Didn't matter though. It was virtually certain that Zhu and Trung expected this to be Doctor Wang's last house call. No way Zhu would let Wang live to tell the tale of the great General Trung hiding beneath urine-soaked floorboards wearing black utility pants and a flak vest stuffed with extra magazines of the same 9mm hollow-point bullets that would later be determined to have caused the pink mess on the floor near Parkov's shattered skull.

The only thing that might save Doctor Wang was that they'd need him to drive the truck back out through the gates. After all, the entire plan depended on keeping the fight within the walls of Parkov's bunker-safe igloo-shaped mansion.

Sixteen or twenty guards could be neutralized by three combat-hardened former military men with automatic machine-pistols, plenty of spare ammo, and the element of surprise. But Parkov's estate beyond the well-contained house was vast. Edge had seen the guard shack when the Russians had driven him out earlier. It was not a shack, but a damn armory. Maybe barracks in there too, for quick shift-changes or reinforcements.

Edge had beaten some pretty lop-sided odds before. But a lone gunman fighting his way out through an army of Russian thugs wielding superior firepower on open and unfamiliar terrain was a Hollywood ending but with Vegas odds of it actually happening.

And it would be just one man left over after the battle inside was won.

One man and one woman.

Edge already knew that Trung and Zhu would have to be put down alongside Parkov inside the Russian fortress. Certainly both Trung and Zhu had the same plans for Edge. But even if by some miracle they wanted to bring Edge back to the Metropolitan Penthouse, Edge knew his only chance at victory was on neutral ground.

Besides, Edge hadn't forgotten Benson's warning about the potential for this blowing up and getting American soldiers killed. And leaving Trung and Zhu full of bulletholes along with Parkov and his minions could play well. There was a good chance the Russian Bratva would call in a clean up crew and incinerate all the bodies before news leaked. Sweep it under the rug. Take it out with the tide.

Plausible deniability. No bodies, no mess. Everyone looks the other way, shrugs, walks off like nothing happened. Trung and Zhu and Parkov were abducted by aliens, swallowed by sea monsters, vaporized by solar flares. Poof. Gone. Replace them and move on without starting a war.

Now all Edge had to focus on was his own private war.

Edge wished he'd learned more about General Trung's military history. Edge had tried to work in some conversation during the planning phase, but Trung had not been forthcoming about his skills and training. The General might have taken the bait, picked up the gauntlet, answered the challenge with a recklessness that might suggest a man unhinged. But Edge learned midway through the night that the General was not to be underestimated. He was the real deal. A down-and-dirty killer with the mind of a master.

Edge had learned this not directly from the General but by observing Zhu. The wiry black-eyed man who'd protected Trung for decades seemed to be completely unconcerned about the General's ability to handle himself in combat.

"We stay in the Spear Formation at all times," Zhu had said sharply when they discussed their plan of attack. "Single file. One line. Edgerton is the point of the spear. Myself in the middle. The General stays at the back end, covering the rear."

Edge had glanced at Trung to see his reaction. There was not even the whisper of doubt in the General's eyes. Zhu's middle position was the most protected, least vulnerable position. But Zhu wanted to be in the middle because he considered Edge to be the greatest threat to the General's safety. It also meant that Zhu was confident that the older, heavier General could handle himself fully exposed to rear attacks.

Edge had spent the rest of the night thinking about his own exposure to rear attacks. Certainly the invaders would need all three men alive and active to take down almost two dozen armed Russians. But once the crowd started to thin out, Zhu might decide to take his shot and put Edge down.

Which meant Edge would use the exact same strategy as Zhu.

The moment Edge decided enough Russians were down, it would be time to put Zhu down. It would all come down to timing, instinct, and whoever was quickest on the draw.

No problem.

The problems would only start after Zhu was down.

When it was just Edge and Trung and Emma.

Then things got tricky. Volatile. Unpredictable.

That was stuff that couldn't be rehearsed. Couldn't be gamed. Couldn't be faked.

It would be the moment of truth.

Three fates clashing in one violent event.

Three destinies swirling in one wild dance.

Edge would be going into the most important fight of his life with no battle plan.

No plan but the feeling in his heart.

A feeling that made him wonder if he and Emma were still locked in that silent stare across the crowded, blood-spattered arena on a hot Hong Kong night. If perhaps time had stopped and space had compressed and eternity was unfolding like that cosmic flower, its petals bursting open in an explosion of vivid color, giving the lovers a blinding flash of insight, revealing to them a hint of the great secret.

The secret that revealed itself only to those who risked it all.

Risked it all on a feeling.

The feeling of always.

The feeling of forever.

The feeling of love.

Edge exhaled hard, willing his heart to slow down. All night he'd forced himself to stay focused on the General and Zhu, the mission at hand, the fight in front of him.

But at the back of his mind he was close to losing his cool, losing his nerve, losing his sanity as paranoia and worry raged through his body. He'd been watching the clock, counting down the hours, wondering if Parkov would lose his own cool, lose his own nerve, lose his patience and decide to get rid of the evidence, get rid of Emma.

It had taken all of Edge's power of focus to stop him-

Extracting Emma

self from begging Trung to send some sort of message to Parkov, leak a rumor, flash a sign. But Edge knew that the only rumor that would make Parkov think his plan was working was a rumor that Trung had been killed.

And the General would never agree to that. Edge knew it without a doubt.

Edge also knew that asking the favor would reveal Edge's own vulnerability. His own weakness. His own Achilles Heel. So Edge stayed silent even though inside he was being ripped apart, was an anxious animal who wanted to howl and stomp, rage and roar.

But then the General revealed himself too.

When Zhu mentioned that Doctor Wang's appointment was for late in the afternoon, the General vetoed him with a swift head-shake.

"We go at first light," Trung had said quietly, switching to Mandarin briefly.

Zhu had protested, suggesting that Wang showing up so early without announcing it beforehand might arouse suspicion. But the General shut him down with a grunt.

And then Edge knew that the General shared the same vulnerability. The same concern. The same urgency.

Which meant Edge would win.

Because although both men felt the thrill of competition, the bloodlust of battle, the drive to destroy one another, in the end it wasn't about Trung or Edge.

It was about Emma.

It wasn't a story of two powerful men going to war for the spoils of victory.

It wasn't a story of soldiers and whores, red rooms and wars.

It was the story of a woman.
A woman who was many things to many men.
But to Edge she was just one thing.
Just one damn thing.
She was his.

28

She was the cause of this, Zhu thought as he watched his once-proud General lay his bulky body beneath the filthy floorboards of Doctor Wang's animal ambulance. The wood floor smelled like every beast in the jungle had taken a piss on it this morning. Zhu was disgusted by what was happening here, and the stench was the least of it.

Not once in thirty years by his side had Zhu questioned the General's decision making. There were times when Zhu suggested different tactics or formations, yes. But a General's job was to make decisions for the good of the soldiers, for the good of the cause, and for the destruction of the enemy.

Except now the General was lying down next to the enemy like they were brothers in arms, comrades in a coup, partners in some perverted plan. It took all of Zhu's considerable self-discipline to hold himself back from drawing his weapon and shooting Edgerton first, the General next, and himself last. Doctor Wang could toss their bodies into the sea. Or perhaps feed them to some ailing beast in his pet hospital.

But of course Zhu could not act yet. Because of all the players in this game, the one who needed to die first was not here right now.

Emma Chang.

Now Zhu closed his eyes tight and fought back the stab of regret. He wished he'd voiced his doubts about her to the General earlier. Warned him of the subtle danger of letting that woman get too close to him.

Get inside him.

But regret was not something that Zhu allowed to cloud his own judgment. Right now the entire operation was in Zhu's hands. Every military officer knows that he must be ready to take over the command of his superior at any time.

That time had come with General Trung.

The man had lost control of his faculties of reason and common sense. He might have to be put down like an old dog gone mad.

Zhu would take no pleasure in it. He wished it were not necessary. But there were thousands of men and women in this operation. This was not the Army, but it was still a military-style operation with clear hierarchies.

And clear duties of men in that hierarchy.

Edgerton first. Emma next.

Then Zhu would make a final assessment on the General's fate. If Trung shrugged off the sight of Emma's dead body, if he laughed and then flashed his brilliant white smile, if he congratulated Zhu on thinking with a cool head, then perhaps the old dog would not need to be put to rest.

We shall see how it plays out, Zhu thought as the strategy settled his savage mood into the cool ruthlessness he needed when moving into combat mode. Either way, his priority right now was to protect the General until Edgerton was dead.

"Move there," Zhu barked at Edgerton, directing him away from the General.

Edgerton sighed and shifted over one spot. Zhu screwed up his face and lay down between the General and Edgerton. He stared up at Doctor Wang blankly as the skinny tiger-man replaced the floorboards over the three surly sardines armed with German machine-pistols.

The world went dark.

The cab door slammed shut.

The truck's engine roared to life.

The tiger-wagon started to move.

29

"Move the tigers, please," Parkov shouted to the guard closest to the cage. "Open the trapdoor and let them into their habitat."

The tigers had been making that buzzsaw-like sound in their throats. They'd been pacing their cages restlessly, so much so that the mama tiger had pulled her babies away from her nipples and stood up to sound her throaty raspy growl.

Emma wondered if the two tigers had sensed that she was stalling for time. Maybe they understood that this man wasn't her mate. Perhaps the incongruence confused them.

After all, animals weren't burdened by the convoluted mating rituals of humans. They were so close to the fundamental forces of nature that it made no sense why a human animal would bother playing sex games with any creature other than their true mates. They weren't tortured by the sophisticated games of drama and intrigue that men and women played with their big brains that tried to overrule what their bodies already knew instinctively.

Extracting Emma

Emma's own instincts were strong and alive now. Instincts she didn't think she had, but now understood were innate and inborn, natural and beautiful.

The instinct to tease.

The instinct to tempt.

The instinct to tame.

To keep a man at bay with her words and gestures, her eyes and her lips. Just like those birds where the male must dance before he is granted access, Emma was using everything she'd learned from the women of the night, pulling out every trick that her inborn mating strategies offered.

She was playing for her life. Just like so many women had done through the ages, would continue to do as the eternal dance between man and woman played out over and over again.

Yes, she was playing for her life. But she was also having the time of her life. She had entered that strange zone that she'd seen alive in the women of the night but never truly understood till now.

It was a feeling of power. A sensation of control.

Using sex to control violence.

But the clock was ticking, Emma knew when the tigers were ushered out and Parkov turned his gaze back towards her. He was obscenely large beneath those shorts. His toes were splayed out and gripping the carpet like some strange creature of dark fantasy. His head looked larger and shinier than before.

Parkov glanced over at the guard standing near the door to the back rooms where she and Edge had made savagely beautiful love, where she'd blacked out in the throes of passion and awoken up to the brightness of love.

And it did feel like love, Emma thought as she watched Parkov say something to the Russian guy who'd treated them with some degree of civility, maybe even sympathy.

"Go to the back and wait for me there," Parkov said to her gruffly.

Emma gulped back a sick feeling of dread. The tigers had helped Emma by delaying any serious petting by those sausage-thick fingers of Parkov. But maybe they'd also broken the spell that Emma had felt herself spinning over the man. She'd responded enough to make him believe he might succeed in arousing her like he wanted. But now he seemed agitated, irritable, impatient.

Like perhaps the balance between sex and violence was starting to swing the other way.

"It's so much nicer out here," Emma offered, changing legs in her cross-kneed position, parting her thighs with lingering slowness, shamelessly hoping her scent would affect him like in some adult fairy tale where she was the witch and he was the ogre.

All she had to do was trick the ogre, keep him under her spell. Just long enough till her lumberjack-prince stormed his way back to her, cutting through the dark forest in search of his witchy little princess.

"Nyet," snarled Parkov. "The men should not see me fuck a China whore. I have a reputation to consider. Come. Move your big arse. And I want your jeans off when I arrive."

Emma took her time standing up. She was worried now.

What if Edge really was dead?

What if he really was gone?

What if he didn't feel like she felt?

Didn't feel like this was worth fighting for.

Didn't feel like this was worth dying for.

Didn't feel like this was love.

30

This feels like love, Edge thought in the darkness of the truck bed floor.

It was a strange thought for an American Special Forces man to consider when lying sardine-like alongside two Chinese Army men beneath the floorboards of a tiger-ambulance on its way to a Russian mobster's igloo-shaped fortress on an island in the South China Sea.

Edge almost laughed, but the stench of tiger-musk mixed with the aroma of organic unmentionables kept his lips closed tight and his breathing shallow and quick.

But the thought spun through his mind again as Doctor Wang spun the truck off the highway and onto the coastal road where Edge had met Benson. The word love hung out there like a billboard in the highway of his mind.

Of course it was love, Edge decided.

Because if it wasn't, what the hell was he doing here?

That settled the question in his mind. But then Edge chuckled inwardly when he recognized there was no question to settle.

Because love was a feeling, and a feeling wasn't a question.

Extracting Emma

It was an answer.

An answer to why Edge was doing this. Why he was doing it with a smile on his face, a song in his heart, a buzz in his head. It felt like his entire life had been leading up to this one moment, fate and destiny poised and ready, sex and violence caught in limbo, a moment of perfect motion and deadly balance, like a killer whale high above the waves in mid-hunt, just before it turns its glistening body in time, snaps its blood-stained jaws in space, comes crashing down in a violent explosion of foam and froth, chaos and carnage.

The image of everything hanging in poignant balance was still in the SEAL's mind when the truck slowed to a stop.

Edge heard muffled voices outside. The truck-cab's door opened, then closed.

Footsteps. More voices.

The back door to the wagon opened above them.

Edge held his breath. Closed his eyes.

Imagined he was a ghost. A mirage. An illusion.

Russian voices came down through the floorboards.

Muffled tones.

No urgency.

The doors slammed shut. The truck's engine rumbled to life again.

The game was on.

31

The game was up.

Emma stood in the circular corridor with the red walls. She faced the three rooms, two of which she knew very well.

The red room where she'd ridden Edge's tongue like a witch on a fleshy broomstick.

The gymnasium where she'd screamed like a banshee being tortured, then sighed in the protective arms of her savior.

The third room was the bathroom. Emma considered locking herself in there. It would buy some time.

Not much, though. Maybe like three minutes before Parkov kicked it open with those big bare ogre's feet.

"Speaking of ogres," Emma muttered as she remembered Edge wielding that dumbbell like a club. "Maybe it's time to go all-in on the violence part."

She glanced back at the door to the outer room. It was still closed. She could hear Parkov saying something in Russian to the guard outside.

Do not come in unless I call for you, she hoped he was saying.

Emma hurried into the gymnasium. She gasped when she entered. It smelled like Edge. It smelled like them. No wonder Parkov had emerged from his workout all worked up. Emma was getting a little worked up herself.

There was a fleeting glimpse of something shifting inside her. Crossing over. Phase change of some sort. Sex mode off. Violence mode on.

Or maybe both modes on at once.

Emma went to the dumbbell rack and reached for the eighty pounder. She couldn't even move it with one hand. She moved down the line. She could lift the twenty-pounder with one hand, but swinging it might dislocate her shoulder, she thought.

Ten pounds was the Goldilocks weight. She gripped it tight, then took a practice swing.

She thought a moment, then opened the door wide, all the way until it clicked into the little socket on the wall and stayed open. That Russian guard had opened the door just a crack and peered in before entering. She wanted Parkov to stride right in, expecting to see her big butt.

That would be the last thought in his mind before she knocked his brains all over those black mats.

Emma gulped as her mind spun forward. She wondered if a ten pound weight would actually kill Parkov.

What if she didn't hit him properly. A glancing blow that only pissed him off, made him kill her immediately.

"Should I just let him fuck me," Emma muttered, blinking away the vile thought of Parkov grunting and muttering in Russian, those feral feet gripping the floor-mats as he pumped his stubby cock into her. "That might buy me even more time. Maybe he'll last a long time. Maybe I can get him to fuck me all day, give Edge as much time as he needs."

There was that trick the hourly girls in Bangkok had told Emma about. You press that spot between his asshole and balls. Real tight. Keep him from coming. Keep him going. The girls used it so the customers wouldn't complain about paying for an hour when they were done in three minutes. Customer satisfaction was important in every business.

Now Emma felt her heart pound behind her breasts. She would have to let him fuck her, she realized. It wouldn't be so horrible. Women spread their legs for money all over the world. Emma had met thousands who felt no shame, no guilt, no filth, no fuss. She could do it to get what she wanted.

After all, she'd been prepared to do it with the General.

She'd been mentally preparing years before she ever stepped into the General's penthouse.

Years before the General's massive shadow ever fell across her naked body.

She'd wondered what it would feel like to take the thrust of a man she'd hated for years, whose death was a gift she begged for every night, whose pain would feel like pleasure to the darkest parts of her mind.

But Trung had never been inside her, Emma thought as she remembered what Parkov had said about the General and that unfortunate woman who'd felt Trung's shaft inside her for a moment and then died for the privilege. She wondered if the story could be true.

She wondered if she *wanted* it to be true.

The thought made her double over as her gut clenched like a hundred knives stabbing her insides. She caught a glimpse of herself in the wall of mirrors. Doubled over like that witch. Bent over like that whore.

Emma stared at the image of herself with that dumbbell club. Then she straightened up and laughed. She cackled and made a face at herself. She faked a moan and bucked her hips.

She pretended the dumbbell was a knobby cock.

She rode it and fucked it. She licked it and sucked it.

She felt herself slipping into madness like a sunset sinks into the sea. Slow and easy, not fast and furious.

"It's all over, isn't it?" she whispered as she tried to hold back a heaving sob. "He's going to fuck me and then kill me. It's been twenty four hours since Edge left. Fourteen hours since the General returned to Macao. Edge is dead or gone. The General doesn't know about me or doesn't care about me. Either way, nobody's coming for me. Nobody's starting a war for me. Who the hell did I think I was? Helen of fucking Troy? Armies sailing across oceans to claim my precious pussy? Men dying in droves for the right to sniff my coveted cunt? Am I just another of those working girls who think the man who pays the rent wants to buy the entire house? That he actually wants to take the whore to the grand ball? That it's actually possible to be the prostitute and the princess in the same lifetime?"

Parkov's bare footsteps padded along the outside corridor. Emma felt despair take hold of her heaving heart. The dumbbell felt incredibly heavy in her hand.

Her shoulder hurt. Her body ached. Her head throbbed.

She let the dumbbell thud to the floormat.

She let that sob break through.

It was over.

She was alone.

She was forsaken.

"For fuck's sake," came Parkov's voice from just outside the open door.

He didn't enter. He had stopped.

He huffed out a rumbling breath. Emma could hear the Russian guard saying something to him from the door to the main room.

Parkov snorted out another exasperated breath. He barked something in Russian, then stomped back toward the main door. Emma heard the door clang shut behind him.

Then silence.

She didn't speak good Russian, but she'd picked out a couple of words.

Two words.

Doctor.

Wang.

32

Doctor Wang's only job outside of driving was to fall flat on his face.

Edge had described the enclosed corridor between the garage and the main house to Zhu and Trung. There was a metal door at the end with a camera above the frame. The door opened into that small area where the tattooed thugs had searched Edge and smashed his phone. It was imperative that the metal door stay open long enough for Edge and Zhu and Trung to fight their way out of the garage and down to that area.

And it was Wang's job to keep that door open.

"You can trip, faint, fake a seizure, or just stop to tie your damn shoelace," Edge had informed Wang while Zhu translated. "We need three or four seconds. Five tops. If we can't get there in five seconds, we aren't getting there at all."

Wang had agreed with a sullen nod. Whatever Zhu had threatened him with was rock solid. The Doctor was completely resigned to his fate. It had made Edge wonder about all the choices that had been made that brought so many people to this one event.

An event from which very few were going to walk away.

Edge stayed silent as the truck pulled into the garage and stopped. The blast-proof and hopefully sound-proof garage door whined shut in the distance. Edge listened for footsteps. He'd been trained to estimate the number of hostiles just from listening to their feet on the ground.

This was easier because there were voices attached. Lots of voices. Too many voices.

"Shift change," Edge whispered after he picked up a few Russian words. He also picked up the familiar voice of the guy who'd been somewhat decent with him and Emma.

The guy was leaving to go home after a double shift. Clearly his choices were going to result in him walking away from what was about to unfold. Edge wondered if that nameless thug's own fate had turned in his favor because he'd chosen to be decent.

Maybe, but Edge wasn't going to make any such guarantees of decency or mercy.

This was war. He was a warrior. You flip that switch. Get into the zone.

You don't rethink your choices once the mission starts. You stop to think, the guy who doesn't need to think puts a bullet in you.

Edge heard the garage door whine open, then close again. He held his breath and prayed that Doctor Wang was still going through the first pat-down, that he was still in the garage. If Wang was already faking a heart attack or twisted ankle at the second door, then this mission was over.

Edge heard Wang's voice. He was still in the garage. He was explaining why he needed so many supplies for two tiger cubs. He said the big tigers might need to be tranquilized. That they might not enjoy watching him manhandle their newborns.

Edge relaxed. Zhu grunted softly in the dark beside him.

Zhu had instructed Wang to pack his medical kit full to the brim with potions and pills and syringes big enough to shoot Stinger missiles from. It was a good idea. It would take a long time before the Russians in the garage would give him the OK to move on to the body-cavity check past the second door.

"Good work," Edge whispered to Zhu in the dark.

Zhu grunted again. Edge wondered if they were becoming buddies.

Nah. Edge had plenty of friends. He liked the kind that didn't want to shoot you in the head.

"Now," said the General softly.

Immediately all three men pushed up on their floorboards. They'd lined up their positions perfectly beneath three loose boards. The boards came up silent and smooth.

The three men pulled their black silk masks up over their noses and mouths. Edge stepped silently to the side of the aluminum shell where Zhu had carefully drilled a small hole and installed a tiny fisheye lens.

Edge peered through it, scanning the walls around the door to the corridor leading inside. He wasn't trying to count the guards. He already knew their positions from his earlier visit. Footfalls and voices had confirmed that it was the same setup. Two guards on either side of the door. Two more to search the Doctor and his bag of tricks. Two more back near the blast-door leading to the driveway.

Edge used hand signals to let Zhu and Trung know the guards were positioned as expected. Then he gave a thumbs up when he found what he was looking for.

The black painted metal box with thick wires leading in and out of it. Edge had taken note of it during his first visit. It was the nerve center for the cameras and alarm system.

Edge wasn't concerned about the cameras too much. They weren't connected to the guard shack. They were of course connected to the screens in the waystation behind the second door, but once Edge and gang were into the corridor, things would happen so fast the cameras wouldn't matter.

Nobody was gonna be watching TV with 9mm bullets bursting all over the place.

So cameras were no problem. The alarm system was the problem.

It would certainly be connected to the guard station at the gate. There would be an emergency call button to summon backup. An intercom system as well, probably routed to the waystation inside the second door. Direct line from the inside guard station to the outside guard shack.

But it wouldn't be as simple as shooting the crap out of that metal box and expecting everything to go silent and dead.

The box was bulletproof, fireproof, and probably blast proof to some degree. Edge would have loved to have his Navy SEAL toolkit of plastique and tiny detonators, but there would be no time for that anyway. The moment Edge and the gang sprung out of the tiger-wagon, it would be bullets for breakfast.

So the only line that needed to be cut was the cable carrying the alarm and intercom signal to the outside. Edge decided it was the black wire that ran along the top corner. It led towards the outside door. It was the only one reinforced with a plastic corrugated sheath to protect it from rain and the elements. Edge would have to sever it with surgically precise shooting.

Zhu and Trung crouched by the double doors of the wagon. Their H&K machine pistols were drawn. Safety mechanism disabled. Full magazines with the extended clips.

Trung was facing the door. He was smiling. Brilliant white. Eyes were shining like golden tiger-eyes in the dark.

Edge nodded to himself. Trung was the enemy and he would fall tonight. Did he know that? Was that part of why he'd accepted this mission? Was there a part of the dark and distinguished General that wanted to go down with his weapon still hot, the smell of gunsmoke in the air, the battlefield littered with bodies?

Then Edge glanced at Zhu.

Zhu had been watching Edge all this while.

He was ready too.

Now they just had to wait for Doctor Wang to walk

into the corridor before getting started. That was the signal. The opening bell. The starting gun.

Edge glanced through his peephole again. Doctor Wang was closing up his bag. The search was done.

The door to the corridor opened.

Doctor Wang stepped inside.

Edge pulled away from the peephole.

Spear formation. Edge was the point of the spear.

He stepped past Zhu and Trung.

Kicked the wagon door open.

Sent a line of 9mm bullets towards the guards at the far door leading outside.

Their bodies slammed against the solid metal with muted thuds.

Blood dragged down against the black metal door like swatches of red paint as the bodies slumped to the ground, eyes rolled up in their heads, mouths hanging open like hungry zombies.

The first guy Edge had killed was Gargoyle.

Bullets for breakfast.

And breakfast was served.

33

General Trung had served the Chinese People's Liberation Army for three full decades, most of which were as a commanding officer. But his fondest memories were of the early days when he was given the dirtiest jobs, assigned the riskiest missions, sent into the deadliest zones of the worst wars.

Those memories returned like he was living them in the flesh, and Trung howled with delight as he watched a Russian thug convulse from the six bullets the General had just put into the center mass of the thug's thick body.

The Russians wore bulletproof vests beneath their dress shirts, but the hollow-points that the German-made H&K pistols spat out burst through the Kevlar and ripped wide holes through skin and tissue, big as meteorite craters on the moon. The General whooped in triumph, stomping on a dead man's chest as he followed Zhu and Edgerton into the covered red-walled corridor.

Edgerton had blown out the alarm cable that led out of the garage with a single three-round burst of precise marksmanship. Zhu had just put down the two Russians who had searched Wang's black medicine case

Three bullets in each man. All head or neck shots. Zhu was very clean. Very efficient. Still sharp like he was in the old days by Trung's side.

Not by his side but at his back, Trung reminded himself when he saw how Zhu somehow managed to keep an eye on Edgerton while making his shots count with the Russians.

"We're going in," shouted Edgerton, putting down the last Russian manning the door.

The SEAL fired in stride, barely taking aim but sending a diagonal line of three bullets across the goon's upper body. One bullet smashed through his cheekbone. The other through the center of his throat. The third shattered his collarbone.

Instant death. No hesitation. The SEAL was elite, no doubt. Too bad for the United States that he couldn't control his fists when dealing with fools that outranked him.

Too bad for you too, came the whispered warning in Trung's head.

The General's ears were ringing from the gunfire. His temples were throbbing from the adrenaline. His heart was pumping hard as he thundered down the long corridor behind Zhu and Edgerton.

Doctor Wang had done his job. He was on his knees, about to be hauled out of the doorway. But the Russian gatekeepers had dropped Wang at the sound of the shots. One of them was yelling in Russian and hitting a button on the side of the wall repeatedly.

It must be the alarm. And it must not be working,

thought the General as he leaned to his left and fired past Zhu and Edgerton.

Zhu flinched, but Edgerton merely turned his head halfway with the lazy confidence of a man who believed no bullet could hit him unless he chose to let it happen.

Trung's shot was a single bullet. It hit the Russian alarm-pusher in the side of his head, right above his left ear. His skull exploded in a puff of pink mist.

Edgerton killed the other gatekeeper with another three round burst to the upper body. The SEAL was past the dead guards before the second guy even hit the floor.

Edgerton had already opened the inner door and was charging into the main arena, firing deadly three-round bursts.

Zhu had leapfrogged the screaming Doctor Wang and had joined in the main event.

General Trung just bulldozed right through the crawling doctor. There was a crunch of bone and a scream of pain. The General figured Doctor Wang would not be using his right hand for surgery anytime soon.

By the time Trung entered the main arena, seven of the twelve guards were already down. Trung shot the eighth Russian in the right eye, put another bullet in one of the downed men who was still coughing up blood, then rammed his elbow into a Russian thug's tattooed neck, crushing his windpipe as the guy leaped out from behind a high wooden bar.

The bar had three large glass vodka samovars in a neat line on the black-glass top. The infused flavors were peach, tangerine, and red chili. As Trung looked at the large Thai red peppers floating in the vodka-infusion, a stray bullet whizzed past his ear and smashed into the glass.

Trung whipped around and dropped to his knees as the samovar exploded above him. Vodka and glass spattered all over his silk cloth mask. The vodka was pungent, and the chili pepper infusion made Trung gag. He ripped off his face mask, then cursed when he saw that the cameras were still rolling.

There was no one to watch the footage right now, but certainly it would be saved in a digital file for the viewing pleasure of whichever Russian next-in-command was tasked with clean up and investigation. Trung aimed at the camera and blasted it off its perch. Not that it mattered now. The damage was done.

The General cursed again when he tried to shoot at a wounded Russian and got no response from his machine pistol except the metallic whir of an empty weapon. The always watchful Zhu put the thug down as the General expelled the empty magazine and reached for another from his vest. His palm was sweaty, and it took a moment to slam the magazine into the gun. Trung quickly took up a firing position, but there was nobody left to shoot.

Trung relaxed when he heard the stillness in the air. It was the deathly silence of a smoky battlefield after the fighting stopped. The gunsmoke was thick and acrid.

The General scanned the room for Emma. She was not here. Neither was Parkov.

Trung's gaze fell on a metal door far in the back, near a leather recliner and sofa. Edgerton was already running towards the door, ejecting his own spent magazine as he ran.

Then shots rang out through the hazy, smoke-glutted room.

Zhu was firing. He fired off another volley of shots, holding down the trigger in automatic mode until the gun spun empty. Trung blinked in the smoke. He looked for Edgerton.

Edgerton was down.

34

"Down on your knees," said Parkov. He pointed the long speckled nose of the black handgun directly at Emma's head. "Slow. Easy. There we go."

Emma did as he asked. She placed her knees on the black mat of the gym, then slowly sat her ass back on her ankles.

Parkov was behind her. She could see his reflection in the mirrored wall to her left. He was sitting on the same exercise bench where Emma had gotten the greatest neck rub in the history of civilization. Parkov was pointing that long handgun at the back of her neck. It did not feel as nice as Edge's gaze aimed at the same spot.

"What's happening?" she asked Parkov.

"Shut up," he snapped. "You just shut up, yah?"

She saw him run his hand over his shiny head. He was sweating more than he had after his so-called workout. It was probably best that Emma shut up, she decided.

She'd heard the gunfire break out just a few minutes after Parkov had stomped off to yell at Doctor Wang for his early house call. She hadn't been sure what was happening.

At first she'd wondered if Parkov had decided to execute Doctor Wang for poor customer service. But soon it was clear that it was not about Doctor Wang. There would be no need to empty every single weapon in the building into Doctor Wang. Not unless he had drunk an invincibility potion made from tiger-blood.

"Shit," Parkov muttered. "Damn."

Emma stole a glance in the mirror. Parkov was patting his pockets. Then he looked around wildly. Slapped his pockets again. Muttered out some Russian curses.

No phone.

No backup.

"Want me to go get your phone?" she offered. Not that she expected him to say yes. She just hoped he'd tell her what was happening out there.

Tell her what all the shooting was about.

What all the fuss was about.

Not that she needed him to answer that question.

Not when the answer was humming in her head.

Screaming through her spirit.

Singing from her soul.

The fuss was about her.

Edge had come for her.

Edge was here to take her home.

Edge was . . . um, where *was* he, Emma suddenly wondered as everything went silent in the battlefield out there and everything inside her mind and heart and body went insane with alarm bells clanging and train whistles blowing and emergency lights flashing and tires screeching and whales bellowing and cats wailing and hounds howling and window panes shattered by stones and Emma's life being shattered because she'd dared to hope, dared to dream, dared to think this was more than what it seemed.

"Seems like it is over, Miss Chang," whispered Parkov from behind her. "They are all dead."

35

Playing dead was hard, but it was damn near impossible when you'd taken a hollow-point 9mm bullet in your side and now there was burning flesh exposed to acrid air, when it felt like someone had caked salt on a hot knife and was smearing it on your wound.

Somehow Edge stayed still as a rock, keeping his head down and his eyes closed. He'd dived to the floor the moment he saw Zhu raise his weapon.

But Zhu was quick, and his H&K was set to fully automatic. It sprayed bullets like a garden hose turned all the way up. Edge felt one of the bullets graze his left side as he fell to the floor. The hollow-point tip collapses on entry, tearing a much wider path through flesh.

Edge had glanced at his wound before going still. He needed to see the color of the blood.

It was bright red like a sunrise. That was good. It meant his liver was intact. His kidneys were fine. Either of those organs get hit and you bleed black as sin.

Edge knew he'd been lucky to take just one bullet. Luckier that it hadn't hit bone. Hollow points ricochet off bone. The bullet zigzags its way through flesh and tissue. You could shoot someone in the forearm and the bullet might come out the guy's neck, destroying everything in between.

Now Edge listened for Zhu's footsteps. Zhu would come over to make sure Edge was dead. Edge had seen him finish off the Russians. He was cold and efficient.

But was he lucky, Edge wondered as he heard Zhu move amongst the bodies of the dead. He heard the sound of metal on metal. He knew Zhu had emptied his magazine. Hopefully the bastard was taking his time to reload. Hopefully Edge could stop himself from going into shock before this fight was over.

"I wanted him alive, Zhu," came General Trung's voice. He was speaking Chinese, but the words were simple enough. "I wanted him to know that he had lost Emma to me."

Zhu didn't reply. Edge heard him spit in disgust. He kept walking.

But he hadn't reloaded yet.

Trung complained once more. Zhu spat again.

Trung barked out a curse, then started walking across the room. Edge knew the General was heading towards the door leading to the gym and bathroom and sauna. Parkov had to be back there somewhere.

With Emma.

The thought of being so close to her gave Edge just enough resolve to hold still even though his wound burned as if Satan were licking the raw flesh with his sandpapery tongue. Edge bit down on his tongue, trying to listen for Zhu's quiet footsteps.

Zhu was close enough now that Edge could feel the man's shadow fall across his body

Eyes still closed, Edge kicked out viciously with his left leg. His steel-reinforced boot connected with the side of Zhu's knee, and the man yelped and went down.

Instantly Edge was on top of him. He slammed his fist into Zhu's face. Hit him dead on, twice, bam-bam.

Zhu's nose exploded in a blood-spatter. His yellow front teeth broke off at the roots. Edge drew his hand back and prepared to ram his knuckles into Zhu's cheekbone, push the bone shards back into his brain, end this fight.

But Zhu somehow managed to turn his head. Edge's fist smashed into the ground.

Edge roared, more in anger than pain. Zhu was thrashing under him, trying to get a punch in. But the blood and tears because of his smashed nose messed with his vision, and so Edge gripped the bastard by the throat and squeezed with everything he had.

He felt Zhu's throat compress. Another two seconds and Zhu would be dead.

Less than two seconds later, three bullets slammed into the floor just inches from Zhu's head.

"Enough," came the General's steady voice. Edge felt the gun press against the back of his skull. "Get off him, SEAL."

Edge groaned as the adrenaline drained away and the pain in his broken knuckles and his burning side roared in like the surf on Coronado Beach.

Edge slowly got to his feet, breathing hard and heavy,

big gulping breaths as he backed away from the groaning, bloody Zhu.

Zhu took a minute to reset what was left of his nose. He reached into his mouth and did something with his teeth. Then he turned to the side and spat. There were broken bits of his yellow shark teeth in the bloody saliva. Edge figured they would grow back if he lived long enough.

Trung kept the gun pointed at Edge. He nodded towards Edge's flak vest with his spare magazines. Edge had dropped his gun when he'd hit the floor. It was empty anyway.

"Take off the vest," Trung said with a sigh. "Empty your pockets. I cannot trust you with weapons or ammo anymore. You understand."

Edge grunted. He grunted again as the vest brushed against his wound. He dropped it in a heap on the floor. Emptied out his pockets. There were two more spare magazines in his cargo flaps.

"Let us go see about Emma, yes?" the General said, flashing his brilliant white smile and gesturing with his gun towards the door to the gym and bathroom. Then he glanced back at Zhu. "Take your time, Zhu. It is just Parkov. And he will have Emma, so no sudden moves."

Zhu muttered something in Chinese. Edge turned and started to walk towards the door.

Then Edge stopped when he heard the sound of a fresh magazine being slammed into an H&K machine pistol.

It was Zhu. He was bloody and broken, but his gun-hand was steady. His black-pearl eyes were focused. His finger was on the trigger.

"Don't," said the General, turning his own weapon towards Zhu.

Zhu blinked. He kept the gun pointed at Edge, but his gaze flicked to the General.

"You would kill me to save your enemy?" Zhu gasped. "Thirty years by your side and we have come to this, General? You are so far gone over a . . . a whore?"

The General was silent. He kept his gun aimed at Zhu's head. Zhu kept his gun-hand steady on Edge.

The standoff lasted for six full seconds.

Then the General sighed. He lowered his weapon.

Zhu grinned with what was left of his mouth. He turned his gaze back to Edge.

Then his eyes went blank. His eyelids fluttered.

Then he dropped the gun. Dropped down to the floor. Started writhing like a fish. Bloody foam started pouring out of his lips.

"Zhu!" shouted the General. "No!"

Edge stared in shock. He couldn't understand what was happening.

Then Edge's gaze went down to Zhu's left knee.

The same knee that Edge had shattered with his vicious steel-reinforced kick.

The same knee over which Zhu's pants had a little zippered compartment.

Edge thought back to that moment in the penthouse when Zhu had caught Edge looking at him.

Many people had made choices that had led to their fate this bloody evening.

Zhu had made the choice to take the vial of poison from his jacket and put it in the secure zipper compartment.

Game over, Zhu.

"Benson would say that's cheating," muttered Edge. "But all's fair in love and war."

Edge spat on the convulsing man's bloody face. He turned and strode towards the back door.

Edge didn't give a damn about the General shooting him in the back. That wasn't how this story was going to end.

Maybe it was the blood loss and the mind-numbing pain, but Edge was soaring now. High as a fucking kite.

He got to the closed door and then stopped. Reality pushed its way into his pounding head. He sighed, stroked his beard, then turned to the General.

"I need a weapon," he said to Trung. "You'll need me to rescue Emma."

Trung walked up, that brilliant smile back on his distinguished face. If he was still upset about Zhu, it didn't show.

"What if I do not want to rescue Emma anymore?" said Trung through that disconcertingly unreadable smile. "Logic says I should shoot you in the head. Then go in there and shoot Parkov and Emma both twice in the head. Then I go erase the video. Take Doctor Wang. Crawl under the floorboards of his truck. Ride away into the sunset like an American cowboy. Hooyah, yes?"

Extracting Emma

Edge watched Trung's eyes for any sign, any signal, any hint of a flinch.

There was nothing. He was stone cold unreadable.

But he was here.

He was right here, right outside the last door.

Almost past the final threshold.

There was no way General Trung was going to cut his losses and retreat.

Edge wasn't going to let him retreat.

Because Edge needed the General too.

The General gave Edge the best chance of getting Emma away from Parkov.

And that was all that mattered.

Edge took a breath, let it out slowly. He nodded, then shrugged as coolly as was humanly possible with the wound in his side.

"No," said Edge. "No Hooyah for you. No sunset rides for you. No victory for you. Not without Emma by your side. You know it. I know it." Edge took a long breath as he considered his words carefully. "And Emma knows it."

Now the General flinched. His pupils dilated. His smile changed form.

He stroked his smooth, square chin. Raised his head, looked down his nose at Edge like now Edge was the unreadable trickster.

"One bullet," said Edge softly. "I'll chamber one bullet in a gun. No magazine. You have to trust that I'll put the bullet in Parkov, not you. You have to trust that my priority is Emma alive, not you dead. If this ends with me dead and Emma alive, that's still OK in my book. It's still Mission Accomplished for this SEAL." He paused. "What do you say, General?"

Edge shrugged, narrowed his eyes, stroked his beard and grinned like a madman. That woozy lightheadedness made him feel like he was floating through the clouds, waving at Benson who was riding by on a flaming chariot drawn by snickering unicorns.

"You still get to ride off into the sunset, but maybe not alone," Edge said with a strangely whimsical intensity. "Maybe Emma chooses to go with you. Who knows how the story ends, General. No way to know unless we walk through that last door, step past the final threshold, take the tiger by the tail, dance with the devil, poke the bear, prod the poodle, take the bull by the balls and squeeze, take the turtle by the shell and hurl." He chuckled. "Not sure if those metaphors translate well, but you get my drift. We aren't retreating, General. We're going in. Now, give me a gun. Give me one bullet. And I'll give you a plan."

36

"I hope this was not a rescue plan, SEAL," Parkov called nervously towards the gymnasium door. "Because it has already failed."

Footsteps had stopped outside in the corridor. The door had been pushed open a crack. Nobody had entered.

Emma held her breath as the door moved open another inch. A slanted shadow appeared on the floor mats. The shadow was tall and very wide. Emma blinked away a bead of perspiration.

Then the shadow moved forward.

The door creaked open on its metal hinges.

The figure stood bathed in the overhead light.

It was General Trung.

Parkov gasped from behind Emma.

"You?" he muttered. "The General himself?

General Trung walked into the room like he owned it. He flashed his brilliantly unreadable smile. Trung was in black utility pants spattered with streaks of blood, some drying, some fresh. It was not the General's blood. Emma was uncertain if she was relieved or disappointed.

Trung wore a black silk tee shirt that showed off his

massive pectorals. The heavy muscles twitched as Trung flexed them as was his habit. He looked very tall and formidable. The streaks of red blood on black canvas sent a ripple up Emma's spine. There was an air of supreme confidence around him that made Emma gulp and glance down and then up again.

The . . . the *General* had come for her?

Not . . . not Edge?

Where . . . where was Edge?

Suddenly Emma's world turned upside down. She wanted to die. She considered turning to Parkov and taking that long gun barrel into her mouth. It would be over fast. So fast she wouldn't have time to think.

Think about what she was feeling.

Emma's head spun as her world slowly turned right side up again. Edge was dead. The General had killed him. It was over. She should end it.

But Emma couldn't move. Another bead of wetness rolled down her cheek. It came from the corner of her left eye. It rolled down to her lips. It was salty. She was crying.

"Relax," said the General in Chinese. "I am here to take you back."

There is no going back, Emma thought as a cold deadness spread through her insides.

She waited for the deadness to kill her, but it did not kill her.

She was still here.

What did that mean?

Emma didn't know.

She didn't want to know.

She was beyond knowing.

Beyond caring.

The General's golden gaze flicked to her face. His eyes were bright and alert. There was something warm behind those eyes. It made her uncomfortable. Not his eyes but the feeling it created inside her. It made her want to vomit. Things were turning around in her head and body and heart and mind.

Then the cold deadness came back to her. It felt nice, she decided.

Emma preferred being dead inside. Now she didn't have to think. She could just be an empty shell. A doll with arms and legs and a little wooden slit at the bottom but no soul inside.

Emma smiled thinly like that cold dead doll with its wooden face and painted-on lips.

The General's smile remained unchanged. Emma wondered if he was just a soldier doll with a painted-on smile just like her. The thought made her giggle inside her wooden head. She could feel things unraveling inside that hollow skull. She kept the smile on her face. She imagined her soul fluttering away like a butterfly waving goodbye.

"Say goodbye to Mister Parkov, Emma," said Trung in English. "We are leaving."

He held out his hand, big palm upturned. Emma stared up from down on her knees. Things felt so surreal and strange. She felt her arm reaching out to his in slow motion. There was no other feeling in her entire body. It was all dead wood and molded plastic.

Parkov had been silent for some time. Emma moved

her plastic eyeballs to the side and glanced at the wall of mirrors.

Parkov was still there, but he appeared to have turned into a wooden doll just like everyone else in the room. Emma felt herself start to giggle again. She caught herself just in time.

Then something caught her eye. Not in the mirror but behind the General.

A shadow moving beneath the closed door.

Just for a flash, then it was gone.

Emma blinked. She swallowed. She felt something come alive in her. That coldness was receding. The warmth of life was returning. The plastic was melting.

Now Emma's mind snapped into focus. It occurred to her that the General had closed the door behind him after stepping into the room. She wondered if Zhu was outside the door.

Then she wondered if Edge was outside the door.

She swallowed a lump in her throat, told herself not to hope, not to dream, not to imagine a future that was almost certainly lost. If it were Edge outside, it would mean that the General and Edge had *both* come for her.

Together.

They'd both come to save her.

Both come to take her.

Both come to claim her.

The thought sent a flash of heat through Emma, burning away the last shreds of plastic, the last splinters of wood.

Now she was flesh and blood again. White flesh and red blood. Hard bone and soft curves.

Extracting Emma

"Come," said the General, his thick fingers curling back on his big open palm. "We are leaving."

Parkov made a clucking sound with his tongue. Then a clicking sound with his gun.

"You are crazy," Parkov whispered. It was the first words he'd spoken since the General walked into the room and the shadow passed beneath the closed door. "You come here *yourself*? For *her*? You storm my fortress and start a war for Emma?"

The General looked at Parkov. He said nothing. No offers. No threats. No bribes.

Now the shadow moved beneath the door again. This time Parkov noticed too.

"Who is that?" Parkov yelled. "Open the door, Trung. Open it or I swear I will shoot you and then shoot this bitch. Open the fucking door!"

The General took a long, slow breath. He turned and strolled to the door.

The shadow beneath the door was moving erratically.

But not just moving.

It was also *mewling*.

"My kitty!" screamed Parkov as Trung pulled open the door and quickly stepped aside to reveal a newborn white tiger cub mewling loudly for mama.

It was too young to walk properly, and it was slipping and sliding on its paws.

Paws that were stained with blood.

Blood that was all over its snow-white belly as it rolled over and mewled again.

Parkov shoved Emma aside and barreled out the door, sliding to his knees and taking the blood-soaked cub into his big hairy arms. He kissed its face and feverishly checked the cub's belly-fur for the wound.

There was no wound.

Parkov looked up and cocked his head. He frowned.

Then his head exploded in a burst of pink brain and white skull and red mist that hung in the air like bloody confetti.

And Edge stepped out of the shadows, smoking gun in his hand, blood-soaked shirt sticking to his side, green eyes shining with love.

Emma screamed and leapt to her feet. She raced past Trung, screaming with joy and relief and concern and love.

Then Emma screamed in pain when she felt her scalp almost rip away from her skull as Trung savagely grabbed her hair as she ran by.

He spun her around by her hair, then dragged her out through the open doorway as she kicked and clawed and howled and spat.

Edge shouted something, but went silent when Trung pressed his gun barrel into Emma's cheek.

Emma went silent too. She gazed up at Edge. He glanced at her, then looked at Trung.

Then Edge tossed his gun to the floor. Emma stared at it, only now noticing that it had no magazine in it. There must have only been one bullet in the gun.

Trung flashed his brilliant white smile. He pointed his gun at Edge.

"Move back twelve feet, please," said the General.

Edge nodded and did it.

Emma watched Edge step back, well beyond the distance where he could disarm the General like he'd done to that Russian doorman.

Emma started to panic when she saw the General's eyes go cold.

Edge seemed unconcerned. His face eased into a smile. He gazed into Emma's eyes.

"I love you, Emma," Edge said to her calmly as he smiled and bled.

"I love you, Edge," Emma sobbed, not sure why he'd just said that, why he was looking at her like that.

Edge dragged his gaze away from her.

"You keep her alive. That was the deal," Edge said to the General. He took a breath, stood tall and proud, looked directly into Trung's eyes. "Now get it over with."

The General chuckled. "Very dramatic and quite brave," he said. "But you know it is not over yet. It has only just begun."

37

Edge began with the top of the empty tiger cage. He studied the joints where the steel bars met, hoping to see a missing rivet or a loose connection.

Nothing.

Then Edge checked the padlock that Trung had clicked into place after sliding the deadbolt across the cage door. The lock was triple-cast steel. Too strong to break, even if Edge were at full strength, with all his blood and all his flesh and no broken knuckles from where he'd punched the floor trying to kill Zhu.

Edge studied the combination buttons. He poked a few of them, but it was pointless. There were more combinations than stars in the universe. He sighed, then gripped the vertical cage bars to test the frame's strength.

The cage was sturdy enough that he couldn't even rattle it. Not with all his weight and all his strength.

Not with every fiber of the fight in him.

Not with every ounce of the love in him.

Which meant he had to look out through those steel bars.

Witness what was happening on the arena floor.

Watch his world turn upside down.

Get ripped apart at the seams.

Blown apart at the heart.

"Ah, finally he turns his attention to us," came Trung's voice.

The General had been standing still as a statue, Emma down on the floor by his feet. Her hair was open and all over from how the General had used it to drag her out here. Her cheeks were red, streaked with tears and the mark of Trung's big right hand.

Emma had tried to fight him and Trung had hit her. She'd scrambled to pick up a gun and shoot him, and he'd hit her again. The blows were hard and solid. They carried the weight of his massive body.

They also carried the fury of his jealous rage.

"*I* am the one who saved you!" the General roared after her first attempt to fight him. "And yet you look at *him*? You look at him like *that*? Like you *love* him?"

"I *do* love him!" Emma had shrieked, her face red with rage, her eyes burning like fire.

"No," Edge had hissed urgently as he slammed his shoulder into the cage bars. "Just do what he says, Emma. Tell him what he wants to hear. Just fucking survive. Stay alive. I'm coming for you. Just survive, dammit!"

Emma had cast a defiant glance at Edge, then made the mad scramble for a dead Russian's gun. The attempt ended with a brutal kick from the General's right shin. It almost lifted Emma off the floor. All the air was pushed out of her. She went down flat on her stomach, gasping like she was choking to death.

Edge had almost broken his shoulder from ramming it into the cage bars. He'd howled and cursed, reached desperately through the bars for a weapon.

But the General had cleared the area around the tiger cage. And after Emma's attempt to grab a gun ended with her gasping for air on the floor, Trung slowly walked around the open room and gathered all the guns he could find. He methodically carried them behind the bar with the vodka samovars and placed them in a pile.

It was like some lumbering caveman gathering firewood as his captive cavewoman awaited her fate. Edge was going mad with rage and worry. Only when he saw Emma finally suck in a hearty lungful of air did he release some of the worry and replace it with even more rage.

That vicious kick had taken most of the fight out of Emma. She was hunched over, barely able to sit upright. Her black hair flopped down across her face. Her shoulders sagged. Her eyelids were opening and closing.

Edge took several long breaths. He knew his wound had used up some of his reserves. He was running on pure adrenaline now. Rage was the primary fuel in his engine right now.

But rage blocked clear thought. Edge was going to damage himself if he kept hurling his bleeding body against a cage designed to contain a five hundred pound beast of pure muscle. Edge needed to think with a clear head.

Five hundred pound beast, came the thought again.

Now Edge whipped his body around and stared at

the wooden trapdoor at the back wall. It led to that enclosed outdoor space with the steel-mesh roof. Doctor Wang had been sent out there to snatch one of those tiger cubs for the Parkov ambush.

Five hundred pound beast, Edge thought for the third as he glanced at that steel padlock and the latch across the cage gate.

He did some quick math in his head. Five hundred pound weight moving fast would create momentum that generated thousand of pounds of force. Yeah, that would be a pretty good battering ram.

"Survive," Edge whispered as he turned back to Emma and saw the General advancing on her. "Just survive, Emma. I'm coming for you."

Then Edge ran to the back wall.

He pulled up the trapdoor just enough to roll out under it.

A moment later he was gone.

38

Emma rolled onto her back and stared up through her blurred vision. She felt something strange against her legs.

Breeze. Cool breeze.

It was the air-conditioning against her skin.

Her bare skin.

She stared up at General Trung. She was on her back. Her legs were up in the air. The General was pulling her jeans off past her ankles.

Emma stared in disbelief as Trung sniffed the crotch of her jeans so hard that the denim was pulled into his mouth. When he pulled the jeans away, that brilliant smile was back on his face.

His gaze dropped down to her naked thighs, then crept up to her dark triangle.

Emma gasped and turned over onto her side, curling up in the fetal position, hands between her legs. Her body was throbbing with pain. It hurt to breathe, but she told herself she had to breathe. She had to survive.

Survive, Edge had said to her. Say what you need to say. Do what you need to do. Stay alive until I come for you. Just stay alive, Emma.

"You think they are still alive inside you?" came Trung's voice.

It was thick with an arousal that Emma had never sensed in the cold General. She turned her head and looked up at him.

"His soldiers," Trung said through that manic grin. He sniffed her jeans again. "I smell them on your cunt. He sent them all marching in, eh? But he will be flanked by my red army. They will launch a rear attack. Smother the SEAL's soldiers. Take back my territory."

Trung started to undo his belt.

The buckle came loose.

The thick leather dropped away.

He took a step closer. Emma curled up tighter. She moved her head to look for a weapon. There were no guns in sight.

Then she saw something.

A black bag that was standing upright. It looked like a medical kit. A doctor's bag.

Doctor Wang.

Emma felt a surge of hope come with the next painful breath. Her ribs were bruised, maybe even broken.

But she was alive.

She was here.

She would survive.

Emma gasped as the General grabbed her ankles and dragged her along the floor. He was pulling her directly in front of the cage. He wanted Edge to watch. But he was too occupied to notice that Edge wasn't there. She tried to struggle to keep him occupied, but she was too bruised and broken to put up much of a fight.

She would have to keep his attention some other way.

Emma took a long breath and exhaled slowly. She reminded herself that she'd been prepared to give the General anything he wanted in return for what she wanted. All those years she'd wanted to find her sisters, close that wound that she thought would fill whatever hole she felt in herself. But now she wanted something more than she'd ever wanted that.

She wanted Edge.

She wanted the future they'd seen in each other's eyes in that wordless gaze.

And she'd do anything for that.

Give anything for that.

Endure anything for that.

And so when the General placed his big palms on her knees and started to pry her legs apart, Emma relaxed and opened up for him.

She looked up into the dragon's hungry golden eyes.

She smiled upon his savagely lined face.

The plastic smile of that wooden doll.

That wooden doll with the wooden limbs and the wooden slit that had no feeling for the wrong man.

Held no meaning with the wrong man.

Was a weapon in the right hands.

And as the General parted her petals and crossed her thresholds Emma closed her eyes and stretched her arms out wide like a snow angel, a ballerina doll, a porcelain princess.

She held the General there without a word. Reached for the black bag, but it was just beyond her outstretched fingers. She tried to creep her fingers over to the bag. She tried to inch her self along as the General huffed and puffed and grunted and growled.

Emma was barely aware of him inside her. It meant so little to her that it almost made her cry out in joy.

Because now she understood that the General had no power over her.

He never had any power over her.

Other than the power Emma herself had given him.

Given to some image of him she'd created in her own mind.

For ten years she'd built him up into this mythical monster of a man, this dragon who'd stolen her princess-sisters and gobbled them up, this beast who'd destroyed her family and still roamed the earth destroying more lives.

But now as she smelled his stench and heard his gasps, she realized that Trung really was just that boy in a soldier's uniform. Just like Emma had given up her power to some self-constructed image of General Trung, this man had just given his power away to some self-constructed image of Emma Chang.

His consort or wife or lover or mother or sisters.

Emma didn't give a damn.

It had never been about him.

It had never even been about her mother or her sisters.

Those had just been waystations along the road to her own fate.

Choices that led her to this moment in time, this position in space, this event in history.

Her own history.

Her own story.

Her own ending.

And as the princess held the dragon in place with her body and expelled him from her mind, a great sound of cages crashing open and tigers roaring wild and heroes bursting forth exploded through the silence of the battlefield.

Emma watched like it was all happening in slow motion.

She watched Edge, beard wild as he came through the back wall carrying a tiger cub in his arms, his eyes wide, his grin wider.

She watched as two five-hundred pound white tigers raced after Edge.

She held her breath as Edge dropped the cub in front of the locked gate.

She exhaled when Edge dived out of the way.

Then she moved as the tigers smashed open the gate.

She pushed Trung off her and scrambled for the black bag.

Reached inside and grabbed something big and thick.

Pulled it out and saw it was a syringe thick as a dildo, sharp as a spear.

She leapt to her feet.

Edge had the General in a headlock from behind.

The General's eyes were big and bulging like that dragon in her dream.

His cock was thick and spurting like that snake in her nightmare.

His pectorals twitched and thundered as he fought for air.

And Emma aimed her dildo-dagger right between those twitching tanks.

She plunged it deep into the dragon's heart.

Pulled it out and plunged it in again.

Fucked him good and deep with her spear until he ejaculated red jets of blood.

She stabbed him six more times before Edge broke his neck and then hurled him across the room.

Trung whirled around like a spinning dervish, sending blood and semen all over the bodies of the dead, his heart and cock both spitting and spurting as he swirled in slow circles, then fell onto his back.

Emma watched as the light faded in the dragon's yellow eyes.

She sighed as the past faded into the shadows.

Smiled as the future opened up before her.

"We go now, please?" came a nervous voice. It was Doctor Wang. "Tigers all good. Others all dead. It is time to go."

And as the dragon lay still and dead, the soldier lifted his precious princess off the battlefield.

He covered her with his arms, shielded her with his shade, showered her with his love.

Then he carried her to their waiting chariot.

Carried her to their waiting future.

Carried her all the way home.

∞

EPILOGUE
ONE MONTH LATER
AXELROD RANCH
MARIETTA, GEORGIA

"It's about time you got back from wherever you were hiding out, Benson," Edge whispered. "You were supposed to give Emma the locations of her sisters one month ago."

Benson grinned and patted Edge on the back of his dark blue suit.

"Wanted to save it for a wedding present," Benson said with a wink. "This way I don't have to buy you two anything."

Benson turned as Emma came over in her white satin dress and white cloth shoes. Her face was glowing in a way that made Edge think about the positive pregnancy test that Emma had shown him last night. It sure as hell made him forget about Benson for a moment, maybe even forever. He watched as Benson whispered something in Emma's ear, then slipped an envelope into her hand.

Emma's face flushed with color. She nodded, gave Benson a long hug. Then she looked at Edge and tried to smile.

"Relax," said Benson as Edge wondered if he should break the guy's nose for upsetting Emma on her wedding day. "It's good news. They're both married and living in Singapore with their families. They remember very little from all those years ago. They were never separated, and they ended up marrying two soldiers who'd taken them under their protection early on. The soldiers were brothers who were smitten with Xie and Po. They wanted them for their own, and saved up enough to buy them off Trung. They've had peaceful, happy lives ever since then. Don't worry, I haven't said a thing to them about you. They don't know about you, Emma. You can decide if and when and how you reconnect. Take your time. They aren't going anywhere."

Emma's face relaxed. Edge watched her expression, then nodded and turned back to Benson.

"Just like you took your time getting the information to us," said Edge. He stroked his beard, which was trimmed to a manageable size so it would fit into the frame for the wedding pictures. "Makes me wonder about you, Benson."

Benson raised an eyebrow, but stayed silent. They both waited for Emma to get distracted by one of the three hundred guests who were spilling out into the lawn and patio and even the stables.

Edge nodded as Ax and Bruiser wandered by with beers in their hands and grins on their faces. It had only been a month, but Edge already felt like he was back amongst brothers.

And Emma felt like she had a new family too after meeting Amy, Brenna, Cate, and Diana. Edge could tell she was happy as a clam. Smiley as a sticker.

Cody and Dogg swung by for some fist bumping action. Emma was surrounded by Diana, Cate, and Brenna. Amy was saying something to the barmen about cutting off the Marines before they started taking their shirts off and challenging the SEALs to wrestling bouts in the mud outside the horse stables. Nancy Sullivan was directing arriving guests and introducing people to one another. Pam Edgerton was one of the guests, and Nancy had been talking in hushed tones with her about maybe joining Darkwater to help with operations.

Edge waited as Benson snagged a champagne flute off a passing waiter's tray. Then the former SEAL grasped the former CIA man by the arm and led him out to the patio,

"You lied, Benson," Edge said softly as the warm Georgia breeze carried the scent of barbecue to them.

Benson calmly took a sip of champagne. "You'll have to be more specific. I've lied to about sixty people in the last hour alone."

Edge tried to hold back his smile. "Over breakfast in Macau. You were eating dim-sum with a western omelet and orange juice."

"You're right. I did lie," said Benson very seriously. "That wasn't orange juice. It was an invincibility potion made from juniper berries and tiger-blood. Now, are we done here? I need to go talk to your best man Fox and see if he wants to join Darkwater."

"You leave Fox alone," Edge warned. "He's nothing like me, Benson. Total straight shooter. Disciplined like a schoolboy. Honest as the day is long."

"Perfect," said Benson. "Because the rest of you Darkwater boys are loose cannons. I need someone I can trust. He's a done deal. You want to tell him or should I?"

Edge rubbed the back of his neck. He took a breath and sighed it out. "First tell me the truth, Benson. You lied to me about finding Emma's sisters. That's why you stalled for a month. You were scrambling to track them down and make good on the lie."

"Then it wasn't a lie, was it, dear boy," said Benson with a wicked smile.

"How'd you finally do it?"

Benson took a breath, then shrugged it out. "The Russians destroyed all the bodies so it wouldn't start a war. But there was some footage of Trung without his mask. I used it to blackmail Chinese Intelligence into launching a massive search to match Emma's DNA."

Edge chuckled. Then he looked into Benson's wise gray eyes.

"Why'd you lie?" Edge asked softly.

Benson stayed silent. He looked away, shrugged, then turned his ancient gaze back towards Edge like this was another test.

Edge nodded. "You were trying to help us," he said softly. "Make it easier for us because you weren't certain we understood how the grand game was played. You wanted to steer us away from having to decide between killing Trung or letting Emma go back to him so she could get to her sisters." He paused a moment. Glanced at Emma inside the house. She was glowing even brighter. "Because you understood that it wasn't about her sisters or her mother or any of that. It was about her own journey." Edge stopped, blinked, gazed out over the lush green pasture. "Her journey home. Her journey to me. To us. To this."

Benson gazed out across the pasture alongside Edge. The two men didn't look into each other's eyes. They were hard men. Or so they told themselves.

They stayed silent as the warm breeze blew across the open fields. Then the patio door opened and Emma stepped out.

"Thank God," Benson said, exhaling loudly. "I thought I was going to have to see a Navy SEAL start blubbering like a sentimental schoolboy."

Emma giggled as Benson planted a kiss on her rosy right cheek before walking back into the house. Emma glanced after him, then turned back to Edge.

"I called them," she said. "Just now. Video chat."

Edge stared at her. "Just like that? You just called your long lost sisters and told them . . . hell, what *did* you say to them?"

Emma was silent for a long moment. She blinked away a tear. She smiled away a sob.

"I said a lot of things," Emma whispered. "I said I loved them even though I'd never met them. I said our mother was willing to die for them, but nobody would let her do it. I said the bastard who separated us and killed our parents with his evil was burning in hell. I told them about you and asked them about their husbands. So yeah, I said a lot of things. And there'll be so many more things to say when we meet. But right now, on this wonderful, magical day, I was really just saying one thing to them."

Edge watched her eyes. They were maple-red and shining in the sun.

"Thank you," Emma whispered. "I was saying thank you. That's what I was really saying to them. Thanking them for giving me a reason to start my story. Thanking them for surviving, because that gave me a way to end my story. End it my way. End it our way."

End it the only way.

The only way it ever ends.

With always.

With forever.

With him.

And with her.

∞

FROM THE AUTHOR

Thank you for reading.

Fay and Fox's story is next. Get *Finding Fay* and the rest of the Darkwater Series here:

wntrs.co/darkwater

And if you'd like a free copy of ***Darkwater Confidential: The Secret Story of Benson and Sally***, you can download it here:

wntrs.co/darkwater-free

Love,
Anna.
mail@annabellewinters.com
wntrs.co/join

Printed in Great Britain
by Amazon